THE
Boyfriend
EXPERIENCE

JORDAN'S GAME
HUSS

JORDAN'S GAME
BOOK THREE

DEDICATION

*For the Oaklees of the world.
You know who you are.*

JA HUSS

CHAPTER ONE

JORDAN

Lawton Ayers is dressed for success. He's got the suit, the tie, the watch, the shoes, the haircut, the cufflinks, and the pair of designer shades. We're sitting outside today. It's officially spring, so the Tea Room owner, Chella Baldwin, has outdoor seating. It's really just a small area separated from the sidewalk by yellow velvet ropes hanging off black poles, and there are only half a dozen tables, but it's nice. Really fuckin' nice.

"So what do you think I should do?" Law asks.

"About?"

"The fucking TV show I've been telling you about for the last ten minutes!"

"I mean, what do you want me to say, Law? It's pretty much in the bag, if you ask me. You're what TV people look for, right? Young, good-looking, professional, wealthy."

"Yeah, but there are a lot of guys who fit that demographic."

I side-eye him for using the word 'demographic' to describe himself. He's way too focused on all the wrong things if you ask me. "Just be you, man. You're a fucking salesman. And you're not even selling them a house. You're selling them *you* selling other people houses."

He stares at me for a second. Tilts his head a little. "Home TV made a name for itself by selling people, so you're right there."

"Exactly," I say. "Nothing to worry about."

"But," he continues, "all those other shows have couples, ya know? Like, teams. I don't have a team. I just have me."

"You've got a team. Get your partner in on it. They'd love Zack. That guy is fucking hilarious. People would tune in just to watch him talk shit to you."

"No," he says. "Zack said no way was he going on TV. Says just thinking about it makes him itch. He's flat-out refused to be a part of it. Which is why I had to start a whole new company. Rocky Mountain Millionaires. That's what I'm calling the show, too. I need…"

He hesitates.

"What? You need what?"

"I need," he says, leaning across the table like he doesn't want anyone to hear him, "I need an edge. I need these Home TV people to see me as one of them. I need… a girlfriend."

I sit back in my chair, smiling.

"It's not fucking funny," he says.

"I said nothing."

"You're thinking it. You're thinking, *Oh, the great Lawton Ayers has finally come to his senses. He needs a girlfriend.* And how many times have you tried to fix me up—"

"And you said no," I finish for him.

"And now he's here, begging me for help."

I hold my hands out, like… I called it. "So you want me to find you a girlfriend?"

"A pretend one," he adds quickly. "A prop. For appearances only. Someone who could show up for this pitch next week and wow them."

"A looker?"

"Yup. She's gotta be pretty."

"A businesswoman?" I add.

"That would be helpful. One in real estate would be perfect, except—"

"Except you've already done the dirty and disappeared afterward with all those ladies."

He sighs. "I've asked everyone. Every girl I know in the business."

"Did they dump a drink in your lap? Or slap you in the face?"

He shrugs. "Both."

"So," I say, feeling smug and not trying to hide it. "My warnings were right." I lean forward and point at him. "I told you to stop fucking around last year, but did you listen?"

"I don't need the lecture, OK? I just need help. I want this deal. No... I *need* this deal. I'm bored, Jordan. Fucking bored of this shit and I'm not even thirty years old yet. I can't just sell real estate for the rest of my life. It's depressing to even think about it. I need more. I want this show. We're in the final stages of negotiation. I'm this far away," he says, holding his thumb and forefinger about half an inch apart, "from getting what I want. I just gotta close."

"And then what? What if you do get the deal and they like her? What then?"

"I give her a cut. She shows up when I need her and disappears when I don't. I won't screw her over. This is business."

I pause for a moment. To make him think I might say no. Of course, I'd never say no to a game. Especially when it involves one of my best friends. But this game is a little tricky, so I gotta tread carefully.

And the truth is… I accepted his invite for coffee at the Tea Room this afternoon because I was gonna ask *him* for a favor. It's like the stars have aligned.

"I have a game," I say. "In play. Well, about to be. And a girl. The perfect girl for your little business venture."

"Who?" he asks.

But this is where it gets tricky. Oaklee Ryan is a handful. I've already given her profile to six other men and they've politely backed away. She's beautiful, so it's not her looks. And she's successful, so it's not her drive.

But her personality is… well, she's what I like to call unpredictable. Or crazy, if I'm being honest. She's fuckin' crazy.

But I only have one more day to get this game started or she gets a refund. And she paid seventy grand for a twenty-four-seven two-week stint. Seventy grand of liquid cash that I already have plans for. That I *need*. In fact, I need Lawton for that as well. I need both of them on board to get what I want.

So maybe I can get two games and the money all done in one deal?

"If I help you, I need a favor in return."

"Shoot," Law says.

"You know the Club?"

"Turning Point? What about it?"

"I need you to find out who bought it."

"Why?"

"Because it's been sitting empty for more than a year now and… and… well, what the fuck is going on over there?"

"Why do you care?"

"I just do. Can you find out?"

"Probably." Law shrugs. "Shouldn't be too hard. It's all public record."

"I know, but it's just a shell company. I need you to find out."

"Shouldn't your guy be doing this?"

"I don't want this inquiry to be traced back to me. So I need you to do it."

"You thinking about buying it?"

I am thinking about buying it. But that's a conversation for another day because there's a lot of baggage that comes packed with that admission and I don't feel like talking about it yet. So I just shrug and change the subject back to him. "You ever go to that brewhouse over on Wynkoop?"

He laughs. "Which fucking one? There's like a million of them down there now."

"The one with the water tower."

"The old grocer building? Red brick, five stories tall. I live right behind that fucker. Can see that water tower from my patio. What's that place called again?"

"Bronco Brews."

"Right. How'd they ever get away with that name, anyway? You'd think the Broncos would be all up in their shit."

"They were, but that place has been called Bronco Brews for almost seventy-five years. So they won. I know the owner. They hired our firm for that lawsuit about ten years ago, but then the old man died and his daughter took over. Oaklee Ryan is her name. And it just so happens she called me up last month looking for a game called…"

He waits for it.

"The Boyfriend Experience."

He smiles. Which is cute. And good luck. Because this smile means he's obviously never met Oaklee Ryan. "So what I'm hearing is…"

"You be her boyfriend, she'll be your girlfriend, everybody's happy."

He's nodding his head enthusiastically, but then he frowns. "Wait. Oaklee Ryan. Why does that name sound familiar?"

"No clue," I lie.

He snaps his fingers. "Oh, yeah. I remember now. She started some protest a couple years ago trying to have all the old mansions declared historical buildings so they couldn't be sold off to developers. She cost me a major deal—"

"But all that's in the past," I say, trying to smooth things over. "She's not into that hippie shit anymore. In fact, she renovated her brewhouse last year and she got a crash course on property values since then. She's not who she was."

"Then why have you been holding onto this game for a month?"

He's quick, I'll give him that. Lawton Ayers didn't become one of Denver's most successful luxury real-estate agents because he's slow. "I've been looking for the right guy. She's picky. In fact, she might not like you, so I'll have to run this by her first."

He looks offended. Which is also cute. "What's not to like about me? I'm fuckin' perfect pretend boyfriend material."

"That you are, Law. That you are. I'm sure she'll love you. So you're in? You can handle the boyfriend experience?"

"That's like… what? Dinner and dates and shit like that?"

"Exactly," I say.

"OK, but makes sure she knows what I need in return. I need polish. I need personality. I need a partner who will go in there on my arm and those people look at us and say, 'Now that's a Home TV couple!' And that meeting is next week, so get this deal done today."

With that he slaps the table, stands up, buttons his suit coat, and drops down a twenty. "Call me," he says over his shoulder as he leaves. "Tonight."

Oaklee Ryan isn't so easy.

"Who?" she says, her face buried in her computer screen. We're in her office on the top floor of the Bronco Brews building in Lower Downtown. I can see the mountains, the Pepsi Center, Union Station, and Coors Field as I pivot my head and look out her floor-to-ceiling windows.

"Lawton Ayers. He's a real-estate agent. Not just any real-estate agent, either. He's like… top fuckin' notch, ya know? He's the perfect pretend boyfriend for you."

She pulls back from her computer, slides her glasses down her nose to peer over them. At me. Practically glaring. "Real estate?"

"He's fine."

"I don't need fine. I need great."

"He's better than great, Oaklee. He's rich as fuck. Sexy as fuck. Intelligent, fit—"

"How fit? Like huge biceps fit? Or lean fit?"

"Does it matter?"

"It does to me," she says. "And I'm the one who paid you, so yes. It matters."

"He's…" I shrug. "I mean, he's got a nice body. I'd fuck him."

"I'm not asking about his sex appeal, Wells. I'm asking about his fitness level."

I hate the way she always calls me Wells. It's like she sneers it every single time. I haven't been taking it personally because Oaklee sneers every word that comes out of her mouth. She's practically dripping with cynicism.

But I'm starting to think she doesn't like me.

"Why? You gonna make him your triathlon partner? You gonna make him ride a bull? Bike up Pikes Peak? Why the fuck do you need to know this?"

She smiles. She's very pretty when she smiles. Her hair is long, blonde, and wild. Not curly, not straight—but large, round rolling waves that almost take on a life of their own when she moves. It's like a metaphor for her, I realize. On the verge of something. Always on the verge of something.

I've seen her with it tied back and on those days she looks… tame. Like a dog on a leash or a lion in a cage. But today it's loose, so she's wild, I suppose.

She has no choice but to be wild. That's just who she is. And that's why every guy I've sent to her has given me a very firm no, thank you.

Her eyes are brown. Which isn't something you see too often with blonde people. And not just any brown, but a very light brown. Her cheekbones are prominent but not sharp, but her chin is round and so is her nose. So it doesn't make her look... handsome. No. She's not handsome. Everything about her is *pretty*.

"Because I have a very specific image in mind and I'm paying for the fuckin' game," she says, answering my question.

Everything except her mouth, that is.

"I sent you an email. Can you at least look at it and see if he's good enough? Because I gotta tell ya, Oaklee, he's your last chance."

"What's that mean? I paid you seventy—"

"I'll give it back," I say, holding up a hand. "I don't want to," I grumble to myself. "But I will. I'm not gonna cheat you, for fuck's sake. I'm just... I wasn't aware that you had a reputation around town."

Her mouth drops open. She is aghast. "What?"

"For being bitchy, OK? That's not me talking. I love you, Oaklee." I pause to smile here. "You're the best." *And I need your money,* I don't add. "But look, you're one of those strong women, right?"

"Right," she says, folding her arms across her chest, eyeing me with something close to contempt.

"You got money, you got a business, you're very beautiful. You don't need a man."

She narrows her eyes at me. "I paid for a man."

"I know, I know, I know!" I say, holding my hand up, pressing it forward into the air to enunciate each word. And then I sigh. And frown. And point to the email she didn't open on her computer screen. "He's your man. And if you don't like him—well, Oaklee, I'm gonna have to give you your money back and call it a day. Because I'm out of men. And believe me, I want your money. I need it for something specific. But Lawton is my last guy, OK? So take him or leave him."

She leans back in her chair, making it creak. Not looking defeated. Not at all. Just... resigned. We both stare out her office windows. It's late afternoon and you can tell there's rain coming soon because the sky is that slate-gray color of spring thunderheads.

"OK," she says. No drama. No explanation. Just, "OK. When do we start?"

"He's all yours," I say, relieved, but keeping it out of my voice. "How about I have him stop by here for dinner tonight?"

She looks at me then, squinting. "He can pick me *up* from here. But I didn't pay seventy thousand dollars for a pretend boyfriend just to be taken to dinner at my own brewhouse."

"Of course," I say. "He'll pick you up and take you out."

"OK," Oaklee agrees. Then she turns her head a little as she smiles—like she's trying to hide it from me—and says, "Deal."

"There's just one more thing," I say.

"What now?"

"He needs help with something."

"Who?"

"Lawton," I say.

"No, from who?" she clarifies. "From me?"

"Yes. See, he's got this meeting with the Home TV people next week. He's putting together some pitch for a real-estate show and he needs a partner."

She blinks at me. Three times slowly. "What?"

So I explain. And I expect all kinds of reactions from Oaklee Ryan over this little snag, but she is surprisingly calm. In fact she's almost thoughtful. Contemplative as I fill her in on his stupid idea. She doesn't even ask about his long-term expectations—which, if you ask me, are also stupid. She only says, "Will this interview be taped?"

I shrug. Because I have no clue. But then I say, "Probably," just to cover my bases.

She thinks about that. Poker face in place. Then she nods her head and says, "Agreed. I'll throw in the Girlfriend Experience as a bonus."

I smile, cautiously. Because there's too many ways to interpret that little comment for it to be a comfortable smile.

But the deal is done, that money is mine, and that's all I needed. So I just say, "Then let the game begin."

CHAPTER TWO

LAWTON

"Yup," *I say* into my phone.

"It's on," Jordan says. "She agreed to be your partner for the interview next week and you've agreed to give her a boyfriend experience. She's expecting you tonight at seven. So just show up at the brewhouse and like... pretend you're strangers and shit. Like stare at her, and introduce yourself—"

"I don't need pointers on how to meet a girl, asshole. I know how to pick up a girl."

"Yup," he says. "Understood. Just... be careful."

"Careful? Why?"

"I gotta go. But if you have any issues, call me, OK?"

I'm still wondering what *careful* means when I get the hang-up beeps. "Fucker," I say, putting my phone down.

"Who was that?" Zack asks. I can see him through my open office door, leaning against the copy machine looking like a model on the cover of *Le Mans* magazine. Short dark hair, expensive suit, watch that costs as much as most people pay for a car catching the afternoon sun on his wrist.

"Jordan," I say. "He found me a partner for the meeting next week."

"Who?" Zack laughs, folding his arms across his chest.

"A woman," I say. Which makes Zack snort. "Owns a local business, young, attractive, go-getter. She's gonna make the perfect girlfriend."

"Don't do it, man. This is a very bad idea."

"I want this show."

"I get it," Zack says, walking into my office and dropping into a chair on the other side of my desk. "I do. I mean, I'm looking for something more as well. But lying to get on TV?" He shakes his head. "It's gonna blow up in your face. You have to know that."

"I think I can pull it off. And besides, I've got a week to feel this girl out and see if she's a good fit."

"I can see the headlines now," Zack says, making one of those sweeping headline pantomimes with his hands in front of his face. "'Lawton Ayers lies to Home TV. Marriage is a sham.'"

"I'm not gonna marry her, for fuck's sake. We're just business partners. And hey, every tabloid wants a good breakup story. We'll make ours spectacular."

Zack laughs. "I can't wait to see this all come apart. She's gonna break you. Take you for everything you've got. Then stomp on your face with a three-inch heel and—"

"So dramatic," I say, rolling my eyes. "I've got a contract all ready for her. Gonna pick her up tonight. In fact," I say, getting up from my desk, "I'm taking off early so I can go home and shower. Gotta make a good impression."

Zack gets up and walks back to the copy machine, gathering up his papers as I grab my briefcase. "This is gonna be fun," he says. "Your stupid plan is the highlight of my life right now." Then he disappears into his office and closes the door.

"Yup," I say. "My life is looking pretty damn good compared to yours, you sorry fuck."

Zack plays everything safe. He's one of those people who buys a Porsche and then drives the speed limit. He's one of those guys who never fouls another player in basketball. His motto is: *Character is who you are in the dark.*

Which I totally appreciate as a business partner, but no one follows that straight and narrow to perfection. Everyone wobbles as they walk the line. And I'm not lying to the Home TV people. I'm just… exaggerating my relationship with this woman, that's all. Besides, by this time next week when I take that meeting, I'm sure we'll be on the same page. We'll be halfway through the game and we'll know everything there is to know about each other.

Yup. In the bag, man. In. The. Bag.

I'm pretty sure this whole boyfriend experience is about sex. I mean, why else would she be doing this? She wants something weird—and that fits into Jordan's whole game thing, right? Yeah, she wants something weird, something she can't just get from any guy, and she wants a man to offer that to her so she doesn't have to ask.

That's pretty much how these games go.

At least I think that's how they go. Jordan never talks much about them, but it's all standard, I'm sure.

So the way I see it… I get free sex, a pretend girlfriend, the perfect interview with the Home TV people, and all I gotta do is bring her flowers and open her car door for two weeks.

My drive home is short because my loft is only a few blocks north in Lower Downtown, commonly called LoDo in these parts. Right now I'm living in an investment property I bought last fall when it was in foreclosure. I spent the whole winter fixing it up so I could sell it in the spring, but this is feeling a little more like fate than luck. I mean, that Oaklee chick's brewhouse is practically right next door to me. I can fucking walk over there tonight.

By the time this whole boyfriend thing is over I'll probably have a buyer and the TV show and... yeah. *Rocky Mountain Millionaires* living, here I come. I have a place in mind up in the foothills. Gonna sell all my properties down here in the city, buy that sprawling acreage, and start a whole new life as the Home TV go-to guy for mountain real estate. I'll be just like that guy who sells the private islands on their channel.

I cannot fuckin' wait.

I take a quick shower, finger-comb my hair, and stare at myself in the mirror, wondering if I should shave. I shaved this morning but there's a shadow there. Kind of a sexy shadow if I do say so myself. So I leave it. This girl runs a brewery. She probably likes a rough jaw.

At six forty-five I leave the loft, hop down the six flights of stairs to street level, and walk up the alley to her front entrance.

Even though my street address says Wynkoop Street, I'm kinda situated behind her building a little. I have a great view of that water tower. It's like eye level with my penthouse when I'm on my rooftop terrace. And there's a whole wall of windows just below it.

I wonder if that's her apartment?

Her building is old. Like over a hundred years old. But now that I'm paying attention to it, I do remember there was a renovation going on last year. I was waiting for listings to come up, since I figured she was turning that place into apartments, but... that never happened.

The front side of her building faces Wynkoop Street. Which is kinda famous for the brewhouses. Hell, our former governor used to have a brewhouse down here on Wynkoop. And over the past decade or so, they've popped up everywhere.

The new competition didn't seem to hurt Bronco Brews any. I see her labels and taps all over the LoDo bars. And that renovation must've cost her millions. So she can't be doing too bad.

God, where has this girl been all my life? She's so... perfect.

The front of the building has a street-level entrance, but I stop and look up before I go inside. There's scaffolding up there and I wonder if she's gonna do work on the façade?

But then the sound of people draws my attention back to the night's goal and I go inside. The lobby is huge, two stories tall, and is flanked on both sides by elevators. Directly in back, just past the grand staircase winding up to the second floor, is a wall of windows that showcase several rows of giant copper brew tanks and staff bustling back and forth.

On my left is a small bar—presumably for people who are waiting for a table in the restaurant on the right. Which is packed. I'm talking packed with people. I hit up one of the hostesses as she's grabbing menus to seat a party. "I'm looking for Oaklee?" I say over the noise of the crowd. "I have an appointment with her."

"Are you Lawton? She's upstairs in her office. Take the elevators to the top floor. You'll find her."

"Thanks," I say. But she's already gone.

I walk over to the elevators, press the call buttons and then step inside. When the doors close the cacophony of conversation fades, then disappears completely as I ascend.

I used to be a party guy but the last ten years or so have mostly been about work. So this relative silence is a welcome relief.

A ding signals the opening of doors, and I step out into… an apartment? Jesus Christ, does this elevator lead directly to her apartment?

There's a wide living room surrounded by windows on all sides and I catch a glimpse of my terrace.

"Is that Lawton Ayers?" a woman's voice calls from… somewhere. The space is a wide-open floor plan and the few walls I can see don't reach all the way up to the tall two-story ceilings.

When I look up at the beamed ceiling I notice a loft space and my eyes follow the perimeter catwalk railing made of stainless-steel cables until I spy bedrooms. Three, I decide. Her decor is simple and homey. A large u-shaped overstuffed brown leather couch facing a stacked stone fireplace takes up one corner, while a long wooden dining table takes up another. There's a large room-sized rug surrounding the couch—brown and white cow pattern. Not real hide, but that one accent is enough to pull the room together. Give it a *feel*. Western. Very Colorado. Almost cowboy, but missing all those cowboy things you find in ranch homes. Like a buffalo over the fireplace and pictures of hunting dogs on the wall.

Instead the walls along the catwalk are decorated with framed posters of her beer labels. Original artwork, probably. They are all very graphic in their design. An orange bucking horse on a brown background with lots of black swirly typography. A pink punk rocker on a black background with pink typography. And more. Every brew I've ever seen in the local bars—and many I've never heard of—all displayed along the walls.

Her history, as art.

The kitchen is in the center of the floor space. Black soapstone countertops with painted taupe-gray cabinets.

Stainless-steel appliances and one of those industrial stainless-steel farm sinks that matches the stainless-steel finishes on the cabinet pulls, light switch plates, and backsplash tiles.

It's totally custom from top to bottom. She put a lot of thought into her design. And it's nice, I decide. Something I'd pick. If I were renovating a house for myself and not for some future generic buyer. Something that merges with the view outside.

And speaking of the view—Jesus Christ, she can see all of Colorado. Which makes me laugh. The entire front range is laid out in front of me, including the imposing Mt. Evans on the west side, Pikes Peak to the south, Long's Peak to the north, and in the east... sprawling Denver suburbia.

This apartment has to be worth millions. It's so unusual, so big, so... perfect. I'd list this place for two million, easy. Maybe more.

"Holy shit," I finally say. "This place is incredible."

"You are Lawton, right? Because if not, you need to leave."

"Sorry," I say, walking towards her with my hand outstretched. She's average height. Her hair is long, dark blonde, and unruly. Like she's been at the beach and the wind has tousled it.

Or like she just rolled out of bed.

Or like someone just fucked her hard.

I snap out of it. "I just got lost for a moment. Your view..." And then I get lost in her eyes. An unusual caramel color, with hazy patches of green that catch the light. And she has thick, pouty lips—with a slight dent in the middle of her lower one that, for some reason, is inexplicably sexy. Her face is soft, but not round and her body is slight, but not skinny. Athletic, I decide.

She smiles tightly as she shakes my hand. "The view. I know. It's the only thing anyone sees when they come up here."

That's not true at all. Not if she's around. The view is definitely beautiful, but Oaklee Ryan is downright breathtaking. "But... do you *live* here?"

"Both live and work." She shrugs. "It's been my home my whole life. But I did this last year."

"But that elevator just comes right to the top like that? No key?"

"I keep it open during business hours and I was expecting you. It locks when I need it to."

"Oh, well, good. I was worried about your safety for a second."

"Sweet," she says. Then nothing.

"So," I say, rubbing my hands together. "I'm your boyfriend."

She looks me up and down like she's not sure if that's accurate. "Hmm."

"What?"

"I'm just thinking..."

"About?"

"If you're right for the job."

I squint at her. "I'm totally boyfriend material. I can play your game. I mean, I guess I could've come up here and played like I got lost looking for the bathroom and found you instead. The woman of my dreams." I wink at her. "Made it a little more mysterious like Jordan told me to... but the view," I say. "This place... it caught me off guard."

She cups her chin with her hand. Thinking. Wondering. "Well, I have doubts. So tonight is an interview."

"An interview?" Which makes me laugh.

"Yes." She waves a hand over at the kitchen where I now notice there's a row of beer bottles lined up on the countertop. Sitting in front of each is a short glass. Like the kind they probably give you downstairs when you order one of those flight display sampler trays. "To see if you're what I need."

"What do you need?" I ask, waggling my eyebrows. "I mean you don't need to get me drunk, if that's what you're getting at."

"Oh, for fuck's sake." She sighs, rubbing her forehead with her index finger and thumb. "This probably isn't going to work. I mean, you're handsome and all, but I need more than handsome. I'm sorry."

"Wait," I say, putting up a hand. "We had a deal. I need a girl—"

"I know all about your needs, Mr. Ayers. That's the only reason I said yes. It was… intriguing. But I just don't know if you're up to this."

I laugh. "Up to what? Treating you nice, bringing you flowers, opening the door and pulling out your chair? I can handle it, I assure you. And I can handle the beer too. What do you need? Should I taste each one and tell you which one I like best?"

I walk over to the beers, pick up the bottle opener, pop the first cap off, and pour it into the glass using proper beer-pouring technique. It's a dark beer. Like fuckin' mud. Not really what I go for. And now that I read the label I see it's called Mountain Mud. Which should've been my first clue. But… fuck it. In for a penny, right?

I take a sip, the foam collecting on my upper lip, then swallow it down and think for a moment.

Oaklee has her arms crossed in front of her very nice breasts, her mouth not quite smirking, but definitely not smiling, either. "Well?" she says.

"Nutty," I say, wiping the froth off my lip. "And thick. Maybe a hint of vanilla too. It's a brown ale? Or a stout?"

"Brown," she says. And maybe... just maybe, she smiles. "So you're a craft beer guy?"

"Not really. But this is Colorado. There's a craft brewhouse on every corner these days."

"Yes." She sighs. "Which is part of my problem."

"I don't get it."

"You don't need to. Yet."

"OK, wait a minute. Let's back up. Jordan told me you bought the Boyfriend Experience. What's that got to do with beer?"

"Everything," she says. "But I'm not going to waste my time explaining if you're not the right man for the job."

"What's the job?"

"Boyfriend Experience," she snaps.

"I feel like we're talking in circles. So again, what's that got to do with beer?"

"Just taste the next one."

"Fuck it," I mumble, popping the top off the next in line. This one's called Anarchy Orange IPA and the label is the pink punk rocker on the artwork I noticed earlier. IPA is more my style, so I pour and take a long sip. "Hell, yeah. This is great. Citrus with a lot of hop. Dig it."

Now that *was* a smile.

"See," I say. "I'm the right guy."

"Next."

"You're trying to get me drunk, aren't you? So you can take advantage of me later. I'm on to you, Oaklee Ryan." I shoot my finger at her and wink.

"Just taste. Your flirty jokes are wasted on me. I'm all business."

"Whatever," I mumble. I'm trying to be friendly and she's just... not. Like I'm not good enough for her. Like she's not interested in me at all.

She's lucky I need her or I'd walk out.

I pop the top off the next beer—which is called Assassin Sour Saison and has a red ninja on a black label. I pour the light brew into the glass. It's very bubbly. I take a sip as she watches. "Nah," I say, setting the glass down. "Maybe some people like that, but I'm not one of them."

She shrugs. "To be expected. Not everyone likes a sour, and this saison has so much carbonation it's more like champagne than beer. It's my favorite."

"Figures," I say. Because I get the feeling that's how this is gonna go. Regardless of how much I like her kitchen design, her view, and her faux cowgirl-esque décor, we are opposites. "So did I pass, or what?"

"You might do. At least you're honest."

"So... tell me more about you."

"No." She snorts. "This is a job, Mr. Ayers. I paid for you and in return you do as I ask."

"Wait, there's something in this for me too. So don't get too bossy, partner. I need you to be on your best behavior next week for my meeting with the Home TV people. Jordan explained?"

"He did. And that's fine. I clean up nice."

"I'm not talking about your looks. You look just fine. I'm talking about your attitude, which definitely needs adjusting."

27

"You don't get to adjust me." She snorts. "I paid seventy thousand dollars for you."

"Jesus fucking Christ. Are you serious? Who the hell pays that much for a sex fantasy?"

"It's *not* a sex fantasy, it's the boyfriend experience. There will be no sex, Mr. Ayers. Not between you and me anyway."

What's that mean? I wonder to myself. 'No sex between you and me?' Does she have a boyfriend already?

And I know it's irrational—I mean, I don't even like her, for fuck's sake—but if she has a boyfriend… well, that might piss me off. "Call me Law, OK? No one calls me Mr. Ayers, not even my clients."

"Fine. *Law.* I have very specific needs, OK? You might even call them… tasks. That's what I'm paying for, so are you agreeable to that? Or what? Because I'm in a hurry and I need this game to start immediately. I've been patient with Jordan, but I'm not really a patient girl. So you'll do. And in return for your signature on my contract I will be your… whatever it is you need for that meeting next week."

It occurs to me that I should be getting paid for this. And for like two seconds I consider hitting Jordan up for a percentage of the profits.

But one more look at Miss Ryan's scowling lips and I reconsider. She's obviously wealthy, she's professionally successful, beautiful in a way that's hard to describe, smart, probably ruthless, and she's one hundred percent local. In like every way. She's the total package as far as my needs go. So I set my ego—and my sexual expectations—aside, and say, "I'm in. Where do I sign?"

CHAPTER THREE

OAKLEE

Lawton Ayers is exactly what I expected from Jordan Wells. Which is both good and bad. Good, because he's handsome in a way that threatens other men. Rich— also threatening to other men. And smart. Which most men don't care about one way or the other, but I do. I like a smart man. Means he can think on his toes. Change tactics mid-stride and see opportunities a dumbass might miss.

And believe me, that's gonna come in handy.

But he's also... well, how to put it. Arrogant? Yes. Just like Jordan. He's one of those guys who has everything, which means there's a chance he'll bow out at the last second and leave me hanging. Like... maybe he's too good for a job like this, ya know?

But that contract is iron-clad. I made sure of it. And even though Jordan Wells is a pretty damn good lawyer, he wrote it up under a false presumption.

"We need to get rid of the suit," I say.

"What?"

"Like... don't you have jeans? And a t-shirt? I mean, I can take you shopping if necessary, but I'd rather use what you've got."

"You? Take *me* shopping?" He laughs.

"Why is that funny?"

"I think it's supposed to be the other way around, right? You want the whole *Pretty Woman* experience."

"She was a prostitute, Mr—"

"Law," he snaps.

"I'm not a prostitute, *Law*. I don't need your credit card. I don't need to be taken to a fancy luncheon on a polo field. I need. A man."

"I'm a man."

"Indeed you are. I have doubts about this, I'd like to make that clear up front. So if you have doubts, you should probably leave now. Because once we sign this contract, you're in. There's no going back. I *own you* for two weeks."

"Can I at least read the contract?"

"Of course. It's in my office and I'll get it now. One moment."

I turn away and walk around a wall partition to my office. The contract was drawn up by Jordan over a month ago. There are enough details in there to make it clear what I need, but it's vague enough to keep a good lawyer like Jordan from asking too many questions. I don't think Law here will be a problem, but... there's always a chance he'll catch on before he signs.

I've interviewed several men since Jordan drew it up, but none of them got past the beer test. If Lawton Ayers has one thing in his favor, it's that. So despite my hesitations, I grab the file off my desk, snatch up a pen, and walk back out to the living area. He's opened another bottle and he's pouring it into the glass.

"I've had this one before," he says, after taking a sip.

It's our signature beer called Bucked Up and has the iconic bucking horse on the label.

"Do you like it?"

"When I drink beer, I get this out of habit if it's on tap. So yeah, I guess you can say I like it." He pours a second glass, presumably for me, and then turns, both in hand, and says, "Let's drink."

"First the contract," I say.

"Buck the contract." And then he laughs. "Get it? Buck instead of—"

"I get it, Law."

"God, for a hippy chick you're pretty uptight, Oaklee."

"Nobody says I'm a hippy. Who said I was a hippy?"

"You know," he says, taking a long drink from one of the glasses. "That whole 'save the mansions' campaign you had going a while back."

"It had nothing to do with free sex and flower children. I was trying to preserve the neighborhood."

"Is that why you renovated your historic building?" He's smirking at me now.

"I took great care in preserving the historical elements when I updated, thank you."

"You're changing the façade. How's that preserving?"

"I'm not changing the façade. I'm having a bucking bronco painted over the brick."

"Oh." He laughs, then takes another sip of his beer. "Excuse me. *Defacing* the façade. My bad."

"This building had a bucking horse painted on it back when it was built in nineteen twelve. It was home to a place called Mustang Grocers. The new mural will look a hundred years old by the time we're done next week and from the outside, my building will look exactly the way it was in nineteen twelve. So don't worry. It's going to add a lot of value to the neighborhood. I hired more than a dozen consultants before I made any changes and the property values on this block have all gone up in the last six weeks."

"I know," he says, finishing his glass of beer. It's a sample glass meant for tasting, so only five ounces. But still, the alcohol content of Bucked Up is eight point eight percent.

I'm not sure he realizes that. I'm not sure I should tell him. In fact, maybe getting him drunk will loosen him up. Make him more agreeable. I'm almost out of time. And Jordan did say he wasn't going to find me another prospect. It's this guy or nothing.

I need him, I decide. He'll have to do.

"I own a penthouse just over there," Law says, pointing. "You can see my terrace from here. I bought it last year and now it's almost worth double."

I stare out the window, looking in that direction. Interesting. The fact that we're neighbors. And convenient too.

Then I turn to face him and smile. The first real smile I've unleashed on him all evening. "See?" I say. "Like I said, property values are skyrocketing."

"What do you know about real estate?"

"I know enough, but it's not the point."

"Well, to me it is. I have that meeting next week. And if this all works out you and I could be partners in this TV deal. So I'd like to know if I'm wasting *my* time here as well."

He tilts his head at me, eyes shining with what? Mischief? Daring? I don't know but it's kind of adorable. They aren't special eyes. Just brown, and not brown like mine. Just boring brown. But that damn twinkle in them does something to me.

And you need him, the inner monologue says. *At least as much as he needs you. So don't get distracted by his dreamy eyes.*

So I say, "LoDo real estate has been steadily climbing since two thousand twelve. The gentrification of Five Points just east of here has property values hitting half a million for the first time in the history of that neighborhood. The average listing in LoDo is seven hundred thousand. This building is now worth in excess of seven million dollars *without* my penthouse apartment. And when I'm done renovating the other floors and put the condos up for sale it will top seventy-five million. So you tell me. Are you wasting your time here, Mr. Ayers?"

He smiles. No. He smirks. Pleased with my outburst. "Law," he says in a low voice. "And no, I think that will do, *Miss* Ryan."

"Oaklee," I say, playing his game.

"Do you need an agent?" he asks.

"For?"

"Your building? The condos? I've been watching this place. Waiting for the listings."

Well… that's interesting. I should've thought of that. Should've opened with that. And the fact that I missed an opportunity to bait him with the lure of being the listing agent for my new condos instead of agreeing to be his stupid TV show partner… well, it disturbs me.

It's a sign of how distracted I've become with my little… problem.

"You haven't passed my test yet, Law. So why don't we start with *my* business and we can talk *your* business later."

He stares at me for a few seconds. I can practically see his mind racing with possibilities. Calculating how many units I have here—thirty-five—how much they might go for—starting price of four hundred fifty thousand and capping out at nine hundred for the fifth floor—and what his take-home might be on that.

Almost six million dollar signs flash in his eyes. "Bring it, Oaks. Test me all you want."

I place the contract on the kitchen counter, go to the fridge, bring out a new flight tray of testing beers—this time with the labels all hidden with brown paper wrappers—and set it down in front of him.

"A blind taste test?" He chuckles. "You really take this shit seriously."

"Afraid you'll fail?" I ask, tilting my head and smirking back at him.

"Not in the least. Let me guess. I gotta pick which is which." He nods his head to the now empty flight tray. "I think I can do that by color alone, Oaklee."

"Perfect," I say, popping the top off the first beer. "Then we should be good to go in about two minutes." I pour the first beer into the tasting glass and hand it to him.

He does a fake cheers gesture with the glass and takes a sip. "Bucked Up. No doubts at all."

I grit my teeth, pop the top off the next one, pour, and hand it over.

He says, "Anarchy Orange, bitches. Love that one. I might need to take a case home."

Which makes me wilt a little. No. Not a little, a *lot*. But I pour the last one, even though he's saying Mountain Mud before he takes a sip. After the sip, after he wipes the nut-brown froth off his lips, he says, "Did I pass?"

I nod. Sad. "Yup, you did. Do you want to sign?"

He stares at me for a few moments, trying to figure out the change in my mood maybe. But then he nods and says, "Yeah. Sure. Let's do this."

CHAPTER FOUR

LAWTON

That test.

I can't stop thinking about it. We signed the contract. I wrote in the part where she agrees to be my partner for the TV show and she initialed that addendum without comment. But there's something wrong here. I can feel it.

That test was way too easy. I mean... she should've picked several of the same type of beer, not three that can be identified by color and smell alone.

I've got her website open on my laptop as I lie in bed, absently looking between the lights of her penthouse from the view out my window, and her site.

She's got several IPAs. Several citrus ones, in fact. Why didn't she line all those up and make me figure out which one was Anarchy Orange? And she's got three dark beers. Two stouts and that brown Mountain Mud. She could've lined those up and made me choose. I don't see any other saisons on her menu, but that one wasn't even one of the tests. And Bucked Up—hell, anyone could identify Bucked Up. It's as common as Coors in this town.

It makes no sense.

And then she got all quiet after the blind taste test. Like she was... upset.

But about what?

That I passed her stupid test?

How could I *not* pass?

Which makes me wonder about the other men she's interviewed for this contract. How could they have possibly fucked this up?

Unless it was her. Right? Her attitude. Her money. Her confidence.

I mean, there are a lot of men out there who hate a successful woman. Maybe that was it? Or maybe she's just too... unpredictable for them?

She's definitely a wild card.

But her knowledge of the real-estate market is impressive. She's perfect for these TV people. I mean, total fucking knock-out, number one. Smart. And she seems like a ruthless businesswoman.

But that test.

And her take-no-prisoners Wild West persona.

I do a search for Oaklee Ryan and find several local news articles about her on page one. Mostly about the brewhouse. Her father's obituary several years ago. One article in *Westword* about her new renovation project, two about the mural going up on the front of the building, and many—like dozens—about the awards her craft beers have won over the past several decades. Several international ones too.

Except... none of them are recent. She hasn't won an award in three years. Not even the Denver BrewBest Fest last month.

Not since her father died, I realize.

Maybe she needs a beer guy to help her come up with a new idea?

But then why the boyfriend experience?

It just makes no sense. None of it.

So I stare at all the pictures of her online. She's got a look. Urban cowgirl. Lots of them feature her wearing short flowing skirts with old cowboy boots with t-shirts bedazzled with rhinestones. The kind you see women wearing at the rodeo. Some of them have her in jeans—toes of her boots peeking out from under the hem. And only one has her dressed up in something I'd call socialite elite.

That was for a party her father threw just a year before he died to celebrate the opening of an art gallery dedicated to western artists. He was a handsome man. White hair, fit body, well-groomed short beard and the same don't-fuck-with-me look in his eyes.

They look like wild animals caught in a pen. Mustangs, maybe. Broncos, both of them.

And then I wonder if he named her Oaklee after Annie Oakley?

Which makes me laugh and hope it's true. I can picture my Oaklee with a rifle in her hand shooting cans as a little girl. Wearing a cowboy hat that gets blown off her head as she takes aim on some rural outdoor shooting range.

She sent me home after we signed the contract. Looking sad and maybe a little desperate. My only instructions were to pick her up in the lobby of Bronco Brews tomorrow at noon wearing jeans and a t-shirt.

When I asked what we were doing she walked to the elevator, called it, and said goodbye with a wave of her hand.

She owns an empire. Like… a true empire. That building is incredible. That water tower is original too. And her father was something of a philanthropist during his later years. He was a big supporter of the arts—hosted a local music festival every summer from nineteen eighty-two until the late nineties. And they have a scholarship fund at Colorado State, University of Northern Colorado, and the University of Colorado Boulder for microbiology students.

Which I thought was weird until I saw an article that states she has a master's degree in microbiology from Colorado State and put two and two together to realize… that's what makes beer, right? Yeast is what gives beer flavor.

She's not one of those I-love-beer-so-I-think-I'll-start-a-brewery people.

She's a fucking scientist and fermentation is something she understands. Lives and knows deep down, like an instinct.

And she came up in the business. Her becoming a brewmaster was almost inevitable.

My email dings, so I switch screens to bring it up and find a message from the acquisitions department at Home TV with the details of next week's meeting.

It's a form letter, I'm sure of that. Explaining the details. Time, date, place. Shit like that. And the little paragraph they send at the end of every single email I've ever gotten from them telling me to study their successful shows so I understand what they're looking for.

I know what they're looking for. We've had more than a dozen phone conversations since I started this process. More emails than I can count. And lots of back-and-forth with the lawyers to get to this point.

This is my chance. We're so close to the end and all I have to do is close the damn deal with this one final meeting.

They love my idea. They have several shows about mountain homes but none of them are based on the hosts and all of them focus on the houses. They have one short season, maybe two. Then they cut them loose, find another angle, and try again.

They are desperate to find that critical combination of personality and wow factor. They want something fresh. Something relevant.

They've said that to me many times and I've assured them I've got what they need.

And they've mostly been on board, but with a healthy dose of caution mixed in. Like they *like* me, but they don't *love* me. And they're going to decide one way or another at this final meeting.

And Jordan hit it on the head. They want me, but not just me. They want a couple.

And Oaklee Ryan is perfect. She is everything I need to get the *Rocky Mountain Millionaires* show off the ground. Hell, she's a fuckin' millionaire too! Not in the mountains, but that's what I bring to the table. I'm the one with that dream. So all I gotta do is fit her oval peg into my round hole…

Which makes me chuckle. Because sexual innuendo and all that.

Except she made it very clear there's no sex involved in this boyfriend experience.

And then there's that flashing red sign again.

Why? She makes no sense at all.

The test, the contract, the game… none of it adds up.

What is her angle?

I slap my laptop closed, exhausted, then place it on my bedside table and turn over so I can see the lights from her window down the alley. A few seconds later, they go out, and I picture her getting into bed. Thinking about me. Thinking about what we might do tomorrow. I wonder if she thinks I'm as interesting as I think she is.

Probably not. This is business to her. As it is to me. So it doesn't even matter if she likes me.

I close my eyes, shut out the view of her apartment, and drift off thinking about how my life will change next week.

How I can sell off all my city real estate, buy that place up in the foothills, and start a whole new life far, far away from the city. I envision a life of traipsing through the mountains, looking for homes, and empty lots with the perfect building sites next to rivers, and finding other people their perfect piece of the Wild West.

City life will be a thing of the past. The rat race over.

And all of this is now in reach. This plan is perfect and Oaklee Ryan is my ticket to freedom.

The next morning I find myself standing on my terrace, coffee cup in hand, looking over at Oaklee's penthouse. I can't see the street because my building is set back and my penthouse is on the far side of that, but I get glimpses of people rushing past the entrance to the alley. It's Saturday, so families are out early to eat breakfast at one of the many restaurants on this block. The sun is shining, the temperature mild—gonna hit high sixties today—and there's no sign of rain coming in over the mountains.

And I have a girlfriend to share it with.

That makes me laugh.

I mean, for all intents and purposes she is my girlfriend. We will be spending the next two weeks doing pretty much everything couples do.

What *do* couples do?

I take a sip of coffee and ponder this. And at the same moment I see Oaklee emerge from her apartment through a sliding door, phone to her ear, as she paces back and forth and waves her hands around in exaggerated gestures.

Hmmm.

She looks pissed.

I take another sip of coffee and consider yelling to see if I can get her attention. Then decide to just watch her instead. She's wearing a long white button-down shirt. Like a man's shirt, I guess. Which elicits an unreasonable feeling of jealousy in me that I quickly swallow down.

We're not that kind of couple.

Underneath the shirt she's wearing shorts and a tank top. It's a little chilly this morning for that, but she's so busy talking on the phone, I doubt she notices the cold.

She certainly doesn't look over here—which causes a stab of disappointment. Because it feels like I've thought about nothing *but* her since we met last night and she clearly has other things on her mind.

I glance over my shoulder, find the wall clock in my living room, and figure I'd better get ready for our first date.

So I leave her to her business, go back inside, and set my coffee cup in the sink and consider her instructions.

Wear jeans and a t-shirt, she said.

Hmmm... I'm not a jeans guy. I mean, I don't always wear suits on the weekends, but I do often enough that my wardrobe starts to worry me.

So I go to my closet, ponder what I have, and decide on a pair of Joe's Jeans I got from Neiman Marcus last summer when Zack invited me to go boating up at Grand Lake with him.

He laughed at them, but these jeans are the shit. Dark denim, straight-legged, not skinny, and they make my junk look good.

I think Oaklee will appreciate them.

I grab a white Balmain t-shirt with the logo splashed across the front from the drawer, steam it real quick because it's got a crease down the side, and slip it over my head.

Shoes… hmmm… sneakers, I guess. I have a pair of Burberry in house-check style, so I slip those on and take a look at myself.

Yup. I totally got this look.

Oh… a belt. I need a belt. I have a thing for belts so I spend a lot of time on this choice, eventually deciding on Burberry (in house check) because it matches the shoes.

I leave my place at ten minutes to noon because I'm punctual that way, and hop down the stairs with a spring in my step that it hasn't had in a long time.

Oaklee Ryan. I might like her. This will, at least, be fun, I think.

And hey, if we get that show we'll be partners. I might feel this way for years if that happens.

When I get to the lobby I'm pleasantly surprised to see Oaklee waiting. She's talking to one of her hostesses, so she doesn't notice me right away. I ease my way through the brunch crowd waiting for a table in the lobby and wait for her to turn.

Which she does. And immediately frowns.

"What?"

"What the fuck are you wearing?"

I look down at my outfit. "What do ya mean? You said jeans and t-shirt."

She's wearing her usual. Short ruffly skirt that flutters against her bare thighs, cowboy boots, a tan tank top, and a cropped army jacket with embroidered patches of her beer bottle labels.

"What the hell? Balmain Paris?" She scowls.

"What? This shirt is fuckin' cool."

"That shirt is stupid." And then she sees my shoes. "And what the fuck are you wearing on your feet?"

"Burberry," I say, starting to get pissed off.

"Oh, my God." She presses her fingertips into her temples and looks down at the floor.

"What?" I ask. "What's the problem?"

She lifts her head, looking me straight in the eyes. "You said you live close by?"

"Yeah, in the next building over. Why?"

"Take me to your closet."

CHAPTER FIVE

OAKLEE

"It's not personal," I say. For like the hundredth time. "I just need a specific look, ya know?"

"I get it," he says. But it's more of a growl. His teeth are clenched, which I take as a bad sign. And his knuckles are white as he twists the handle on his door and opens it up to wave me in. "After you."

"Oh, this is nice," I say, looking around at his place. "Very homey."

"It's stage furniture," he replies. "I'm getting ready to sell the place and all this is included in the asking price. So don't waste your time complimenting me on the design. I didn't pick it and I didn't—"

"Jesus," I say, interrupting him. "I get it. Not your style."

It's a loft, like my place, and it's a penthouse. But nothing like my penthouse. It's small, for one. I mean, even comparatively speaking. I get it. I own my building and I have the entire top floor. Plus I use it as an office. There's no other four-thousand-square-feet apartments in this neighborhood.

But this place is small. "How many bedrooms?" I ask.

"Just the one. Most people can't afford more than one bedroom in LoDo. I want it to sell fast and this one will."

"OK." He's touchy about the square footage disparity between us. I get it. "Let's see your closet."

"Right this way," he says, once again waving me forward. Which is nice manners. Not necessary for this boyfriend job, but a good perk. Lawton Ayers obviously had a good mother.

I walk into his bedroom and the first thing I see is the view. Which almost makes me laugh because I roll my eyes every time someone comes up to my place and remarks on the view.

It's not like he has a great view, though. This apartment is in the back of the building and faces the alley. There's only a peekaboo view of the mountains because my building—specifically my penthouse—is really what he's looking at.

"Huh," I say.

"What?" he asks, flipping on the light in his closet.

"You can see my place from your bedroom."

"I told you that last night."

"Yeah, but it never occurred to me that someone could actually see into my place, ya know?"

"Privacy in the city is a myth. Which is why I'm getting the fuck out of here. No space. Can't stand it."

"Oh," I say, turning away from the window to face him. He's standing in the doorway of the closet, kinda backlit so a shadow falls across his face and blurs his features. "Where are you moving to?"

"Indian Hills. You know where that is?"

"Kinda," I say. "Somewhere up there." I wave in the general direction of the mountains. "Why so far?"

He tilts his head at me. "That's right. We haven't talked about my end of the deal in all this. Well, I guess now's as good a time as any. The TV show I'm pitching is called *Rocky Mountain Millionaires*. You know those shows on Home TV that feature million-dollar log homes and shit?"

"Kinda," I say again. Because I'm not really a Home TV watcher.

"Well, that's what I'm doing. They have other shows that feature high-end real-estate agents. So my show is something in between. We only deal in mountain homes and only high-end buyers. It's a fantasy show. For people who want to get the fuck out of the city and live a different kind of life."

"People like you," I say.

He nods. "People like me."

"Interesting," I say.

"How so?" he asks.

"Well." I chuckle a little. "You're the kind of guy who shows up in a Balmain Paris t-shirt and Burberry sneakers when I say to come dressed in jeans and a t-shirt."

"Just because I'm a professional doesn't mean I don't enjoy the outdoors. This is Colorado, for fuck's sake."

"Look, I don't know why you're being combative with me over clothes. I told you a hundred times. It's—"

"Not personal," he says, interrupting me. "Yeah, I get it. So what should I wear, *boss?*"

I smile. Tightly. "I'm going to ignore your attitude and get back to the job at hand, OK? Let's see what you have."

He stands aside and does a little bow as he waves his hand to the closet.

Which is... a very. Nice. Closet.

"Wow," I say, easing past him. Our bodies touch, my stomach brushing across his as I maneuver my way inside, and for a second I get a whiff of his aftershave. It's a manly scent. Like sandalwood or something.

I stop, our bodies still touching, and glance up at him. When our eyes meet he squints at me.

I know we're thinking about it. Sex, that is. Because he's attractive and I'm looking pretty sexy right now in my boots and skirt. But neither of us says anything.

So I inhale deeply, push past him to break contact, and take in the closet.

Two whole separate spaces. All custom high-end dark-wood cabinetry in one room and a dressing room with mirrors and a low bench in the middle of the next.

There's racks of suit coats. Like two dozen button-down shirts that are starched to perfection, slacks hanging, and a whole wall of shoes lined up along the shelves. I'm pretty sure if I had a ruler with me, everything in here would be spaced two inches apart.

"Hey, what's this?" I say. My eyes are immediately drawn to a black leather jacket hanging up towards the back of a row of coats.

Law laughs. "Leftover from my teen years."

"You should wear this today," I say, grabbing the hanger and taking it down.

"Shit. I was fifteen when I last wore that jacket. Won't fit. I doubt I could even get my arms in the sleeves."

It's a biker jacket. The old kind with zippers and shit. Heavy, and worn, and there's two patches on the front. One is a black skull flanked on either side by ravens on a white background. The other is of a white motorcycle on a black background. Both of them say Shrike Bikes. When I turn it around to see the back, there's a large anarchy symbol centerpiece patch and nothing else.

"Were you in a…"

"Gang?" he says, finishing my sentence once again. "You could say that."

"Hmmm," I say, trying to picture him in that light, find it impossible and take off my little army jacket so I can slip the jacket on, because there's no way I can't. "Fits me," I say, smiling over at him.

He shrugs. "Take it with you if you want. I've got no use for it."

"Really?" I say, walking into the dressing room so I can see myself in the full-length mirror.

"Sure. That's what boyfriends do, right? Give their girl their jacket to wear."

I look at him and we both laugh.

Law isn't so bad, I decide. And this is a new light to see him in. Bad-boy teenager. "So what kind of gang were you in?"

"Fight club. MMA style though, not bare knuckles like the movie."

"Bad boy, huh? I might've gotten you all wrong, Law."

"People usually do." He sighs.

"You know," I say, "there's a Shrike Bikes showroom just down the road over in Five Points. I know a few of the guys over there. The owner has a little bar attached and he has all my beers on his taps. We made a little deal a few years ago. We could go over there and get you a new jacket."

"So we can match," he says, winking at me.

"Yeah," I say. "We could match. How perfect would that be?"

"Is that the kind of boyfriend you're looking for, Oaklee? Outlaw partners?"

I nod. "It is. That's the kind I need for this game, anyway."

So he shrugs. "Whatever you want, then."

"You could get a t-shirt too."

He makes a face. "You want me to be a walking billboard for Shrike Bikes?"

I wince. "Yeah, can't do that." I take another look at his closet. Desperate to find something suitable. "Do you have any concert shirts?"

There's a wall of dresser drawers in the small hallway between the two closet rooms. He turns to them, opens a drawer and starts looking.

"How about this?"

It's an old, old Johnny Cash shirt. Like so old, it's gray when it so clearly started out black. And there's little holes in the front near the collar. Like it's been washed so many times the fabric is falling apart. "Is that a leftover too?"

"Yeah." He nods. "I think I wore this every day for a month once when I was sixteen." And then he laughs. Like he's thinking back on those days and finds them better now that they were in the past.

"It's perfect. Do you have your leftover boots and some ripped jeans?"

"Nah," he says. "I mean, I got some Chucks I could wear. I never wore boots back then."

"Ripped jeans? Preferably faded?"

"Nope again. I'm a different guy now, Oaklee. I wear suits."

"Hmm," I say, disappointed. "Well, throw on the t-shirt, change the shoes, and we'll call it good."

"Where we going?" he asks, tossing the shirt to me—which I catch out of instinct—and then grabs the back of his shirt behind his neck and lifts it over his head.

I wasn't ready for that. In fact, the entire process—from the moment his fingertips find the shirt and lift up—my eyes track down to his stomach as he reveals it in what feels like slow motion, but clearly isn't because this is reality and not some movie.

He. Is. Cut.

Cut, bitches.

The lines… oh, the lines of his muscles. They are something to behold. Rolling hills and valleys of taut muscles. And the way they move as he pulls the shirt over his head is… is like a ballet. Something choreographed. Something beautiful.

"Oaklee?"

"Huh?" I say, forcing my eyes to meet his. Finding myself reluctant to do so.

"The shirt?" he says, hand outstretched.

I expect him to be smirking. Ya know, because he caught me looking. But he's not. He's just… unaware, I think. Unaware of the fact that the sight of his bare chest just made me breathless. Completely oblivious to my obvious ogling. Because he says, "So where are we going?" as he slips the Johnny Cash shirt over his head.

"A party," I say. "And not the garden kind you probably go to over in the Country Club neighborhood. The beer kind. Which is why I need you to look a certain way."

"Got it," he says once the shirt is on. And then he toes the stupid Burberry sneakers off his feet and turns to the wall of shoes to hunt down his Chucks.

They are old, and torn—like the shirt—and the laces are already tied just the way he likes them so they slip on easily. He smiles after that and walks into the dressing room, where I'm still standing wearing his aged leather jacket, to look at himself in the mirror. Like this shirt and these shoes are old friends he's happy to meet up with again.

"God, I feel so different."

"You look different too."

"Better?" he asks, reaching for a pair of sunglasses on a nearby counter and slipping them on.

I nod, unable to reconcile the two versions of this man. The preppy millionaire he was five minutes ago and the hot bad boy he just turned into before my eyes.

"So you don't have a boyfriend? Why?"

"What?"

"Well, you hired me to be your boyfriend, so clearly you don't have one. But you need one for this party?"

"Ye… sorta. I guess you could say that."

"Trying to make a guy jealous?"

"No." I shake my head.

"Liar," he says. And now he *is* smirking. "You like the bad boys, admit it. And for whatever reason this bad boy you've got your eye on isn't interested. So you need me to be his stand-in so he understands what he's missing."

"No," I say, more forcefully this time. "That's not it."

"Whatever," he says, walking out of the dressing room and then leaving me alone in the closet as he disappears into his apartment. "I'm gonna find out what you're up to sooner rather than later, ya know. There's no use lying to me."

I follow him out, find him in the kitchen jingling his keys in his hand. "Ready?"

I nod yes as he opens his apartment door and waves me through. Always the gentleman, this guy.

We're down in his underground garage heading towards his car when I realize I'm still wearing his jacket. "Oh, shit," I say, stopping. "I've got your jacket on."

"Keep it," he says, clicking the alarm on his key fob. The lights of a black BMW blink twice as the alarm chips off and he opens the passenger door for me.

He definitely has nice manners. If I ever meet his mother I will be sure to compliment her on his upbringing.

I slide in and he closes the door gently as I find and secure my seatbelt. But my eyes never stop tracking him as he walks in front of the car to get in on his side.

How did this man get so hot in the span of ten minutes?

Is that all it takes for me? A stupid t-shirt and some sunglasses?

No, Oaklee. You saw his body, dumbass. You're shallow as fuck.

"Now you really do have to tell me where we're going." He chuckles. "Otherwise we'll never get there."

"Golden," I say. "There's a bar up there having a beer-tasting party."

"Oh, cool. So you've got a few beers in there?"

"Nope," I say. "Not exactly."

CHAPTER SIX

LAWTON

As we get on the 6th Avenue Freeway towards Golden Oaklee is quiet. It was kinda fun back at my place. I saw her looking at me when I took my shirt off. I mean, I did that on purpose. I've been working out five days a week since I was seventeen so I've got a nice body. And I'm not being conceited either, it's just fucking nice.

People don't notice it much though. Probably because I wear suits. Like they know I'm big—a little over six-two and my shoulders are so wide every dress shirt in my closet was custom-made. T-shirt sleeves stretch around my biceps and the chest is always too tight. Which makes it look like I'm showing off, and I'm not. That's just how things fit me.

This shirt is especially tight. I mean, I've had it since I was a teenager and the only reason I didn't rip the fucker getting it over my head is because it was huge on me back then.

So people can't help but notice I'm big. But I just carry it well, I guess.

Yeah. She looked. Good and hard.

Which makes me smile. Then glance over at her to see if she's noticing my smile—but she isn't.

"What's on your mind?" I ask.

"Huh?"

"You're quiet all of a sudden. You're probably thinking 'He's out of my league,' right?"

"What?" This makes her laugh.

"Well, I'm kind of a catch."

"And I'm not?" She actually snorts.

"No, I didn't say that. You're a total catch. But I get it. I'm probably not the kind of guy you date, right?"

"What makes you say that?"

"Well, you're dressing me up like a… like a biker or something. Is that who you normally date? Is there some angry biker waiting for me at this bar in Golden?"

"No," she says, shaking her head. "I mean, yeah, I like the bad ones, I'll admit that. But that's not why we're going."

"So why are you doing this? You don't need to buy a boyfriend. You've got thousands of people coming through your brewery every week and chances are most of them are dudes who'd be more than a little bit excited about dating Oaklee Ryan. So what's really up with this game?"

She sighs but doesn't look at me. Just stares out the window as we make our way west up into the foothills.

I take the hint to change the subject. I'm a patient guy that way. I'm gonna find out what this is really about soon enough. So I say, "I looked at a place up in the Golden foothills. Was pretty nice too. Too nice, maybe."

This gets her attention. "How too nice?"

"You know. Fancy shit. The house I picked, the one I'm gonna make an offer on if I get this TV deal, is more… homey, I guess. It's not a log cabin but it's got raw edge beams, and the trim is that cool knotty pine. Not too knotty though," I explain. "Because there's a difference in quality."

She huffs a laugh through her nose and turns her body a little so she's facing me.

"This Golden house had a pool, and tennis courts with lights and shit. And it was in a gated community of sixty-acre ranches. The one I chose is only ten acres of land but it's all surrounded by forest. You can't see anyone. And this one is a little smaller. I just like the finishes better."

"It's funny," she says.

"What is?"

"Hearing a guy talk about home finishes."

"Real estate." I shrug. "It's my life."

"Does that… disappoint you?"

"I dunno. It's all cool, I guess. I mean, it certainly pays the bills. But I'm gonna be thirty this year and I'm starting to think about doing other things."

"Mid-life crisis at thirty, huh?"

"There's a part of me that thinks… I was never this guy, ya know? This ten-thousand-dollar suit guy. This thirty-thousand-dollar watch guy."

She looks at my watch, which she didn't balk at like she did my clothes, and gasps. "Are you serious about the watch?"

I shrug. "Every successful man needs to tell time, right? Why not do it in style?"

"So you are this guy then. The suit guy."

"Can't I have a nice watch and live up in the mountains?"

"You can do whatever you want, I guess."

"How about you? You always see yourself as Oaklee Ryan, brewmaster?"

"I grew up in that building," she says. "I knew how to brew beer long before I got my degree. Long before I was old enough to drink, that's for sure. And I like certain parts of it. I like finding new yeast and discovering new flavors.

57

I like thinking up new names and designing labels. That's all pretty fun."

"I looked you up online. You guys have won lots of awards."

She huffs again, only this time it's different. Cynicism, I think.

"But not since your father died," I add. Because it was left unsaid and we're both thinking it.

"That's... not my fault."

"What do ya mean?"

But she just draws in a long breath of air, lets it out slowly, and stays quiet.

"How come you don't have a beer at this tasting? At this bar we're going to?"

"I have my reasons."

"Is this part of the game?"

"Why do you ask so many questions? I'll let you know when you need to know, OK?"

"Fine with me," I say. "We can talk about the meeting next week then. How about that?"

"Cool. Tell me everything."

"So..." I begin. "You know how Home TV is built around personalities?"

"I guess," she says. "I'm not really one of those girls who lives for renovation shows."

"It's not a renovation show. It's a real-estate show, but only for the über-rich looking for mountain homes in Colorado. Like a second home in Vail or Aspen, get me?"

"I get you," she says, the tension easing out of her body as she relaxes against the door, facing me again.

"So I've been negotiating this deal for like a year now and we're finally in the final pitching stage. I haven't met anyone yet so they're flying to Colorado for the tour, right?

I take them around, show them my idea, give them a taste of what I'm selling, convince them I'm a guy people want to see on TV and all that good shit. But Jordan—our sex-game mutual friend—mentioned that they like partnerships and I don't have that. My business partner is antisocial. He's refusing to do this with me even though he'd be perfect. So Jordan mentioned you as a prospect. We could be partners. And to be honest, you're kinda perfect, Oaklee. Just the way you are. Like… this game with you is like luck smacking me in the face. You've got everything these people are looking for. You're pretty," I say, holding up a finger. "Smart." Holding up another. "And successful." Ticking off number three. "But not just successful. Lots of people are successful, ya know. You're like *creatively* successful."

"So I complete you." She laughs. "Is that what you're saying?"

"Yeah." I laugh back. "Yeah. That's what I'm saying. You complete me. Just the way you are. Like… I can't think of a single thing I'd change about you going into that meeting. Just be you, man. We got this. We totally got this."

"Do I have to be on TV with you?" She wrinkles her nose at this.

"Probably. I mean, this is a real business deal, Oaks." I don't know where that nickname just came from, but I like it. It takes her by surprise too, because I think she's blushing. "You have so much… color to you. They're gonna want you. Like they're gonna see you and think, *OK, she's nice to look at.* But then they're gonna learn about you and think, *We need this girl now.* Because you're just… interesting."

"Well." She chuckles. "I've been called a lot of things and interesting has never been in the top ten."

"What's in the top ten then?"

"Um... well, number one is crazy. Rude comes in a close second. Flamboyant, loud, pompous, dramatic, vulgar, arrogant, tacky, and ruthless rounds out the list."

I smile. "I haven't seen any of that yet. Maybe a little"—I make that gesture with the tips of my thumb and forefinger about half an inch apart—"flamboyant."

"That's because I need you. And you don't know me yet."

"Nah," I say.

"Just wait."

"Is that a warning?"

She nods. But her body has shifted again, her back slightly towards me, her face pointed at the window like the drive into downtown Golden is the most interesting thing ever.

"There," she says, pointing to a bar on Washington Avenue. "That's where we're going. The Opera House Tavern."

"Looks like it's closed," I say, passing it by to find parking.

"It's a private party for local brewmasters. Everyone who is anyone in Colorado brewing comes to this stupid party. I thought I'd have to cancel this year since Jordan was so slow at finding me what I needed. But then you showed up."

"Like Prince fucking Charming," I mutter under my breath.

I find parking a couple streets over and we get out. Golden is nice. Still small enough to feel like a neighborhood, but bustling with students from the School of Mines and those weird river people who think kayaking on Clear Creek is fun. It has an underground feeling of cool, like Boulder does, but without the drug culture.

Plus, the entire town smells like hops right now because the Coors Brewery is just a few blocks over. So hey, if you're gonna throw a party for Colorado brewmasters, this would be the place, right?

We walk down the street back towards Washington in silence. I'm consumed with thoughts of my shoes. The Chucks feel good. Maybe even great. But they feel odd. Make *me* feel odd. It's been a long time since I wore them. I should've thrown them away a decade ago but like the leather jacket Oaklee's wearing right now—I couldn't. They feel like a connection to my past. They feel like that's all I have left of my youth. Of the guy I used to be. The me who disappeared years ago and never came back.

Which is dumb. I'm still in my youth. I'm only thirty. Not even thirty. Not till summer. But Oaklee kinda hit home when she asked me if I was having a mid-life crisis.

It *feels* like a mid-life crisis.

"OK," Oaklee says, bringing me back to the present. "When we get in there, you're my boyfriend."

I try not to laugh, but I can't help it. "Yeah. I mean that's why you hired me."

"I didn't hire you," she says. "I bought you."

I don't even bother to be annoyed at that. She's in a mood and it's got nothing to do with me. It's this party or whatever it is. These people, probably. "So what do you want me to do? Public displays of affection and stuff like that? Brag about our fantasy sex life? Be an asshole and tell them all how much money I made last year?"

She stops walking and turns to me. "Be jealous."

"Of what?"

61

"Me!" She laughs. "What else?"

"What do you mean exactly?"

"Just… you know. Be a jealous asshole. Like glare at all the men and smack me on the ass if I'm talking to one of them." She bites her lip and looks up at the sky. Like she's thinking hard.

"Oh. My. God. I was right. You're here to make a guy jealous."

"No," she says. "No, that's not it. Just… I don't have time to tell the whole story and you wouldn't believe me anyway, so just go in there and act like an asshole. Oh!" she suddenly says. Like that idea she was looking skyward for suddenly popped into her head. "I know what you can do. Mansplain everything."

"Mansplain?"

"Yeah, you know. When men make women feel stupid by trying to explain something. Like… OK, you're in real estate. The way you assumed I didn't understand property values. That's mansplaining."

I point at her. "I didn't do that. And I know what mansplaining is. Just… what am I supposed to mansplain about?"

She looks me up and down. Smiles. And says, "How about fitness? Jordan was right. You are very fit." She lifts her eyebrows up as she says the word.

"Are there gonna be a lot of women in there?" I ask. "Like who am I directing this behavior towards? These guys bringing their girlfriends?"

She huffs. It's sorta cute the way I exasperate her. "Love that you just assume everyone in there is a dude." She rolls her eyes. "And no. Do not insult their girlfriends."

I laugh. "So they are all men?"

"Obviously I'm not a man."

"Obviously you're not my target."

"There's only one other woman brewmaster in Colorado." She makes a face. "Hanna Harlow. Do that to her. And," she says, like this is another great idea she just thought of, "smack her on the ass too."

"What? No. I'm not smacking anyone on the ass, Oaklee."

"Just do it!" she says. "I paid a lot of money for this opportunity, Law. You need to do what I say."

I have a childish urge to tell her she's not the boss of me. But she kinda is. And she did pay a lot of money to have me hang with her for two weeks. So I say, "If the opportunity to smack her ass comes up, I'll do it. But I'm not going in there with that as my goal. Give me something else here. I have no idea what we're doing."

"Just flirt with her, OK?"

"Her? I thought I was *your* boyfriend."

"You are. Just trust me."

And with that she turns and walks towards the door, waiting for me to open it for her.

I follow her, my hand on the door handle to pull it open. But then I stop and clarify because this makes no sense. "So I'm supposed to act like your jealous boyfriend, mansplain biceps curls to this Hanna chick, and then be a douche and hit on her?"

"Exactly."

But there's no more time for talking because she places her hand over mine and pulls the door open.

Inside it's dark and loud. Not with music, though there is some music playing on an old jukebox as we pass through the small lobby, but with gregarious conversation. Lots of men holding mugs, excitedly chatting with one another. All of them sporting beards. Most of them wearing tight jeans. A few showing off tattoos. All of them hipsters.

Hipsters, for fuck's sake. I should've known this. Probably did know this unconsciously. But it never occurred to me how much I'd stand out in this crowd.

I am not a hipster. This Johnny Cash t-shirt and these old-school black Chucks can't hide that fact.

As soon as people notice us there's a chorus of "Oaklee!" being shouted out from all corners of the room. She's very popular, I guess. Of course, if the entire craft beer movement in Colorado has just two female brewmasters, that's not surprising.

She starts introducing me to them. There's a Rosco, a Duke, a Cormac, an Ace, a Beckett, a Bear, and a Jack.

I feel like any minute now we're all gonna break out into song. Start singing *Sugar Boats* by Modest Mouse and then talk about Whole Foods and our cool vinyl collections as we complain about people who drive cars.

Until I realize Law is kinda hipster too.

Fuck.

Their girlfriends are called Beatrix, Magnolia, Tallulah, May, Piper, Frankie, and Juniper.

Oaklee fits right in there as well.

Jesus. We're a hipster couple. I suddenly feel the need to grow a beard and buy some pot.

When I notice the guy named Rosco is wearing some old-school Chucks I feel a little better. But just a little. Because everyone else is wearing chukkas or boat shoes, or old-school Adidas, and I'm left wishing for my Burberry house-check sneakers. Because even though Rosco and I are wearing the same thing on our feet—

that's where the similarities stop. Because he's wearing Bermuda shorts with a button-down Hawaiian shirt.

These are not my people.

And it's very obvious because every guy in here is side-eyeing me with suspicion.

The girls though… they're all over me. And Oaklee. They crowd around her. In fact everyone crowds around her. She is definitely well regarded in this group because from the moment we walked in she commands the entire room with her presence alone.

Everyone has something to say to her. All of them have questions like, "Where have you been?" And, "Why didn't you come to our barista jam last weekend?" And then, of course, "Who is this?"

Which refers to me.

But that's when the door opens again—light forcing its way into the dark room, highlighting streams of dust in the sunbeam.

And now the chorus yells, "Hanna!"

And the whole thing starts all over again.

Oaklee seems to fade to the back of the room. Almost unconsciously. Like she's a wolf and this Hanna chick is a baby goat she wants to kill and eat for dinner.

I look back and forth between them, trying to figure out the dynamic. And just as I'm about to decide they're enemies, Hanna sees her and shouts, "Oaklee!" as she pushes her way through the crowd and hugs her hard. Almost spinning her around with her enthusiasm.

"Frenemies," I mumble under my breath.

"Law!" Oaklee yells from her corner. Which has now been invaded by every female here because it's obvious that Oaklee and Hanna are the ringleaders in this girl pack.

Except—girl packs never have two leaders. Even I know that.

"Where did you get this jacket?" the girl called Juniper exclaims, fingering the aged leather of Oaklee's sleeve.

This brightens Oaklee up as I cautiously approach them. "This masterpiece of fashion belongs to my new boyfriend Lawton Ayers." She hooks her arm in mine and pulls me close. "He wore it as a teenager and kept it for the memories. But it doesn't fit him anymore—as you can tell." She laughs heartily at that. "Because he's built like a lumberjack now."

I raise my eyebrows at her for that comparison. Lumberjack and Lawton Ayers have nothing in common. But it's hipster speak for cool, right? So I go along. "I gave it to Oaklee because it's a precious piece of my past and deserves a good home. I know she'll love it as much as I used to." It's stupid, but it's full of feelings and these chicks dig guys with feelings.

The girls all go, "Aww," and take sips of their beer as they bat their eyelashes at me.

"So where did you two meet?" Hanna asks. Oddly, as suspicious of me as the men are.

And I realize—I have no idea what to say. Luckily Oaklee starts talking and diverts all the expectant looks from me to her.

"We were kayaking down Clear Creek—not together, mind you." Oaklee laughs. "And I got stuck in a tangle of branches that must've gotten caught on some rocks after a thunderstorm." She nuzzles her face into my chest and sighs. "He saved me."

"Aww," they all say again.

Except Hanna. She actually scowls. What is this chick's deal?

"And since then we've been inseparable."

"We're probably in love," I add. Because every face turns to me like I'm supposed to say something like that.

This time they don't say, "Aww." They just look at me. Confused.

"He means… we're married to ourselves, of course. But we might shack up in the future."

"Ahhhh!" They all laugh. "Of course."

Of course? I'm so not cool anymore. Who the fuck marries themselves? Like… was that just an expression? Or do people really do that?

"So what do you do, Law?" Hanna asks.

Ah. Finally. I'm on task. "Real estate," I say. "High-end real estate. That means I only deal with millionaires. I only sell in the trendiest neighborhoods and everyone has pre-approval for a jumbo loan before I take their calls."

Mansplaining and monetary self-righteousness in three succinct sentences. Exceptionally douchebag, if I do say so myself.

Everyone makes a face. Even that guy named Jack, who has sidled over next to his girl, Beatrix.

I just smile at him and say, "What's your deal, Jack? You own a brewhouse like Oaklee here?"

Beatrix, ever the supportive girlfriend, rubs his arm as he glares at me and says, "I homebrew, bro. Run a monthly club for insiders only."

"Ah," I say, laughing. "I get it. Everyone has to start somewhere."

"Yeah," Hanna says. "We all bootstrapped our way up to this level. Not like Oaklee, who was born into it."

I look at Oaklee, because that was a not-so-thinly veiled insult. Like she got her success handed to her.

But she just smiles and says, "Cheers to bootstrappers! Now where's my beer so we can toast each other properly?"

Oh, good. Beer. I need one because the social and cultural expectations in this room are stressing me out.

"Beer! Beer! Beer!" the guys all start chanting. And then the one called Bear—who kinda looks like one if you ask me—is standing on the bar, clapping his hands until they all quiet down.

"We're here today," Bear yells, "to celebrate the best of Colorado brews. Congrats to this year's winners. Jack and his Black Label Stout took first place in the Breckenridge Beer Festival. Congrats, Jack!"

Jack takes a bow and gloats at me. Like this just proves his worth and my comment was stupid, just like my designer Joe Jeans.

"Second place," Bear continues, "goes to Ace and his Gold Digger IPA! Took first place in the Fort Collins Fat Tire Fest!"

Ace whoops for himself and does a fist pump.

And then Bear is yelling again. "And first place, for the third year in a row, goes to Hanna and her Buffalo Brews Buffed Up brew, which took first place in the Brews of Colorado last week!"

Everyone goes crazy for this. Whistling and shouting. Bear even jumps down from the bar to swing her around as he hugs her.

I glance over at Oaklee, who is clapping politely, but her smile is forced.

Yup. These two definitely have history.

But is it jealousy? Because Hanna is the star now, not Oaklee?

"And now for the beer!"

Four of the girls appear with flight trays of glasses filled with what I presume to be this year's winning brews. Each are set up on the bar, one for everyone, and Oaklee grabs my arm and drags me down to the end of the bar where we take up two barstools and look at the tray of glasses in front of us while everyone else finds their own place at the bar, or the tables, and gets down to business.

"You OK?" I ask.

"Yup," she says, jutting her chin to the beer glasses. "Try them. I can't wait to see what you think."

"OK," I say, picking up the first one. It's in a glass that says Black Label Stout, so I can only assume this is Jack's. I sip it, make a face because it's not what I like at all, then set it down. "It's good, I guess. But I like your Mountain Mud better."

Oaklee smiles, then picks up the next beer and hands it to me. "Try this one."

It's Ace's Gold Digger IPA. Which I know I'm going to love before I even take a sip.

"Yup," I say. "That's good."

"Yes, he deserves first place if you ask me. Now this one," she says, handing me Hanna's Buffed Up.

I take a sip and nod. "Yeah, I love it. Tastes like…" But then I stop. Take another sip. Then another, just to make sure. I look at her. She's frowning. In fact, her eyes are very sad all of a sudden. And not because she didn't win this stupid contest either.

She's frowning because…

"This is Bucked Up," I say.

She nods. Slowly. Silently.

"She stole your beer recipe and has been passing it off as hers?"

Another nod from Oaklee. Then she whispers, "She stole my recipe. And this isn't the only one, Law. This is why I need you."

CHAPTER SEVEN

OAKLEE

Everything after that becomes a blur. We stay for a while. A long while. And I get drunk. Because what else can I do at this point? What?

Hanna Harlow was my freshman dorm roommate up at Colorado State. We were both seventeen because our birthdays are in October. We were both microbiology majors—me for the beer, of course. Her for the good of mankind. The CDC is in Fort Collins. On the western campus of CSU, in fact. And that's where she wanted to work. Her dream, before she met me, was to eradicate malaria worldwide.

At least that's what she said.

We were inseparable that first year of college. In fact, we were so tight, so engrained in each other's lives, when we were allowed to move out of the dorm in sophomore year we got a house together.

Of course together really meant my dad paid for it because Hanna said she had no family. Like none. She told me she was on scholarship. A social worker had helped her navigate her way through system while she was in foster care as a kid. Nurtured her. Hounded her when necessary. But that social worker had died just a week before she started school and so poor, poor Hanna was all alone now. All she had was me.

I want to gag just thinking back on it. How stupid I was. How trusting and naive I was. And all the ways she would fuck me over by the time we graduated.

She started stealing my notes first. She struggled in school. In almost every class and especially calculus and microbiology.

I caught her stealing my Calc III notes in senior year. And you might say, *What's the big deal? They're just notes, right?*

But my notes aren't just notes. I am meticulous. I am methodical. I am an expert notetaker. I had dozens of people in Calc II begging to buy a copy of my notes in junior year and I always said no.

I gave them copies for free.

Because I am generous, and trusting, and stupid.

So again. What's the big deal if Hanna took them? I would've given them to her anyway, right?

But isn't that the point? Isn't it? That she felt the need to go behind my back? She went into my room, rifled through my backpack, and took them like they belonged to her.

And they didn't. They were mine.

It was a red flag I should've heeded. A big, fat, flashing neon sign telling me to take a second look at this Hanna girl. And her stupid story of having no family. Which, by the way, wasn't true. But I didn't find that out until senior year when her family—all six of them—showed up for graduation.

I found out later that her parents were farmers out near Sterling. Not huge ones, mind you. Not the kind who make several million dollars a season. But still. They were well off enough to pay her tuition because, yes, that's right. She lied about the scholarship too.

She was no rags-to-riches story. She was no bootstrapper. She came from an upper-middle-class farm family that looked very proud, and very nice, when I finally met them and realized she was a sociopath.

By that time I'd been done with her for a while. We had separate apartments before junior year was over. She was rooming with four other girls in a house on the west side of Shields Street and I was in a condo over the downtown tattoo shop. And boy, did she rub that condo in my face every chance she got.

"Must be nice to have your daddy pay for everything," she sneered when I threw a party and she invited herself over with the new group of friends I'd made since our falling out.

As if.

But I didn't know it then. I didn't realize how much she had lied until school was over. And by that time who could I tell? Everyone was on their way out of town. Back to their homes or striking out on their own.

I went home to Denver that same night. My dad showed up with a bunch of guys from the brewery. They packed me up while I was receiving my diploma, and moved me back to Bronco Brews.

I wrote her off as an unfortunate associate that I'd probably never see again, started working on my masters degree at the CU Health Science Center, and for three blissful years she was nothing but a bad memory.

Then my dad died and she came back.

While I was dealing with the business of his death and generally picking up all the pieces and putting them back together in a new way as I tried to figure out how to move forward—truly alone for the first time in my life—she was making friends with all the other craft brewmasters. And that year—the year my father died—was the first year in eight decades that Bronco Brews didn't enter a single beer festival.

Well... we did. I know that now. It just wasn't under our name. It was under *hers*.

She started stealing our recipes before my dad's body was even cold.

She started with an old brew we had discontinued. So even though I knew that was our recipe, there was nothing I could do. There wasn't even a way to prove it.

But this year she bucked up. Big time.

"I don't get it," Law says. We're driving down the Sixth Avenue freeway towards downtown. I'm good and buzzed too. I drank way too many Gold Diggers this afternoon.

"What don't you get?" I ask, getting a little dizzy as I look out the window and watch the scenery whiz by. He's been quiet this whole time I've been telling him the story.

"Like her audacity, for one. How could she think that no one would notice?"

I huff out a laugh. "Did anyone notice today?"

"But why *didn't* they notice? How could they not notice? I noticed, for fuck's sake, and I'm not even in the business."

"You noticed because you were drinking it last night."

"But they're professionals. It's their job to notice."

"Bucked Up was new thirty years ago. It's the first big beer we ever made. It won all kinds of awards back then, but we don't enter it in festival contests anymore. Why would we? We develop new brews every year. It's already had its day."

He just shakes his head. "Well, I don't think she likes me. This whole plan of yours isn't going to work. She didn't even look at me this afternoon. In fact, she went out of her way to avoid me. I tried to mansplain my workout at the gym and she scoffed."

"Yeah, because I was there. She saw you. You practically declared your love for me. I'm wearing your fucking jacket. It's a junior-high love story as far as I'm concerned and she's going to react appropriately. Believe me, you're going to bump into her in a few days. She'll appear out of nowhere and be all friendly and probably hands-y too. She didn't just steal my notes, she stole at least three of my boyfriends back in college. And she totally copied my senior thesis."

"What do you mean?"

"Like stole it, Law. She found out what my topic was and did hers on the same thing. Then she asked to present first in class so it looked like I stole it from her."

"And people fell for that?"

"Well, she got an A and I got a B+. So I guess they did."

"Maybe she just did better work?"

"The fuck?"

"I'm playing devil's advocate, Oaklee. Don't get mad at me. I'm on your side."

"She's going to make a move on you, just watch."

But he's shaking his head. "I don't think so. I'm not her type."

"You are her type. Her type is my type, OK? So you *are* her type."

He looks at me and smiles. "I'm not your type either."

I huff out a long breath of air because he's right. I don't date real-estate guys. I don't really date, but when I do, I date... bad boys. "Tomorrow we're going down to that Shrike Bikes showroom and dressing you up like a biker so when she finally does make her move, she'll see what she's missing out on."

"So that's your type, huh? Biker?"

"Don't judge me."

"I'm not judging you. I'm just asking."

"Why do you think I don't date? It's because no matter who I go out with, she finds out and steals him away."

"She didn't come on to me today."

"No, of course not. But she will. And even if you think you like her, and it's your job to seduce her—don't fall for it. She just wants what I have. She doesn't want you."

"You realize that's a little bit—"

"Paranoid?" I laugh. "Just wait." I turn my back to him and cross my legs, swinging my foot in irritation. "I'm not paranoid. This has been going on since freshman year. I know her better than anyone. She's fixated on me. On my success, or my luck, or my family, or whatever. She takes what I have, not because she wants it, but because she doesn't want *me* to have it. It's that simple."

"So that's your end game? Get her to fall for me. Then what?"

"The Capitol Hill Beer Fest is next Sunday. You can enter a beer for consideration up until the night before because the tasting is all done live in front of a crowd. So I'm going to enter Bucked Up and see what happens when the tasters all have to sample two of the very same beer. Because I already know she's entered Buffed Up as well."

He scratches his neck, like he's thinking about this. "Is that the only entry you have?"

"No." I sigh. "Assassin Sour Saison is my grand reserve special edition beer this year. That's my main entry. But there's no way she's brewed a saison. She doesn't have the talent to come up with a sour recipe, number one. And she's her only brewmaster. Buffalo Brews is small. She has a very small bar up in Boulder and doesn't employ an entire department for research and development like I do. Oh, and did I mention the name of her label? Buffalo Brews." I huff again. "Do you see how she stole my name too?"

"No," he says, getting off Sixth and heading north on I-25. "You're called Bronco. She's called Buffalo."

"Yeah, but it's similar."

"Not really," he says.

Which just pisses me off. How does she do that? Get people to trust her? Give her the benefit of the doubt? Play devil's advocate?

"Well." I laugh. "There's no denying that Buffed Up is shamelessly copying Bucked Up. And do you know she tried to file a trademark for Buffed Up?"

"So?"

"So? It's blatant brand confusion! She knows people won't know the difference!"

He sighs. And it pisses me off because I'm right, goddammit! I'm not crazy!

"Anyway," I say, brushing off my anger and irritation. "There's no way she's gonna enter a sour saison this year. Even if she knew I was brewing one, she can't replicate it. It's a long, long process. And I've had that recipe hidden in my apartment since I came up with it. I brewed it up myself. I've had those tanks and yeast under lock and key for the past three years as it aged. I have personally overseen the entire process—from yeast incubation to bottling. You're the only one who has even seen the label. She didn't steal that one."

"Which is why I only did the blind taste test on three beers last night, not four."

"Exactly. She doesn't have it. And she doesn't know I have it either."

At least I tell myself that. I need to believe it. Because if Hanna Harlow got her hands on my sour saison recipe I might fucking kill her. Like for real blow her fucking brains out.

"Sometimes I think she knew about me, ya know?"

"No," Law says. "What do ya mean?"

"Like... she went to CSU because I was going to CSU. She knew about me. Somehow. And planned all this."

"Oaklee," he says through a laugh. "That's not paranoid, that's crazy. How would she know about you?"

"I'm the heir to Bronco Brews!"

"Yeah, but so what? I mean, why the hell would she fixate on *you*?"

"I dunno. But it was all perfectly laid out. The roommate thing. And why would she be a microbiology major? She sucked at it. And I could always tell she was never really interested. She only passed microbial genetics because she cheated off me on the final."

"Maybe she really did want to save the world from malaria?" he says.

"I'm not fucking crazy, OK?"

"Whatever," he says, getting off the freeway at Speer and heading into LoDo. "You bought me for two weeks and I need you for the Home TV show thing. So I'll do whatever you want. Even lure your archnemesis into a fake boyfriend experience if that's what's gonna make you happy. But it's kind of a waste of seventy thousand dollars if you ask me."

"Well, I didn't ask you. And I'm not crazy. She's obsessed with me."

He just smiles and stays quiet. Which means he totally thinks I'm crazy.

"You know, this is why I never brought it up to the guys back there at the Opera House. They'd act the same way you are."

"I'm not acting any way, OK? I'm just—"

"Playing devil's advocate, I get it. But you don't believe me, do you?"

He shrugs as he pulls into his parking garage. "I think this girl gets under your skin. I think you lost your dad a few years ago and you're still recovering. She's a good scapegoat. Maybe even a worthy adversary. And it's possible that you're just off your game right now and need an excuse. Something more than you're just... sad. Ya know?"

He looks at me and turns off the car. We sit there in the dark silence of the underground parking garage just staring at each other.

"Fuck you," I say.

"No, *buck you*, Oaklee."

And I can't help it. I laugh.

"You're drunk. I'm gonna walk you home." He gets out of the car, walks around to my side, and opens my door, leaning over me to unbuckle my seat belt. "Come on," he says, extending his hand.

I take it and let him pull me out of the car, then hold his arm to steady myself as we walk down the alley towards my building.

"She's—"

"Stop," he says, cutting me off. "Just forget about her. You've got your stupid sour beer to show her who's boss at that beer fest. Just let it go."

79

"I'm not letting it go. And you're not either. This is your job, Law. You're going to seduce her and find out if she really did steal my Bucked Up recipe."

"How the fuck am I supposed to do that?"

"Make her fall for you, of course. Then pump her for information."

"You do realize that if she is the psycho you claim her to be, she's gonna be on to me, right?"

"She's got one goal. Be me. So she won't be thinking about beer when she's with you. You're going to make sure of that. Tomorrow we're going over to Shrike Bikes and turning you into my kind of guy."

"Whatever."

We walk into the Bronco Brews lobby, which is bustling with a gathering Friday-night crowd, and head straight to the elevators. "I can take it from here," I say, flashing my keycard at the elevator since it's locked up on the weekends.

"Shit," Law says as the doors open, and urges me forward. "What kind of boyfriend would I be if I didn't walk you up to your door?"

"Looking for a kiss goodnight, Mr. Ayers?"

He just smirks at me as the doors close.

A few seconds later they open again straight into my apartment and we both exit.

"I don't like this setup."

"What setup?" I ask, throwing my purse onto the kitchen counter and walking over to the couch to fall into the cushions.

He follows, sits down on the other end of the couch, and picks my feet up, placing them in his lap as he slips my shoes off and begins to massage. "That elevator that leads straight into your apartment. You do realize that once you sell the condos there's gonna be a shitload of strangers with access to it?"

"All the keycards will be coded."

"Not during business hours."

"God, that feels good." His foot massage is no joke.

"You need one of those accordion gates."

"I've looked into it," I say, closing my eyes to enjoy the way his fingertips are pressing into the aching soles of my feet. "And I probably will before the condos go up for sale."

"I know a guy who does them. I'll give him a call for you."

I open one bleary eye to smile at him. "Feeling protective all of a sudden?"

He shrugs, staring at me. "You're young. Pretty. And rich, Oaklee. And while I think your obsession with Hanna is just that—an obsession—you *are* a target. You should take personal security more seriously. Especially since you live up here all alone. Doesn't it freak you out?"

"Not until you put it like that." I laugh.

"Seriously, how big is this place?"

"Four thousand square feet. Give or take."

"Jesus," he says, looking around.

"But it's home," I say. "My dad and I have lived here since I was born. I renovated it, of course. But all the original stuff is still here. I can't leave. Even if I wanted to."

He nods his head and begins massaging my calf. Which elicits a more sensual sensation than the foot.

I just look at him for a little bit. The way he's concentrating on the massage. The shadow of stubble on his jaw. His broad shoulders and the way his muscles move in his upper arms as he works his magic on my tired leg.

I haven't had a massage in ages.

Or sex. I have not had sex in months and that last hookup barely counts. It was quick and anticlimactic. Literally. At least for me.

Maybe I should take advantage of the perks that come with the boyfriend experience after all?

I know I'm buzzed. Possibly near drunk, like he insinuated. Those Gold Diggers were over eight percent alcohol content and I'm pretty sure I drank a twelve-pack. But Lawton Ayers is goddamned handsome. Even if he's not *quite* my type.

"That feels good," I whisper.

He smiles at me, making me notice, for the first time, that he has a little dimple in his chin when he does that. "Yeah. I'm well known for my foot and leg massages. Practically famous."

Which gets me thinking. "So what's your deal? I mean, besides you're going through an early mid-life crisis and want to be a TV star?"

"Ah," he says, laughing a little. "That's a long story for another time."

"I mean, you don't have a girlfriend?"

"Nope," he says, shaking his head as he looks back down at my leg.

"Why not?"

"Why don't you have a boyfriend?"

I shrug "I'm too busy, I guess. To put in that kind of effort."

"Same," he says, looking at me for a moment, unleashing the dimple once again.

"So you just what? Hook up with people?"

"Is that what you do?"

"Occasionally."

"Same."

"Are you going all mysterious on me, Mr. Ayers?"

"I see where this is headed and I don't want it to get out of hand."

"What do you mean?" I chuckle.

"You're buzzed. You're angry at that Hanna chick. And I'm your hired stud for two weeks. So you're thinking… hey, why not fuck him?"

I tsk my tongue. But I don't deny it. Because I am buzzed, angry, and horny. "So you're gonna what? Deny me?"

"Are you asking?"

"Would you say no?"

"Probably not. I mean, you're kinda hot."

"Just kinda?" I say, winking.

"But I'd hate myself in the morning."

"Why?" Now I'm scowling.

"Because you're drunk, Oaklee. And it's not right."

"Ohhhh," I say, getting it. "You're one of those moral men who has trouble seeing the difference between opportunity and taking advantage."

"Are you coming on to me?" he asks.

I nod.

"So beer makes you conveniently forget that this game isn't about sex? That it's not even about you?"

"Well… you're touching me in a way that overrides all my sensibilities."

"Which is the perfect reason why I should get up and go home right now and let you sleep it off."

"So go," I say.

He just laughs.

83

"Or you could be a good boyfriend and put me to bed."

"Don't start something you can't finish. It's not fair."

"Fair?" I laugh loudly.

"Yeah. Because I'm a guy and you're likable. Also crazy. But in a fun way so far. And you're beautiful. Is that what you're waiting to hear? That I find you attractive?"

"More or less attractive than Hanna Harlow?"

"Jesus."

"Seriously."

"Well, the two of you look a lot alike, actually."

"I know! Right? She's even copied my hair! Did you know when I met her she had a pixie cut? And now it's long, and wavy, and wild just like mine!"

"I was joking, Oaks."

The nickname makes me smile. "My dad used to call me that."

"Sorry," he says, redirecting his concentration to the massage. Which feels way better than it should. Like… my whole body is vibrating. Tingles are climbing up my leg headed straight for my pussy.

When they get there it begins to throb.

He's right. I should stop this now.

But he called me Oaks. Like we're old friends. And he's here and there's no awkwardness like there usually is with a first date—even though this wasn't a date.

It sorta feels like a date.

God, Oaklee. Get your shit together.

So I try to concentrate on the conversation.

"No, I miss that nickname. And I do miss him, so you were right about that. Taking over the business was always my lot in life. But not this way, ya know?"

Now his smile is sad. And I don't want to feel sad. Sad is something I'm very familiar with. So I pull my legs up, get on my knees and crawl over to him. Sit in his lap and straddle his legs.

So much for getting my shit together.

"What are you doing?" he asks, staring up into my eyes.

"I'm not that drunk," I say, leaning in to kiss him.

He kisses back. No fight. No words. Just...

His tongue finds mine and they move together like we're old friends. Like this isn't our first kiss, even though it is. Like we've done this a thousand times before, even though we haven't.

"I lied," I say, whispering into his mouth.

"About what?" he whispers back.

"I bought the boyfriend experience for me."

He smiles and I love the way it feels against my lips.

"And you're perfect so far."

"Am I?"

"Mmmhmmm. You open doors. And tell me to wear my seatbelt. And walk me home."

"That's just the standard service, ma'am."

"Oh." It's my turn to smile against his lips now. "Well, I paid for the deluxe package. What's that include?"

"You tell me. What's your idea of the perfect boyfriend?"

I lean back, gripping the firm muscles of his shoulders, and think about this. He just gazes up at me with this stupid smile on his face.

Not stupid, like stupid. But stupid like cute.

Yes. Cute.

"Well," I say, taking him in. "The perfect boyfriend is always on your side, ya know? Even when you're being crazy."

He chuckles under his breath. But his eyes never leave mine. He just stares at me. "What else?"

"And," I say, biting my lip as I think, "he protects you."

"Like he gets you a security door for your elevator so no freaks can find their way up on accident."

I giggle and nod my head. "Kinda like that, yes."

"What else?"

"He remembers things."

"What kind of things? Like birthdays, and anniversaries, and Valentine's Day?"

"Pfft," I say. "No. That's the standard package." Which makes him smile. Big enough to really flash that chin dimple at me. "In the deluxe boyfriend package he remembers things like… how she enjoys cooking for him so he brings home fresh ingredients once a week."

He raises his eyebrows high on his forehead. "She enjoys cooking?"

I nod. "She does. And he enjoys eating it. Even if she does try some experimental dishes every once in a while. In fact, he searches for obscure recipes online and just brings the required groceries home every now and again to show his support."

"Ahh," he says, laughing. "Noted. What else?"

"He dresses up for Halloween."

"Hmmm," Law says. "Like matching costumes kinda dressing up?"

"Exactly," I say, forcing myself to keep a straight face.

"O-kay… is that it?"

"Nuh-uh," I say, shaking my head a little. "There's more."

He waits, but he must get my meaning when I don't answer—and I'm grinning like a dumbass at the thoughts running wild in my head. Because he says, "Right. He knows all her sweet spots that want to be massaged."

I laugh. I can't help it. "He does." And then I lean into his ear, my lips brushing against the stubbled skin of his jaw, and whisper, "He can make her come in seconds if he wants. Or he can draw it out of her slowly over an entire night."

"Which does she like better?" he whispers back.

"Depends on her mood. For instance, tonight... she's wound up tight and just needs a release. The perfect deluxe boyfriend would know that and act appropriately."

I lean back just as he opens his mouth to respond, and place my fingertips on his lips, saying, "Shhhhh."

He stares at me for seven long seconds. His eyes searching mine. Darting back and forth like he's waging some internal war with himself.

But then his hands find their way to the curve of my ass and I close my eyes and say, "You have great hands."

CHAPTER EIGHT

LAWTON

So this is what I'm thinking as all this is happening.

She's drunk.

She's hot.

But she's drunk.

But she's coming on to me.

But she's drunk.

But she paid for the boyfriend experience.

But she's...

Fuck it.

It goes exactly like that. I mean, I'm a dude. I can only wage a war with myself for so long, ya know? She's got her pussy positioned right over my cock. And because I'm just a dude, I'm actually getting hard from that alone. Add in the sexual innuendo and well... you gotta know when the battle is over and it's time to surrender.

So I let my hands slide down her body and cup her ass. This makes her move forward a little, pressing herself on my cock in a way that gets me from half mast to full sail.

The first kiss was pretty amazing. Her mouth is soft and her plump lips pressing against mine might be the most sensual thing I've experienced in a long time. Better than the feel of her rubbing on my cock. Better than the play happening between our tongues.

But the second kiss is even better. It's a little harder. Just a little desperation added in. I suddenly want to hold her everywhere at once. I want to cup her face, and her ass, and slip my hands between her legs because I know her pussy is as wet as her mouth right now.

I like the desperation. The hard, fast fuck is always a winner. But I feel a little guilty. Like I'm taking advantage of this day. Of this contract. Of her.

So I switch things up and bring my hands up to her neck, threading them into her long, wild mane of blonde waves, and hold her close as we kiss.

I like the slow and soft as well and that's what I'm gonna give her tonight.

I mean… fighting it is a lost cause. I'm already gone. The option of stopping is no longer on the table. So I'm gonna make it count. I'm going to pretend she's the only girl in the world. She's my vision of the perfect partner. We're a couple, and have been a couple since time began.

I'll make it perfect.

That's how I'll justify this. That's how I'll make it up to her for being a douchebag dude who can't control his primal urges.

"Oaklee," I say. Because I want her to know I'm with her. Her. Not anyone else. Just her.

"God," she says, whispering the word. "You're a lot hotter than you first appeared, Law."

"That's because you're drunk," I say, laughing as I swipe a piece of hair covering her eyes away and tuck it behind her ear.

"If you say so," she says, her hand grazing against my t-shirt as she reaches for my belt. When she gets a hold of it she looks down and stops to laugh. "Burberry. In house-check. I should've known."

"Matches my shoes," I mumble absently, still playing with her hair. It's soft. Both in texture and in waves. She'd be right at home on the banks of the river that run through the property I'm going to buy in Indian Hills. I can almost picture her there with me. Wearing some gauzy summer shirt and cut-off shorts that have all those white strings hanging off the jagged edges. Her shoulders bronzed from days in the sun. Laughing, of course. Because she has a great laugh. I haven't heard much of it, but what I have heard, I love.

Love. Jesus. Get a hold of yourself, Lawton. She hired you to be a fake boyfriend for her nemesis. She's not into you.

Right.

Except right now she is.

So again… fuck it. Because I don't want to say no. Even if I could, and I have decided I can't, I don't want to.

She's got the belt unbuckled and the button on my jeans popped. The zipper is down and her hand is pressed up against me, massaging my cock as I ponder this quick change of events.

I shouldn't think about it. I should just let all the rambling thoughts in my head go and concentrate on the here and now. Just enjoy it.

But I'm not that kind of guy. I'm not a go-with-the-flow person. At all. I was thinking about tomorrow yesterday and now it's completely different. Because tomorrow I'll wake up here, or alone in my own place, and I'll have to deal with the consequences. There's gonna be those awkward silences as we both remember what we did. There's gonna be some kind of wall between us now. Distance. Uncomfortable distance.

But she kisses me again. And even though I've felt two ways about her kisses already, it's different this time as well. It's not soft, it's not demanding, it's... a lead into something else.

The problem is I don't have a clue what that something else is and it's going to drive me crazy.

"You're driving me crazy," I say unexpectedly.

She scoots herself up closer to me so her breasts are pressing into my chest. Her hand is still between us, but she's lifting up her skirt and—I think—playing with herself.

"I'm driving me crazy too." She laughs.

"Are you sure—"

"Yes."

So I stand up, grabbing her ass to keep her body close, and she automatically wraps her legs around my middle. I want to take her upstairs but I don't really know where her bedroom is and looking for it would kill the mood. So I just reposition her on one of the long ends of the u-shaped couch and ease her back until her legs stop gripping my waist and she lets herself lie back.

I place one hand on each of her knees and go for it. Just open them up as she lifts her skirt out of the way and pulls her panties aside, and go for it.

I'm on my knees, my head positioned, my mouth salivating at the thought of licking her. She repositions so her back is pressed into the cushions and her legs are wide open, and one of her hands is on my head—not guiding me, exactly. But urging me.

I don't need the urging. My tongue flicks against her folds, making her moan and wiggle a little. And I take over the job of keeping her panties pushed aside so she is free to do whatever she wants with that hand.

She slides it along my neck, softly dragging her long fingernails across my skin, and these light, feather touches make my whole body prickle up with a chill of pleasure.

Both of my hands reach up and grab her breasts, squeezing them as I lick her, searching for the spot that will make her moan.

"He can make me come in seconds if he wants," she says. "Or he can drag it out of me slowly, over an entire night."

Her words about what makes a perfect boyfriend.

One hand releases her breast and slides down, brushing across her t-shirt bedazzled in gemstones until I have one finger pressing against the entrance of her pussy.

She's wet down there. Just like her mouth was wet when we kissed. And when I push the tip of my finger inside her just a few centimeters, just enough to part her folds of sweet-smelling flesh, she arches her back and begins to breathe heavy. Her chest rises and falls, the air spilling out of her mouth in ragged gasps, like I really could make her come in seconds.

But I don't want to.

I decide to drag it out slowly.

CHAPTER NINE

OAKLEE

My God, he feels good. His tongue does magical things to me. His finger is gentle as it probes my inner depths. Maybe too gentle. I can feel the climax just waiting. Just hanging out, sitting on the edge of a hundred-foot drop, waiting for him to push me off.

But he doesn't.

Oh, his tongue never stops and his finger keeps pressing. But he won't let it enter me deeply. His tongue always misses my clit, and I know—I just know—he's doing that on purpose. Lawton is a man who knows his way around a woman, I can tell. He knows exactly where my hot buttons are.

"More," I say. "I want more."

But he doesn't answer me. Doesn't stop what he's doing. Doesn't make even the slightest change in his movements.

It's torture with a side of bliss.

It's delightful suffering.

It's playful agony.

And I don't think I can take it. I don't think he's going for making me come in seconds and that's what I want right now. He's going to drag it out of me slowly just because he can.

"Lawton," I groan. "Come on…"

But he just keeps licking. Just keeps pressing. His tongue deliberately missing the one place I want it so desperately to touch. His finger just deep enough inside me so I know what he *could* do, always holding back and never giving me what he *should* do.

"You're teasing me."

Which makes him laugh. The slight puff of air that escapes his mouth is like a vibrator set on the slowest speed.

I grab his hair and press his face into me. I grind my hips, searching for a way to make him slip. Make him relent and give me what I need.

But he pulls back. Withdraws his finger.

I stare at him, aghast. "What are you doing?"

The mischievous smile should be enough, but he takes it one step further and confirms my suspicions. "Taking my time."

My breathing is heavy and quick, my mind spinning and a bit dizzy. My eyes want to close and I want him to go back to licking me, but he stands up.

"More," I say, whispering the words.

"Oh, you're gonna get more, Oaklee. Much more."

He kicks off his shoes and pulls his t-shirt over his head.

I watch, transfixed by his perfectly muscled chest. And then he drags his jeans down his legs, kicks them aside, and just… stands there.

Moonlight is shining through the windows of my penthouse. Illuminating him on one side, keeping him cast in shadow on the other.

He is Adonis. He is David. He is perfection.

His cock is long and hard, lying against his thigh. The tip round and the shaft fat. He is fully erect. Ready for me.

So why won't he just take me?

"Take me," I beg.

He just shakes his head no.

"What are you doing?" I ask.

He says nothing. Just sits down on the couch and pats his thigh. A come-hither gesture. A sit-on-my-lap invitation.

I don't even hesitate. Just stand up, walk the few steps that separate us, and sit down on his lap again, pressing my pussy against his cock to try to entice him into giving in.

"Whoa there, cowgirl," he says, his eyes still twinkling with mischief. "We're not quite ready for that yet."

How? I ask myself. How can he be so calm and in control and ready to go slow when all I want is for him to fuck me hard and make me come?

How could we be so different?

"Take off the jacket, please."

I huff out a laugh. But I have that thing off in two seconds.

"Good," he says, playing with my hair. "Now the shirt."

Now we're getting somewhere, I want to say back. But I don't. Because I don't think he wants me to be playful. I don't think he wants me to do anything but listen to him and do exactly what he says.

So I grab the hem of my t-shirt and lift it up over my head, my breasts rising as I do it. I toss it aside, expecting him to be looking at my breasts and the way they want to spill out of my sexy demi bra, but he's not. He's looking me in the eyes when I find his gaze.

"Take it off," he says.

My bra, obviously. So I reach around, unclasp the hooks, and the tension of the elastic eases, letting my breasts fall out of their tight constraint.

I feel like I can't breathe. He's watching me, still not looking at my breasts. But he's got a small smile creeping up his face. Like this is going exactly the way he planned.

I shrug out of the bra and let it fall to the floor, unconsciously pressing my breasts together with my upper arms.

My nipples are tight, the soft skin stretched as they peak up.

"Play with them, Oaklee," he says. "I want to watch you play with them."

Good God. I feel wetness pooling between my legs.

It's weird being controlled like this. Because even though he's telling me what he wants and what he wants me to do, I feel like I'm giving it up freely.

I play with them. They're not huge by any means. But they are ample. The size of small melons. I massage them with my palms, then tweak each nipple, pinching myself hard enough to make me wince.

How? How is he making me do this?

"Are you multi-orgasmic?" he asks, still not looking at my breasts, only my eyes.

I shrug. "I don't think so. I dunno. I've never had that kind of experience before. I've never had this kind of experience before."

"Do you want me to show you?" he asks.

"Show me?" I ask back.

"How to become multi-orgasmic?"

I nod. Because I would like that very much. So I say, "Yes. Show me how."

CHAPTER TEN

LAWTON

I say, "I'm going to rip your panties now," just as the ripping sound fills the room. She gasps, but I keep watching her eyes. "They were in my way," I add, by way of explanation.

"OK," she replies, two seconds too late to object.

"Now put me inside you."

I can almost hear her heartbeat as the words come out of my mouth. She lags two seconds behind again, my command running through her mind, searching for meaning.

The meaning comes later. There's no rush.

She must agree because she lifts up her hips, reaches for my cock, and wraps her hand around it. I watch her. My eyes never leave hers as she pumps it a few times, consumed by the urge to feel me.

"Stay focused, Oaklee," I say. A gentle reminder that she takes seriously because she draws in a deep breath and presses the tip of my cock up against her wet folds. "Now sink down. Put me fully inside you. And then hold still."

"You're trying to kill me, aren't you?"

I let myself laugh a little at that. "No," I say. "Not at all. I'm trying to make you feel what you deserve to feel when you give yourself to a man. That's all."

"That's all," she says. But not like a question. She swallows hard, places her hands on both of my shoulders, and sinks down just like I asked her to.

Her eyes close and this might be the best moment of the whole day. Watching her feel pleasure as she buries my cock inside her pussy.

When her thighs are flat against mine she opens her eyes again, staying still like I asked. "Now what?"

"Now play with your breasts again. And Oaklee?"

"Yes," she whispers.

"Enjoy it."

She lets out a long breath of air with her smile and says, "Oh, I will. Don't worry about that."

As she begins to massage her breasts once more I slip a hand underneath her flirty skirt and find her clit, my thumb skimming over it as she holds her breath and stops what she's doing.

"Don't stop," I say. "I'm showing you how it's done, remember?"

"Mmmhmm," she whimpers. "OK." And then resumes playing with her breasts.

"Harder," I say. Which she misinterprets and begins to rock her hips back and forth, so I grab a hold of her hip bone and still her as I say, "No, squeeze your tits harder, Oaklee. But stay still until I let you fuck me."

"Jesus, Lawton. What are you doing to me?" But she laughs, and I like the laugh, so I laugh too.

"Trust me. You're gonna thank me in a little bit." And then I get back to business. My thumb continues to stimulate her clit as I watch her squeeze her tits. She closes her eyes once again and I consider that a win. "Do you like it?" I ask. "Does it feel good?"

"Yes," she moans. "I like it very much."

"Then squeeze harder. Feel me, feel yourself, and when you're ready, come for me, Oaklee."

She goes still. Rigid, almost. And in seconds her mouth opens, her eyelids flutter, and her thighs tighten against my legs as she squeezes my cock with her pussy, spilling her release all down my shaft.

I stop rubbing her clit and let her enjoy it. Let the contractions pulsing against my cock slow down, then finally stop.

"I thought you'd last a little longer." I chuckle.

"Can't help it," she says. Her body melts. Practically collapses forward against my chest. Her heart thumping against mine, her breath slowing down, all the while my cock stays inside her, hard and ready for more.

"We're not done. Are you ready for more?"

"I think I might fall asleep." She says this lazily, her words slurring a little. But she's not drunk on alcohol. She's drunk on me.

"You won't fall asleep."

I grab her shoulders, gently push her backward until she's sitting on top of me again, and lift her head up with a finger under her chin. "Look at me," I say.

She opens her eyes and smiles.

"Now put your hands flat on my chest like this," I say, placing her palms down on each of my pecs. "And fuck me."

All her body weight is pushing down on my chest, her tits swaying as she begins to move. I grab them both, straighten her up so the inevitable arch in her back can form, and begin to squeeze her tits the way she just was a few moments ago.

I squeeze them hard. Full-handed one moment, then pinch her nipples the next.

"Go as fast or as slow as you like, Oaklee. Just feel us and forget the rest. Forget all about wanting to come

101

again. Forget about the doubts you have about doing that. Just feel me squeeze you, and fuck me."

Her skin prickles with a chill exactly the way mine did earlier.

And she does all that. She lets go. She gives in.

She starts moving her lower body. Starts drawing her hips up and down, coating my cock with her own climax, and all the while I'm squeezing her tits so hard, she should be screaming.

But she's not screaming. She's moaning. Her hands leave my chest and grab onto my shoulders as her spine buckles outward, then arches inward. This makes me slip just a little bit deeper inside her. Just enough for the tip of my cock to touch her A-spot.

Her body convulses and she gasps, almost as if surprised. Her soft moans become louder as I squeeze her tits harder and harder and harder still, until I'm sure she will have fingerprints on her skin in the morning.

She probably knows this too, but she doesn't care. The only thing she cares about is the way she suddenly feels.

And that's when she comes again.

This time she grits her teeth and closes her eyes tight. A look that lands somewhere between pain and pleasure.

I continue to fondle her breasts, softer now, because I want her to enjoy the aftereffects of her orgasm. But also so she can recover. Be ready for more.

Because there's more. Much more.

"Holy shit," she mumbles, dropping forward onto my chest. Her head resting on my shoulder. "Damn, Lawton. I've never come three times in a row before."

"Twice?" I laugh. "We're not done yet."

She lifts her head up a little so she can look at me. "Is it your turn now? Should I give back?"

Her wicked smile tells me exactly what she thinks "giving back" means. "I'll get there, don't worry. And while your offer is appreciated, my cock is very happy inside your pussy. Tonight is about you. Next time—if there is a next time—it can be about me if you want."

"If?" She chuckles.

I shrug. "Life doesn't come with a guarantee. I know that better than most."

"Hmmm," she says.

"But enough of the talk. Are you ready to go again?"

"Again." She says it almost like a question. "Three times. I dunno if that's possible."

"Oh, it is."

She looks at me, blushes a bright pink—which looks good on her bronze skin—and shrugs. "OK. But I'm warning you, the next time won't be that easy."

I stand up, taking her with me once again. And this is starting to feel like a familiar move between us, because her legs automatically wrap around my middle. Then I turn her around and place her on the couch. "Turn around," I say. "Put your hands right here." I pat the back of the couch. "And your knees right here." Indicating the cushion she's sitting on.

She smiles big. Blushing again.

I decide I like her. I think she's capable of a lot of things. Has a lot of ideas. Most of them probably borderline crazy because of this weird obsession she has with Hanna Harlow. But Oaklee Ryan is one of those fun girls. The kind who keep you on your toes. The kind who make bad decisions based on emotion. The kind who probably make very bad exes because they end up doing psycho things like showing up at your work and texting you forty-seven times in one hour.

But all that makes it exciting, right? And if we get this TV deal, who knows. Maybe we'll never be ex-anything. Maybe we'll be friends, or lovers, or business partners forever.

She maneuvers herself into the position I want, placing her hands on the back of the couch and her ass directly in front of me.

"Nice tattoo," I say, noticing it for the first time.

She looks at me over her shoulder and whispers, "Thank you."

Its lettering spans the entire space between her shoulder blades. Not big and gaudy, like a gang tattoo. But small and feminine in script handwriting.

I lean over to read it out loud. "'The world worships the original.' Who said that?"

"Ingrid Bergman," Oaklee says. "It's supposed to say, 'Be yourself. The world worships the original.' But I think that first part goes without saying, so I left it unsaid."

"Words to live by."

"As I do," she quips back, smiling at me.

I position myself close to her. Letting my cock slip between her ass cheeks as I move in a slow, back-and-forth motion.

"That feels nice," she whispers.

I say nothing. Just concentrate on what I'm doing. Which is trying to hit her clit with the tip of my cock with each small thrust forward.

When I succeed, she moans. Bowing her head to rest it on the soft, overstuffed cushion of her couch. I do it again, and again, and then on the third time, she arches her back, which relieves her of the stimulation.

"Something wrong?" I ask, not bothering to hide my smile.

"It's... intense."

"It's supposed to be."

"A part of me wants you to just fuck me hard. Just slam your cock inside me. I'd come that way, you know. I can tell. I can feel it building."

"And the other part?"

"The other part," she says, relaxing her back again so she can feel me against her clit, "the other part never wants *this* to stop."

"Well, you might have a problem then. Because I can't do both at once. So which do you want first?"

She huffs out a laugh. "You'll probably get three out of me, but not four. No way. After this I'm gonna fall asleep, despite all your best-laid plans."

This makes me chuckle. "Just answer the question, Oaklee."

"This," she says, turning her head so she can see me.

So I continue, and immediately I can see she's on the verge again. On the edge of release. So I ease up and deliberately hold back the next time I move forward.

"Come on," she whines. "You're teasing now."

"You wanted to know how to become multi-orgasmic. This is how it's done. It's a give-and-take. A this-and-that. Win some, lose some."

She shakes her head. "I already had two and I'm ready for number three. That's not multi-orgasmic enough for you?"

"That's a very sad result, Oaks. I'm aiming for six at least."

"Six?" She laughs. Louder this time. "Never going to happen."

"You will," I say. "Have a little faith." And then I pound her. Hard, just the way she asked for it. So hard her tits are bouncing. Slapping against each other just like my hips are slapping against her ass.

It only takes about a minute of that to have her wailing. It's a primal scream. Loud, and long as she moans out, "Fuck. Yes. Fuck. Yes. Fuck. Yes," to the rhythm of my thrusts.

And then... she. Goes. Silent. Biting her lip. Squinting her eyes closed. Bucking her back as one of her legs drops, her foot finding the floor to steady herself.

Her muscles begin to quiver as she comes. Her teeth chattering like she's been out in the cold. Her body a sweaty contradiction.

I let her collapse after that. Sit down next to her and let her curl up into me as her quaking muscles begin to relax and her heavy breathing begins to slow.

I play with her long, long hair. Hold a piece in my hand and use it like a feather. Dragging it up and down her spine to make her shiver. And say, "Let me know when you're ready for number four. I can do this all night."

CHAPTER ELEVEN

OAKLEE

I wake up to birds singing outside my window, and in that hazy state between sleep and waking, I have a dream about...

Sex.

Jesus Christ. I sit straight up in bed, my hair covering my face like a blanket. I swipe it away, making a peek hole to see through, and look over to the other side of the bed.

His side.

Which is empty.

As it should be, Oaklee, the inner voice says.

But there was definitely sex in this bed last night.

I flop back into the pillows, close my eyes, and think about it. How he made me come again, and again, and again. How I was so exhausted by the time we got to orgasm number seven my whole body was practically convulsing from the strain on my muscles. In fact, I feel sore. Not just my pussy. Like all over.

I was screaming. Which makes my face hot with embarrassment just thinking about it. I, Oaklee Ryan, am not a sexy screamer.

Until now.

He took dirty sex to a whole new level.

He. Is a freak. In bed.

Freak.

Uggggh. I flip the covers over my head and smile. Because it was fantastic. I feel like I never had sex before

Lawton Ayers took me last night. Like every other time was just pretend compared to what he did to me. How he made me feel.

I sigh, then throw the covers off and swing my feet out of bed. I look around, straining to hear if he's maybe in the bathroom or downstairs.

But it's just silence. Well, the sound of the city down below, and the birds, of course. There's like a bazillion sparrows and robins nesting on the roof up by the water tower. But I don't think Law is still here.

Some girls might feel sad about that. A one-night stand usually comes with lots of regrets the next day. Either that or the inevitable, *Will he call me again? Or won't he?*

I have none of those feelings. I only have... satisfaction.

Yes. I laugh, standing up to stretch. I only faintly remember him dressing me in this nightie last night before he fucked me one last time. And even though I look a mess when I glance over at the giant floor-to-ceiling framed mirror propped up on the wall near my closet, I *feel* beautiful.

I walk over to it and just stare at myself. At the peach-colored nightie with the white lace ruffle splitting the sheer fabric down the middle to reveal the lower cleavage of my breasts. The little matching panties. My long, bronze legs and my toned arms.

I picture him standing behind me. Maybe putting his arms around me as we stare back at ourselves through the mirror. Maybe he leans down and kisses me on the neck, his reflective eyes locked on mine.

We smile, I think.

Good God, Oaklee. Snap the fuck out of it. He's pretend.

But I sigh again anyway. I don't care. Last night was... wow.

I go downstairs, just to make sure he's gone, and even from the top of the stairs I see that he left a note on the kitchen island.

My stupid, silly heart begins to beat fast and my feet skip down the long flight of stairs and cross to the center where I pick the note up and read.

Oaks,

I imagine you're pretty hungover this morning.

Which makes me snort. Because while I do feel tired and my body is sore, none of that has anything to do with drinking beer yesterday. And for fuck's sake, beer is my life. I drink it every single day in the tasting room. A twelve-pack isn't enough to knock me down.

So I took the liberty of leaving you recovery instructions.

One—drink the bottle of coconut water immediately. It will hydrate you. It's filled with potassium, which you need after the workout I gave you last night.

Two—take the two ibuprofen.

Three—I found your home gym. So I've taken the liberty of putting together a hangover workout. Don't balk, either. This is proven to make you feel better after a hard night of drinking and sex.

I skim the workout, which consists of lots of sit-ups, a healthy dose of push-ups, and twenty minutes on the cycle, then go back to the letter.

Four—drink the second bottle of coconut water.

Five—take a long hot bath. There's a bubble bomb waiting for you tub-side. Nice assortment to choose from, by the way. I chose strawberry shortcake because… well, you're delicious and sweet.

Six—I couldn't help myself. I picked you an outfit from your closet. I feel it's only fair since you get to play dress-up with me.

Seven—Pick you up at one for shopping.

See you then,

The Boyfriend.

Oh. My. God. He's kind of adorable. In fact, I'm thinking he's way too good for that no-good Hanna bitch.

Maybe I should keep him for myself? I mean, I did buy him for two weeks. I could just pretend this is a game for her and make it mine, couldn't I?

I bite my lip as I think about this. I already broke my no-sex rule. He probably thinks I'm an easy slut.

No, he said I was sweet and delicious. That has to count for something. And while I don't have a great recollection of him getting off last night, I know he did.

I know he did.

Didn't he?

Shit. What if I passed out before he got his turn?

I chew on my lip as I think about that. And while I'm doing that, I hear my phone ding an incoming text from… somewhere.

I look around, find my purse on the side of the couch, and dig around inside to find my phone.

Unknown number: *Did you follow instructions?*

Me: *Who is this?*

Obviously it's Law, but I feel like being silly for some reason.

Unknown number: *Look out your window to the east and find out.*

I get up, walk over to the window, open the slider, and step outside.

Lawton Ayers is waving at me from his terrace looking hot as fuck in a pair of tan cargo shorts and nothing else.

"Hey!" he yells.

Which makes me giggle and walk over to the edge of my terrace to look down and see if anyone can hear him.

There's a few people gawking up at him from the alley, but fuck it. I yell back, "I have one question for you."

"Shoot, Oaklee."

Jesus. I laugh. Because shoot and Oaklee—that's kinda funny. "Did you…" But I can't bring myself to yell it across the city.

"Did I come?" he yells back.

I put a hand on my forehead and feel the heat creeping up my cheeks.

"Yes," he calls. "Twice."

I nod my head and smile. "Good."

"You look sexy in that, by the way. And I'm not trying to be a dick or anything, but if you're still wearing that nightie that means you didn't follow instructions."

"I was just about to," I yell.

"Hop to it, Oaks. It's already eleven thirty and I'll be there at one. On the dot." Then he waves at me and goes back inside his apartment, closing up his slider behind him.

Someone whistles at me from the alley below, so I back away and go inside, closing my slider behind me too.

I don't know what to think about this. I just twist the cap on the first bottle of coconut water and take a long gulp. Then I walk back over to the window and look out at his terrace, picturing that whole interaction in my head. Hell, who am I kidding? I'm reliving the whole goddamned night.

Freak. He is a freak in bed. Who'd have thought, right? This fancy-suit real-estate guy could rock my entire world. Seven. Times. In one night.

I absently walk back over to the kitchen island and pop the two ibuprofen in my mouth, then swallow them down with the coconut water and head to my gym. Because working out is a time to think for me.

I do the sit-ups on my giant ball because I like the support, then do half of the prescribed push-up count and get on the cycle.

It's only then that I realize the cycle is positioned so it looks out at his terrace. So I spend thirty whole minutes daydreaming like a schoolgirl about Lawton Ayers. Which is ten minutes more than his orders.

I drink the second bottle of coconut water even though I still feel full from the first one. I feel like he went to a lot of trouble coming up with this hangover cure that I didn't need, so I should honor that by following his instructions. And then I run the bath, drop the bubble bomb in, and know, with one hundred percent certainty, that every time I smell strawberries from this day forward, I will think of him.

The outfit he chose for me is... interesting.

Jeans, which I love. And they are old jeans with rips in all the right places. Worn thin and soft from years of washing and just a little bit loose.

An old brown leather belt that he must've chosen because the leather is worn and has lots of scuff marks on it. Like he knew this one was my favorite, and it is, so he was right.

A t-shirt that says, *Save water, drink beer*—which I forgot I even had—but was actually one I gave my dad for his fiftieth birthday back when I was a teenager. I found it when I cleaned out his room just before the renovation last year and couldn't bring myself to throw it away because he wore this thing at least once a week until he died.

Like Law's Johnny Cash shirt yesterday, it used to be black, but has since faded to light gray and all the hems have long ago given up and turned to nothing but frayed edges.

There's also a pair of boots sitting on top of the pile. My very first pair of Frye boots. Dark brown leather engineer boots with silver buckles near the ankles. They are quintessential biker. I hate to admit it, but Law was right. I'm not proud of it, but I like a bad boy, what can I say. And I attract them with the bad girl look.

He's got me pegged.

In fact it's like Lawton picked through all of the hundreds of items in my closet and found the four things that say the most about me.

How did he do that? How did he know?

I put it all on, tucking in the shirt to show off the belt, then pulling out a little so it flows over my hips in a few places. When I pull the boots on and look at myself in the mirror I feel young again.

I feel *free* for some reason.

So many things hadn't touched me yet back when I was a teenager. My father was still healthy and alive. The business was booming. Like totally going gangbusters. We'd just come up with Anarchy Orange IPA, which I totally had a hand in creating. And we were winning award after award in all the global beer festivals.

How did he know?

It was also before I met Hanna Harlow at college. Before she lied her way into my life and then promptly fucked me over. Before she stole my boyfriends, and my recipes, and my personality.

Before she stole my life.

I turn away from the mirror. Mostly because it's almost one o'clock and I want to be downstairs to let Lawton up when the girls buzz me from the lobby. But also because it makes me sad to think back on those days. It makes me realize how much I've lost these past few years. And it would be tolerable—I could deal with stupid Hanna—if my dad were still here. He'd take care of her. He'd make it all go away. He'd handle things like he always did, protecting me from all the nasty in the world.

But all that paradise is lost and there's no way I'll ever get it back.

I feel like... like I'm alone.

I know I'm not. I have a ton of friends. Acquaintances, at least. I have fifty-two employees and most of them like me. There are one or two old-timers in the brewery I bump heads with every once in a while because we have different ideas about what new brews we'll release each year. But they're still here. They don't quit on me. And I don't bulldoze over them. I listen and we fight it out and come up with a compromise.

And the waitresses all like me. I think. I mean, I can get a little crazy at times. I blow my top every now and then. But they don't quit either. Most of them stay. I mean, you can't expect a person to wait tables for their whole life. Turnover is expected. It's not like the brewmasters who have a career here.

The marketing department might hate me.

Thinking about them actually makes me smile. Because I am forever in their business. Always coming up with new ways to promote. They probably wish I'd be more hands-off, but I enjoy the marketing. And my ideas are good ones.

Mostly.

There was that time I insisted we have a custom Shrike Bike built with the Winter Park Wheat beer label painted on the tank. But I rode it in the Toy Run that year and then we auctioned it off for charity a few weeks later. So that was a hundred grand well-spent if you ask me. It got everyone excited, we made sure two hundred needy kids in Denver had a nice Christmas, and when it was all said and done, the whole thing was a tax writeoff.

Then there was the time I sponsored a wet jeans contest on the roof. There were like a dozen helicopters circling overhead for that. It was great publicity.

Every time I think about it I still have to laugh out loud. It was for the release of a seasonal summer IPA called Full Boner. But hey, if bars can have wet t-shirt contests for women to highlight their tits, then we can have a men's wet jeans contest to highlight their dicks.

Fair is fair.

The entire marketing department took a poll asking what my dad would think about that stunt. This was the first summer after he died. And "Rolling over in his grave" came out on top.

But I wrote in "Laugh like the Devil" as one of the choices and that one came in second.

He would've laughed. I know it.

I have lots of people around me and even though I drive them nuts ninety-five percent of the time, that other five percent is all love. They appreciate my crazy. They respect my talents as a brewmaster. They might not like my marketing ideas, but in the end, they have to admit, my reputation as a wild card intrigues people and gets them in the door.

But I still feel alone.

Especially now. With all this Hanna bullshit going on. I wish my dad were here. I really do. It would be nice to be taken care of again. It would be a relief to be second in command instead of captain of the ship.

"Well." I sigh, walking down the catwalk towards the stairs. "He's not here, Oaks. So you just have to deal with shit on your own."

I descend the stairs and just as I'm stepping onto the creaky hardwood floors the elevator opens and Lawton and another guy I don't know step out.

"How did you get up here?" I ask. But while those words are flowing past my lips, I notice what Law's wearing.

Brown slim-fit khaki pants, a light blue denim button-down with a white t-shirt underneath, and a pair of brown cap-toe oxfords with a lovely distressed-black patina on the leather.

I blink. Three times. Because even though this look really isn't one I typically go for in a man, he looks *hot*.

"Oaklee Ryan, meet Eduardo Montes de Oca. He's an elevator security specialist and he hacked your security in less than a minute."

Eduardo—who is tall, young, handsome, and built a lot like Lawton so I assume they must work out at the same gym—nods to me and says, "Your system sucks," in heavily accented Spanish.

"Oh," I say. "OK. Well, I guess we should fix that."

"Got it covered," Law says. "He's gonna take a look at everything while we have lunch up on your rooftop terrace." That's when I notice he's got a bag in his hand that says Capitol Hill Bagels on it. "Can he have your keycard so he can do a thorough evaluation?"

"Um… sure." I walk over to my purse on the couch, dig through it until I find the keycard, and hand it over.

"Gracias," Eduardo says. Then turns back to the elevator, gets inside, and disappears when the doors close.

"I told you it was horrible," Law says. "But he'll take care of it. Don't worry. By the end of the week that shit will be locked up tight. Now how do we get to the roof?"

I'm a little stunned. Not because it's presumptuous of Lawton to take it upon himself to deal with my lackadaisical elevator security, but because… his whole persona is one of power. He took away my ability to make this decision on my own.

He… handled things.

Just what I asked for before he appeared.

And it feels good.

CHAPTER TWELVE

LAWTON

She points to the stairs and says, "Up there," to indicate how we get to the rooftop terrace. So I follow her, smiling the entire time because she's wearing the outfit I chose.

Last night was... wow. So many words to describe last night. Unexpected comes first. Because I had no intention of fucking her when I woke up yesterday morning. She'd made it pretty clear that this game was not about sex and I took her word on that.

But she was drunk.

And that makes me feel very guilty. Like I took advantage of her somehow.

"So hey," I say, once we reach the catwalk and she heads down it towards a bedroom. "I'd just like to apologize about last night."

She laughs. "Why? It was pretty fun."

"So you remember it?"

"How could I forget?"

"Well, you were pretty buzzed."

"Oh," she says. "Right." Heading into the bedroom.

I realize it's her room. The one I fucked her in last night. The sheets are a mess. Like, totally hanging off the bed. The comforter is just a pile of white bunched up in the middle and most of the pillows are on the floor.

"Excuse the mess," she says, stepping over a pillow as she makes her way towards her bedroom terrace. "I'm not one of those make-your-bed-daily kinda people."

No, she isn't. She's one of those mess-it-up-nightly kinda people, I think.

"The elevator actually goes all the way up to the roof too. That's how people get up there when I throw parties. But there's a ladder that leads up there from this terrace and since Eduardo Whats-his-name is monopolizing my elevator today, the bedroom terrace ladder will have to do."

"Jesus, Oaklee," I say.

"What?"

"That is so not secure!"

She shrugs. "I'm six floors up. Who cares?"

"Well, when people can ride your elevator up to the roof and climb down the ladder that *leads to your bedroom*, I care!"

"You're kinda bossy, Lawton." And then she flips her hair, pushes a hand past the sheer white curtains to find the door handle—which isn't even locked!—opens the French doors, and disappears behind the now blowing-in-the-wind fabric.

I follow. And by the time I get outside she's already climbing up the ladder and I have a great view of her ass in those jeans I picked out.

When she gets to the top and turns around I'm still gawking at her. "Throw the bag up."

I do that and climb after her. When I get up on the roof I just stop. Stand still for a moment looking at the mountains with nothing obstructing them. Then I turn in place and take in the rest of the three-hundred-and-sixty-degree view. "Holy shit." That's pretty much all I have to say.

"Yeah." Oaklee sighs. "My dad made this place when I was still a little girl." Then she turns and points to a painted-white wooden picnic table underneath the water tower. "He used to hang mosquito netting on all sides of the tower and drape white garden lights on the legs for my birthdays. He threw me a private party up here every year."

I picture it in my head and smile. "Sounds real nice, Oaks."

"It was," she says, smiling back, but sadly. "It really was. And one day, when I finally settle down and have my own kids, I hope I can do that for them too."

I take the bag of food from her hand, grab her other hand with my empty one, and lead her over to the table. "Well, I feel kinda proud of myself for coming up with this idea. I don't think much can surprise me about this city anymore."

We both take a seat. Me on one bench, her on the other.

"I mean, I know Denver. I have sold more than two hundred houses since I got my real-estate license eight years ago, in every neighborhood you can think of, but mostly downtown. So I kinda feel like I've seen all this place has to offer. And then you bring me up here and show me how much I've missed. How much more I have to see."

"You live right over there, Lawton," she says, pointing at my building down the alley. "It's not that different."

But I disagree. "My view kinda sucks. No, *really* sucks compared to yours. There's nothing special about a penthouse view of an alley."

"Not true," she says, opening up the paper bag and pulling out the two bacon, egg, and cheese bagels. She sniffs them, smiles and says, "Bacon. One of my four food groups."

Which makes me laugh. "What are the other three?"

"Beer, butter, and beef."

And now I laugh again. "A woman after my heart."

She blushes a little, which delights me for some reason. Then she says, "Your view is of my water tower, Law. That's kinda special, right?"

I nod. Because she's not wrong. And now that I know what this place over here really is—a slice of the romantic side of Denver, mountains stretching the entire front range from north to south, the hum of people and cars down below like a song caught in the softly blowing wind, and the city skyscape just over her shoulder—well, the whole thing is like a fantastical Hollywood backdrop if you ask me. "I bet it's outrageously beautiful up here at night."

"It is," she says, opening up her bagel and taking a bite. She looks around for a few moments as she chews. "I'll bring you up here at night if we have time."

"We can make time," I say. And it comes out slightly...seductive. Like I'm planning to fuck her up here. Which I'm not. I'm pretty sure what we did last night was a mistake. This whole arrangement, from top to bottom, is a business deal. And I should've stopped myself last night. Should've kept it professional. Because now she's probably thinking I'm a giant douchebag for taking advantage of her while she was drunk.

That's how I'd feel if I were her.

"You know," I say, unwrapping my bagel too, "you're not as crazy as I thought you were."

She winks at me. And that wink says, *You don't know me yet.*

"Seriously," I say. "When I got home this morning I looked you up online."

"Why?" She laughs, almost spitting out her food.

"Because I had this vision of you as some hot-headed wild woman, and for the life of me, I couldn't figure out where I got that impression."

"Hmmm. So what did you find online?"

"Well," I say. "You've pulled a lot of stunts over the years. I'm surprised the only one I ever caught wind of was that whole 'save the mansions' campaign."

"Got examples?" she asks. Winking again.

"Lots."

"Was it the wet jeans contest I threw? That was up here. I was on the news that night."

"Found that one, yes." I laugh. "And a bunch more of those. But the best one was when you made pot beer for an April Fool's joke."

She almost snorts. "Oh, my God. That was awesome. My dad laughed for days. We filmed a commercial showing people getting high on a pot stout beer called Rocky Mountain High and it went viral. Three million views on YouTube in two days! And it was so real the Denver cops came and arrested us!"

I can't help, I laugh too. Because I read that online. Her and her father got arrested for illegally selling pot and had to stay in jail over the entire weekend. Monday morning there was a protest outside the capitol building with thousands of people holding signs saying 'Free Oaklee!'

"How did I never meet you before this?" I ask.

She shrugs and chews her bagel. "You're a boring guy, I guess."

"And you truly are wild."

"Guilty."

"But you're taking all this Hanna Harlow stuff pretty well if you ask me. Because you haven't pulled anything crazy on her yet. I mean, all morning I've been asking myself why that is. So... why is that?"

She frowns now, then shakes her head. "It's not fun anymore. Not since my dad died. He's the one who made me wild. He's the one who was always pulling pranks and being crazy when I was growing up. He's the one I was always trying to make smile with my antics. Not anyone else. Just him. And now that he's gone... I just don't feel the same. I don't think about fun stuff like that anymore. I haven't pulled an April Fool's joke since the year he died."

"But you have a plan for Hanna Harlow, right?"

"Not really." She shrugs. "I just thought... I dunno. I could bait her into stealing my boyfriend and that would prove something. But it's a dumb idea, isn't it?"

Part of me hopes she thinks it's a dumb idea because she likes me. Wants to date me for real. Wants to give this a try. Because I kinda like this woman.

But there's another part of me that hopes she comes up with something really cool to get back at that chick. Because while this boyfriend experience stuff might be fake—Hanna Harlow really did steal her beer recipe and pass it off as her own. And she should pay for that.

So I say, "No. It's not dumb. I don't know if it'll work. But it's not dumb to want people to pay when they've wronged you."

"Exactly," she says. "That's what I really want. I want her to pay. I want her to know I know and I want everyone else to know too. I want her to feel shame. Because she's a lying, cheating, backstabbing bitch. And it's not fair."

"No. It's not," I say. "So how about we go over to Shrike Bikes and turn me into your boyfriend."

We walk over because Five Points really is just a few blocks away and the Shrike Bikes store is in a building right across the road from Coors Field. It's actually quite a big building. I've seen this place plenty of times. There's a diner down the road called Cookies that has the best burgers in town. I go there every once in a while. But I've never stopped into this showroom. Other ones, yeah. They have them all over Colorado. And when I was a kid—back in my wild days—I had a Shrike Bike once. It was payment for some fight money a guy owed me and the jacket Oaklee took home last night came with it. I wrecked the bike pretty quick because... well, I was sixteen. It wasn't even legal for me to ride that bike so I had no clue what I was doing.

But I had no fear either. Nothing to lose back then. That was before Elias Bricman found me and changed my life.

I was glad to leave that part of me behind. In fact, just walking towards the building gives me a weird feeling in my stomach. Reminds me of all those days I did nothing but stupid things.

And not stupid things like Oaklee does. *Really* stupid things.

"Jesus," I say, once we walk through the door. "How big is this place?"

There's like fifty bikes on the showroom floor, a bar off to the left, and the buzzing coming from the back— not to mention the pink neon sign that says Sick Girlz Ink—tells me there's a tattoo shop in here too. There's even a shooting gallery—fake, like the kind you see at a carnival, taking up one whole wall to my right. The whole place smells like summer. Popcorn, and cotton candy, and leather. There's also a clothing store in the front, and that's where we're standing now.

I study the wall of boots, then look at the racks filled with customized, hand-painted leather jackets.

"Big," Oaklee says. "I forgot that coming here is an experience. You need boots and a jacket for sure. But get whatever you want. I'm buying."

"You're not buying," I say. "That's ridiculous."

But she's already over in the women's section, browsing through the skirts.

A guy comes over wearing a red and black bowling shirt with an embroidered patch over the left side of his chest that says 'Chuck' in fancy retro cursive writing. "Looking for something in particular?" he asks me.

"Boots," I say.

"For going out? For riding the bike?"

"Bike," I guess, figuring Oaklee wants me to look like a biker, even if I don't actually own one.

"Engineer? Or harness?"

"Show me both," I say. Because I remember wanting a pair of these back in the day. Back when I was poor as dirt. So wild, homeless would not be an inaccurate way to describe my living status. God, how bad I wanted a pair of these boots. And why I never got myself a pair after the money started rolling in... I don't know.

"Brown or black?" he asks.

"Black," I say. Even though I like brown better. I can't wear black biker boots to the office... but brown ones, I could maybe pull that off with jeans. "Black," I say again. Because this isn't about me. It's about what Oaklee needs me to be. "Size eleven."

"You got it, bro," Chuck says. "Be right back."

I browse the jackets while I wait, wondering if Chuck is his real name or that's just the name that comes with the shirt.

Now these jackets are serious pieces of art. They start at four hundred dollars and go up from there because I hear that the Shrike family paints them custom somewhere up in Fort Collins. And... I lift up the sleeve, peek inside, and feel a sense of satisfaction that I knew where to find it. Each one is individually signed by whoever painted it. This one says Spencer. The guy who owns this whole company. It's got three zeros on the price tag.

But the art is magnificent. Not gaudy, either. Not some lame eagle posing in front of an American flag.

No, this is two ravens sitting in front of the iconic Shrike skull. And it's subtle. Like, most of it is painted in metallic blue-black and you can't really see it until the light hits it just the right way.

I slip it on, just to see if it fits. It does. And I'm just about to take it off when Chuck returns with two wooden boot crates branded with the Shrike logo burned into the wood. Whoever does the marketing for this place really has an eye for detail.

127

He sets the boxes down near an overstuffed leather chair and says, "Take your time, bro. I gotta go take care of some folks over there real quick."

"Sure," I say, glancing over in the direction he was nodding. There's like half a dozen people holding cameras. The kind you use for news broadcasts or filming.

Huh. Wonder what that's all about.

But I turn back to the boots because all those people disappear into a back room and there's nothing more to see.

"That jacket is great," Oaklee says, coming up behind me. "I love it. You're getting it, right?"

"Sure," I say, then jerk my arm away when she goes to reach for the price tag. "You're not buying this." I laugh. "So just buck off, Oaks."

She smiles and shakes her head. "These your boot choices?"

"Yup," I say, opening the first crate and taking out one boot.

"Oh, that's pretty," she says, leaning over my shoulder to pet the leather. "Try them on, I want to see you."

So I slip my shoes off, slide the boots on and realize… "Shit. My pants are too straight."

"Oh, I'll go find you some jeans. One sec."

She's gone before I can stop her. Not that I *could* stop her. So I just put the other boot on, ignoring how stupid I look wearing them with straight-leg pants, and walk around, trying them out.

You know you're wearing a pair of quality boots when they feel like they were made custom for your feet.

I try on the engineers next. Which have the same feel, but the not classic biker vibe the harness ones give off, so I pack them back up and decide on the first pair.

128

"Here," Oaklee says, handing me a stack of jeans. "I didn't know your size, so I guessed. Go try them on."

I sigh, take the stack, and walk off to the dressing rooms.

"Looking hot isn't torture, Lawton Ayers! It's fun!" she calls after me.

"Whatever you want, Oaklee," I mumble back.

There are three sizes in different styles, but all of them are faded and ripped. They're a lot like the ones I chose for Oaklee today. Soft, the wash so light, they're almost baby blue. And filled with strategically placed holes that don't look manufactured. When I glance down at the price I get the feeling they *aren't* manufactured. That each hole was carefully made by hand by some seamstress.

I pick my size, strip out of my own pants, then pull them on.

A black leather belt comes flying over the top of the dressing-room door, the buckles slapping against the wooden louvers. "Put that on too," Oak calls from the other side. "And let me see you before you take it off, OK?"

"Sure," I grumble. "Whatever you want, Oaklee."

"Was that sarcasm?" I can sorta see her through the louvers. She's got her eye pressed up against the door trying to get a peek.

"Go away, you weirdo. I'll be out in a second."

But she doesn't go away. I can see her boot tapping on the carpet through the opening at the bottom of the door.

Fuck it. I change, pull my boots back on, and open the door to let her gawk at me.

She covers her mouth with her hand when I walk out, trying to hide her smile. Then she says, "Oh, wait," as she

129

comes towards me, slipping the jacket down my arms. "I actually love the look you have today, but take this off so I can see how it looks with just the t-shirt."

She's tugging on my denim button-down, so I take that off, smiling as I watch Oaklee study the muscles in my arms, and then slip the leather jacket back on over the white t-shirt.

"How's that?" I say. "This the look you're going for?"

She bites her lip, walks up to me, reaches up to thread her fingers through my hair, musses it all up, then steps back and smiles. "You're perfect. No, you're fuckin' hot, Lawton. I love it." She whirls in place, and that's when I see Chuck, standing behind her. Waiting patiently. She says, "We'll take this," as she does an up-and-down motion with her pointer finger at my body.

"You got it, Oaklee," Chuck says. And then he's snapping price tags off the jeans and the jacket and walking away before I can stop him.

I'm about to remind her that she's not paying for this stuff. Not any of it. But decide that's a losing battle and when you want to get your way with Oaklee Ryan, you play her game. So I say, "Hey, aren't you getting anything? You didn't find a skirt you like over there?" I nod my head to the women's section.

"Maybe," she says, biting her lip again. I kinda love it when she does that.

"Go look again. You might as well. We're here, ya know."

"OK." She smiles. "I won't take long, I promise."

"Hey, there's fifty bikes in this place for me to try out. Take all the time you want."

She darts off and disappears in the racks of clothing.

See, now that is how you handle Oaklee. Distract her as you pay for the clothes she thinks she's buying.

I feel like patting myself on the back right now.

But I don't waste time gloating. I head straight for the cash register where Chuck is already totaling shit up.

And that's when I see... *the bike.*

"Ah," Chuck says. "Nice, isn't she? The old man made that for himself about fifteen years ago. But he's selling if you're interested."

"I know this bike," I almost whisper. "I actually remember seeing him ride it once. Some grand opening for a store, I think."

"Yeah," Chuck says. "He's selling a bunch of his older stock to make room for new bikes. I guess the old lady put her foot down and said no more bikes at the farm until he sells some."

"Crazy," I say. "That he'd sell this... masterpiece."

"They're all masterpieces." Chuck laughs. "Hop on and give her a feel while I ring you up."

I'm about to say, *Nah.* But instead my mouth says, "Yeah. OK."

And then my leg swings over. My eyes seeking out every last detail of artwork on the tank. One foot on the floor. One foot on the pedal. Both hands on the grips. "Jesus," I say. "This is damn nice."

"It's got a nice rear suspension," Chuck says. "Floating bitch seat for Oaklee. I've ridden on the back of that bad girl and let me tell you, she will feel like she's flying."

I can picture it too. Me. Her. This bike. The future.

Stop it, Law. This whole thing is fake. Just a business deal, nothing more.

"Hey!" someone calls from the door. "I got a delivery. Where do you want them?"

There's a guy standing off to my left with a hand truck stacked two high with kegs.

"Over in the bar," Chuck says, pointing to the other side of the building.

And that's when I see the label stamped on the keg.

Buffalo Brews.

I look over my shoulder real quick, trying to see if Oaklee is still in the dressing room.

She's not. And I know she sees the same thing I do just by the look on her face.

CHAPTER THIRTEEN

OAKLEE

The skirt is super cute and that's all I'm thinking about when I exit the dressing room stall and start walking over to Law. He's sitting on a bike near the cash register and the first thing I notice is that he looks… he looks… like the man of my dreams.

I giggle at that. And I'm just about to make a joke about buying him that bike just so I can ride bitch with him when I see a guy rolling kegs across the showroom towards the bar.

My mouth is open, my head about to turn to Chuck to ask him what that's all about—but that's before I see the brand printed on the keg.

Buffalo Brews.

"What the fuck?" I yell. There's a ton of people in the store, so I get lots of weird stares, but I don't care. "Chuck! What is going on here? We have a deal!"

Chuck looks at me, confused. "What are you—" But that's when he sees the problem. "Oh, shit. I dunno, Oaklee. Let me go find out."

He leaves the cash register just as Law walks over to me. "Hey, maybe it's not what you think," he says.

"Not what I think?" I exclaim. I'm too loud. And people all over the store are still staring at me. So I gather myself back up and grit through my teeth, "She's trying to get my vendors, Law. It's exactly what I think."

My whole body is shaking with anger. I'm so mad. I want to kill that bitch! I mean, I have been patient with her for all these years. I've been biting my tongue and keeping my mouth shut, just trying to be reasonable, and it's obviously not working.

I need to up my game. I need to put on the warpaint and battle armor and declare war. Because that's what this is.

"Oaklee," Law says, rubbing my shoulder. "Calm down. You're shaking, for fuck's sake."

"Yes," I say. "I am. Because I have never felt such anger in all my life. I looked the other way when she cheated off me in college. I turned the other cheek when she stole my boyfriends. I talked myself into being rational, and calm, and sane because I don't like getting crazy, I really don't. My anger isn't something I'm proud of. I want life to be easy. I want life to be calm. I don't want to be the drama queen everyone thinks I am." I turn to look at him. "And where has that gotten me? Huh? I have had this deal with Spencer Shrike since before my dad died. It's been almost eight years! And she thinks what? She can move in on my territory and take my place now that my dad's gone? I don't fucking think so, Lawton! I don't fucking think so!"

"Shhh," he says, pulling me into his chest and putting his arms around me. "We'll get it handled."

"How?" I ask. "How are we gonna get it handled?"

"Just wait for Chuck to come back and tell us what's going on, OK?"

I don't answer. I'm too angry. I feel like crying, that's how angry I am. "She has no right," I say. "No right to play with my life like this! What did I ever do to her but be a good friend? What?"

Law just holds me tighter and shakes his head. "Just take a deep breath. It's probably not what you think.

Like… maybe that guy is just here to drop off samples or something. For the manager to taste."

"Two kegs for tasting?" I say.

"Oaklee," he says in a calm voice that makes me want to slap him. Then he pushes me away, holds me at arm's length and says, "Just. Calm. Down. I'm gonna go see what's happening and you're going to stay here. OK?"

I look up at him. Feel the tears stinging the corners of my eyes. But I say nothing. Because all I can think about is how I need to get even with that stupid bitch, Hanna Harlow.

"OK?" Law repeats.

"Whatever," I say, pulling away from him. "I'm gonna go change." So I walk off towards the dressing room stall. And he walks off towards Chuck, who I can see is having a conversation with the bar manager. And by the time I get to the stall, Law has reached Chuck, and they start talking.

I watch. Seething. Seeing red. So hot with anger, I'm actually sweating. My hands are shaking and my legs feel weak. So I grab onto a rack of t-shirts and steady myself as I watch the conversation across the store.

I can't hear them and I don't know how to read lips, but I can read facial expressions just fine.

Chuck is asking the bar manager about the kegs.

Bar manager probably says something like, *Hanna Harlow came in here last week and talked us into putting her kegs on tap for a free trial.*

And Law says something like, *But that's Oaklee's tap. She has a deal.*

And Chuck says, *Yeah, we can't do that. There's a deal.*

And bar manager says…

Law is walking back towards me now. Stoic expression on his face. And I don't know him well enough to understand what that means, but I don't have to guess, because the first thing he says to me is, "Hanna Harlow had a deal too."

"Let me guess," I say through clenched teeth. "She offered them a free trial."

"No," Law says, shaking his head, looking a little sad. "No, that's not the deal."

"Then what is it?"

"Let's just pay for this stuff and we'll talk about it outside. Chuck!" he yells, then rips the tag off my skirt and walks over to the cash register. "Add this to the bill and make it quick. We're leaving."

I grab my clothes and purse from the dressing room and walk over to the counter. "What was the deal?" I ask.

Chuck just shakes his head and refuses to look at me as he runs Lawton's credit card.

"I said we'll talk about it outside, Oaklee."

"I want to talk about it now. What's the deal, Chuck?"

But he doesn't answer. Just waits for Law to sign the little machine to finalize the sale and then hands him a receipt and our bags.

"Let's go," Law says, holding onto my arm as he starts making for the door.

I let him lead me because I really do not want to lose my temper in this store. I really don't. But as soon as we're outside, I whirl around and snap, "Tell me what's going on!"

"I will," Law says calmly. "But we're gonna walk home while I do that. OK?"

"You're talking to me like I'm a crazy person!"

136

"I think you have serious crazy potential inside you, Oaks. And I want you to stay calm."

"OMG, it's bad, right? Just tell me!"

"Promise me we'll keep walking and you won't explode in public."

I take a deep breath. We're only a few blocks away from my house and I just want to get there. Like… right now. Because I feel like I'm going to cry. So I say, "I promise," in the most reasonable tone I can muster up.

"OK. So here's the deal. Two weeks ago Hanna Harlow came in asking about room on the tap."

"Mmm-hmm," I say through tight lips. "Got it."

"She was told about your deal and that they only serve Bronco Brews at the downtown Shrike showroom bar."

"OK."

"And she pointed out that Buffalo Brews won Best Brew in Denver this year in the *Westword*."

The *Westword* is the cool free weekly newspaper. All the hipsters read it with their Sunday bagel each weekend. So that contest was no joke. I didn't even enter this year.

"And…" Law says, dragging out the word. "She also mentioned that it was very similar to Bucked Up, so they should just take Bucked Up off the tap and put up Buffalo Brews Buffed Up instead."

I stop walking so I can face him. "And they said yes?"

"Oaklee," he says, still calm. "You promised not to make a scene."

I look around and realize everyone is now staring at me because I was screaming. So I take another deep breath, close my eyes for the count of three, open them back up, and say, "I'm under control. Go on."

"The bar manager said yes."

"Those motherfuckers." I seethe it. But I'm walking again. I didn't scream. I'm in control. "I'm going to kill the Shrikes."

"Now wait a minute," Law says. "Chuck—who I take it is some kind of manager of the showroom?"

"He runs the whole place, yes."

"Well, Chuck told the bar manager not to put it on tap until you had a meeting with them. So they're gonna call you and set that up for next week. But until then, they will only be serving Bronco Brews at the bar. So see, it's all gonna work out."

"No, it isn't. She's gonna talk her way into my tap. She's gonna lie her ass off, and get her way, and I'm going to be left with nothing by the time she's done with me."

"No," he says. "That's not going to happen. Because we're going to come up with a plan. OK? A logical plan. We're going to stay focused, and be calm, and we're going to prove she stole your recipe and tell the whole world about it."

"How?"

"Stop yelling, Oaklee."

Oh, my God. I'm so pissed. But I take another deep breath and growl, "How are we going to prove it, Lawton?"

He sighs. "I dunno yet. We'll host a taste test maybe. Get people in the door and have them do a blind taste test and make them realize it's the same beer."

"That's not going to work! What if people can't tell? What if they say Buffed Up is better? Then what do I do?"

"Look, I'm doing my best, OK? We just need to think about this a little. Not jump to any conclusions and not do anything stupid that could get you sued."

"Sued!" I huff out a laugh. "Let that bitch try!"

By this time we're back over at my building. We walk into the lobby and I force myself to smile and be nice to the waitresses and hostesses as we pass them, making our way towards the elevators. I don't take my crazy out on the employees. That's just not right. So when we get into the elevator I just punch the top floor.

"I cannot believe you just did that," Law says.

"Did what?"

"Punched the button for the top floor and it just accepts it. You didn't even use a keycard!"

"It's business hours," I say.

"Someone could rob you blind, Oaklee. Just go up there and take whatever they wanted."

"Well, I do have cameras. So I'd catch them if they did. Besides, the waitresses all keep an eye on it."

"Not when they're busy, they don't."

"Look, it's been this way for as long as I can remember. No one has ever—"

But I stop talking and in the same moment we both say, "Hanna broke in and stole the recipes."

"That bitch!"

"I told you your security sucked." Law takes out his phone and presses a contact. "Eduardo? How long before you can get the new security in?" He waits, smiles at me and nods his head just as the elevator doors open into my apartment. "Uh-huh," he says to Eduardo.

We both walk out into my apartment and he continues to listen to Eduardo talk. "Well." He finally sighs. "We think there was a breach." Then he looks at me. "Where do you keep your security footage, Oaklee?"

"I only keep it for a week. It gets deleted every seven days. She had to have stolen those recipes years ago. She won't even be on there."

"Right," he says. "OK. But where's your security room? Eduardo is gonna upgrade you so that from now on, we'll know."

"Basement," I say. "There's a locked door at the end of the barrel room. My keycard will open it. It's all in there."

"Got that?" Law says into the phone. I hear Eduardo's faint response and then Law hangs up.

The thought of Hanna Harlow being in my apartment makes me sick. Like… literally, I want to throw up.

I run to the nearest bathroom and that's exactly what I do.

Law comes in behind me, pulls my hair away from my face as I dry-heave, trying to make that sick feeling go away, and says, "This is a sign of a perfect boyfriend, by the way."

Which makes me smile, then laugh. Because he's right. You know a guy is a keeper when he holds your hair as you throw up.

Twenty minutes later I've brushed my teeth, Eduardo has come and gone, running a new security setup by Lawton, and we're both sitting on the couch.

He's got my feet in his hands again. Massaging my toes.

"I feel so sad," I say.

"Don't feel sad," he replies.

"But I do. I mean, I'm so stupid. Of course she broke in here and stole my recipes. I practically handed her an invitation. And oh, my God. What if she got the Assassin Sour too?"

I want to cry. And the moment I think that in my head the tears just pour out.

Lawton reaches for me, pulls me into his chest and says, "We'll fix it. I promise, we will. Just please stop crying." It takes me a while, but he's patient as I let myself run out of tears. And then in the ensuing silence he says, "So where do you keep them? Your recipes?"

"My office. On my hard drive, mostly. But the older ones, like Bucked Up and Mountain Mud, those ones are all in my dad's old files. I don't even think that cabinet is locked!"

"Don't beat yourself up. You're just... too trusting, Oaklee. Ruthless people like Hanna see you as a target and then take advantage of you."

"That makes me sound even weaker!" I huff.

"No, it makes you... sweet."

"Fuckin' sweet! I handed her everything! I didn't even put up a fight! I let her cheat off me in college, and take away boys I liked, and now I've handed her my business! She's probably got every old recipe we have and she's going to release a new one every year until she takes over every Bronco Brews tap in Denver!"

He opens his mouth to say something in response, but then he doesn't. Because he knows I'm right. Hanna Harlow is a sneaky cunt who will run me over then back her truck up to do it again.

"I need a way to get to her, Lawton. You need to get her to trust you."

"She hates me, I can already tell. She didn't even look at me yesterday. Didn't say one word to me at all."

"That's because you weren't really dressed up like her kind of guy, ya know? I don't think she really believed we were together. But now you have the boots and the jacket—"

"Boots and a jacket!" He laughs. "That's not going to make her change her mind about me."

He's right. It's not enough. I need something better. Something more.

"Hey," he says. "You hungry? Because that bagel wasn't enough for me."

"I am not hungry," I say. "I might never eat again, that's how not hungry I am."

"Come on," he says, pushing me off him and standing up. "I'm gonna take you somewhere fun. And believe me, once you get there, you'll eat."

Somewhere fun turns out to be Funsville. And even though I want to pretend this wasn't a great idea, I can't help but smile as we walk through the doors.

It's a bar. It's a restaurant. It's an Eighties arcade.

Funsville is a place you can't not have fun at.

"Hey, Larry," I call out to the owner as we pass by the bar. I do a quick check to make sure Bucked Up is still on tap here. If Hanna Harlow got to Larry, I'm in some serious trouble.

It is, so I sigh with relief.

"Jesus, do you know everyone in Denver?" Law asks.

"That's Larry. He and my dad are—were—old friends. I used to come here all the time when I was a kid, but it's been a while."

Larry comes over to us as we buy tokens and tickets at the machine and says, "Oaklee!" as he wraps his arms around me and gives me a great big bear hug. "You haven't been here in years!"

"I know. So busy these days. This is…" And then I stop, wondering what Lawton is to me. But I say, "My boyfriend, Lawton Ayers." Because he is my boyfriend. I've even got it in writing. For two whole weeks I have someone to count on. And it feels nice, so I'm gonna make the most of it.

Law and Larry chat as I take my tokens over to the skeet ball area and start throwing. Seeing Larry makes me sad because it reminds me of all the great times I had in here with my dad as a kid. And that's why I don't come around. I don't like to think about that.

And it seems like I've been thinking about the past a lot these last two days. Ever since Law started playing this game with me.

But I watch them as they talk. Every now and again they laugh too. Like they are old friends. And as I'm watching I imagine that's how it would be if Lawton ever met my father. Because Larry and my father are—were—a lot alike.

They both have full sleeves on their arms. My dad's tattoos were mostly Wild West things. But Larry's are all old carnival things. A beaded woman. A fat man. Lions, and zebras, and a ringmaster on his back. I know that because we used to go up to Grand Lake with Larry to fish every summer and he'd take his shirt off.

In fact, now that Law is in the middle of his Oaklee's boyfriend morph, they look a lot alike too.

They're both wearing white t-shirts. They're both wearing biker boots. They're both wearing faded, ripped jeans.

But they're still… different somehow.

What is it? Why are they different?

And that's when it hits me.

That's when I figure out why Hanna isn't into Lawton. He needs some tattoos.

CHAPTER FOURTEEN

LAWTON

Even though I don't know Larry personally like Oaklee does, I've been in Funsville plenty of times with Bric. This place has been a fixture in Denver for more than twenty years and Larry here has been its one and only owner.

So I tell him that as I watch Oaklee walk over to the skeet ball and start playing. I say, "My sponsor used to bring me here back when I was a teenager."

"That right?" Larry says, making change for a kid at the counter.

"Yeah," I say, remembering back on those days.

"You were… an alcoholic?" Larry says. "So you two used to meet up here, what? When you had the urge to drink? Not a good plan since this is a bar too."

For a second I don't even understand the words coming out of his mouth. Then I say, "Alcoholic? No." And I laugh because I guess that's what people think when you say 'sponsor.' "No. Elias Bricman was my Boys Without Brothers sponsor. He gave me a scholarship to attend private school and changed my life. And this place was part of it. Because we used to meet up here to, ya know, talk through shit."

"Ah," Larry says, laughing at his presumptions. "Sorry. I'm jaded. Don't mind me."

"No problem," I say. "I guess I never thought of it that way. I don't talk about Bric much. You know him?"

"Who doesn't?" Larry laughs again. He's got an easy laugh. It's nice too. He's got a look about him that says 'don't fuck with me.' And that's how I always pictured he'd be if I ever had an opportunity to talk with him.

But that's not how he is at all.

"I've known Bric since he first moved here as a teenager. Used to come in all the time. And now that I think about it..." Larry does one of those looking-at-the-ceiling moves, like he's trying to remember something. "I know you. Skinny kid. Always wearing a leather jacket. Bad street attitude."

"Yeah," I say, smiling. "That was me."

"You don't look much different now, truthfully. Bric ever make an honest man out of ya?"

"He did," I say. Because one, I get that because I'm dressed like this today it's easy to imagine nothing's changed for me. And two, he didn't say it in a mean way. He wasn't judging me. "I run a multi-million-dollar real-estate agency here in Denver now. But I'm doing a favor for Oaklee this week and she wants me to look like a tough guy."

I shrug and so does he. A mutual, *Girls are all crazy, what can you do?* gesture.

"Well, I'm glad to hear that, Lawton. Real glad to hear that. It's nice when the kids come back and show me who's boss."

And with that he shoots me one more smile and walks off to help a customer near the token machine.

It's weird. How my past has been missing for so long and meeting one crazy girl named Oaklee has brought it all rushing back.

Like that jacket. And the Johnny Cash t-shirt. The motorcycle and the boots on my fuckin' feet.

I look at Oaklee, who is frowning down at a couple of tickets the skeet ball machine is spitting out, and decide... it's kinda cool. That she's taken me on this two-day whirlwind down memory lane. And I still have twelve more days with her. It's not even the sex, either. Though that was pretty goddamned fun and if she's on board, we're totally gonna do that again. It's just... her.

She's got a wild side, I see that. And now that I've known her for two days I can understand how the guys who turned Jordan down for her game would've thought she'd be hard to handle. Or unreasonable. Risky, maybe.

She is all those things in some ways. But in others... she's just a little girl who lost her dad and is getting shit on by someone she once called a friend.

I walk over to her and she smiles at me over her shoulder. "I suck today. Usually I kick ass at this game."

I pick up a ball, roll it around in my hand, then toss it down the lane and it goes smoothly into the center hole.

"Show-off." She giggles.

"I played a lot of skeet ball when I was a kid. Lot of skeet ball."

"Here?" Oaklee asks.

"Yeah, but other arcades too. I was a street kid. Homeless at fourteen."

"What? But your mother did such a good job!"

"What?" I actually let out a guffaw at that remark.

"You have such great manners. I figured... I figured wrong, I guess. I seem to figure you wrong a lot. Which isn't fair."

"Why?"

"Because you have me nailed down, ya know?"

"Well, yeah," I say, picking up another ball and tossing it. It bounces out of the center hole and goes in the gutter.

"My mother didn't teach me anything except I couldn't count on her. I could count on myself. Can't win 'em all, right? I mean... I had it pretty rough and then it got really great because Bric changed my mind about that. He taught me people do care. And you can count on them. And no matter how hard it was back then, I don't ever forget to be grateful for what I have."

Oaklee just stares at me. Nodding. Then she says, "I get it too. I used to have it pretty great, and then it got pretty rough. And the only thing that kept me going was the fact that things could always get worse so I'd better be thankful for what I had left."

"Yeah, that sucks. Sorry," I say. And not just because I want that word to fill the silence as she stares at me. "I really am sorry that you lost your dad. I'm sorry that Hanna Harlow is a dick and took advantage of you. And I'm on board, OK? I'm here to help you and that's what I'm gonna do. We're gonna get her, Oaks. I promise. We're gonna get her back for making your life worse when things were already bad."

She takes a ball and throws it, this time hitting her mark. We watch the ball disappear inside the center hole and then she says, "You don't have to, ya know."

"Don't have to what?"

"Do this. Play this stupid game with me. I mean you have a lot going for you, Lawton, and I'm just fucking it up. I'll still show up for that meeting. Don't worry about that. I'll still do my part."

"Hey," I say, sorta laughing, but sorta not. Because I'm not ready for this to be over yet. I like her too much to quit on her after only two days. "I'm in, babe. In it to win it, no doubts. So you say the word and we'll get that bitch."

She turns away, but I'm almost certain she's smiling as she does it. So I peek around her shoulder and say, "What? Are you laughing at me?"

She shakes her head, but her smile is so big, I swear to God, she looks like a different person. A happy person. Probably more like the person she used to be than the one she is now. The girl who pranked the entire world with Rocky Mountain High beer for April Fool's and went to jail for an entire weekend just to keep the joke going.

"Why are you smiling like that?" I ask.

And then she takes a deep breath, lets it out, and says, "OK, if you're in, that's cool. I want you to be in. And I've got a plan, and you're gonna think it's crazy, so I just want you to know you can back out and say no. I won't get mad, and I won't fuck up your deals and I won't hate you or anything. That's all. I just want you to know that."

She says the entire thing in one breath and by the time she's done, she she's sucking in air.

"Ahhh... should I be worried about this plan? You know, because you basically just scared the shit out of me with that little declaration."

"What do you mean?"

"Well, anyone who has to promise all those things in one breath just to make me understand that this crazy plan is entirely up to me and saying no is OK has something in mind I won't want to hear. So spill it."

"Well, that depends," she says. "On how you feel about pain."

"What?" I laugh loudly this time. "What are you talking about?"

She grabs my biceps, pulling me close to her like she's about to divulge a secret. And then she looks up into my eyes—her caramel-colored ones looking up at me. Wide, and innocent, and very much like they're ready to beg me if it comes to that. "Did you ever think about tattoos?"

For a second I don't understand the connection to what we were talking about and what we're now talking about. So I look down at her, dumbly, and say, "What?"

"Tattoos, Law. I was just thinking… you know, while you were standing over there with Larry, that you really do look like a biker today. Except he's all tatted up and you're not. And yeah, you've got the jacket, so no one knows you're not. But Hanna knows you're not, right? She saw you yesterday in that Johnny Cash t-shirt. So I think—"

"You think she's not looking at me because… what? I'm just some wannabe weekend warrior?"

She pokes her finger into my chest and says, "Exactly!"

"Ah, man," I say.

"Just listen, OK? Hanna likes the guys I date. She's proven it to me over and over again. And even though she hasn't actually stolen a boyfriend from me since college, she does date them after I'm done. It's like… it's like she goes out of her way to find my ex-boyfriends and then she brings them places she knows I'll be. So I know, I just know… if you had tattoos she'd really think we were together. I mean, I don't know what she thinks we're doing together now, but she must feel pretty confident that I'm not serious about you. So we need to make her think we're serious."

"And tattoos will do that?" I say, giving her the stink eye.

"Yes!"

"I don't know," I say. "And it's got nothing to do with pain, either. It's just… Bric always warned me about the body art, ya know?"

"Bric?" she asks, confused.

"Elias Bricman. He owns... well, a lot of shit. Used to own a... a private club over by the capitol building. That's how Jordan and I know each other. Bric is the common denominator. He found me when I was sixteen, shook the thug right out of me, and set me up with a scholarship to a private school. I never looked back, ya know? And he was glad I'd never gotten a tattoo like a bunch of the other kids he was sponsoring. Said it would be easier in the real world if I didn't mark myself up like that. Announce who I was to the world before they got to know me and shit like that. So... I dunno. It's a big deal to me."

She nods. Frowning. "I get it. No problem. It was just an idea. I'm sure the jacket will be fine." And then she smiles. Weakly. And turns back to the skeet ball game.

And I hate that. I hate that I've disappointed her. I hate the frown, and the worry lines creasing her forehead, and that look in her eyes. That look that says things can always get worse. Because I used to feel like that too. And people who live by that creed know. No matter how good things get, life will always be there to kick you when you're down.

So I say, "Now hold on a minute. I didn't say no. I just said it's a big deal. I mean, I've never even thought about getting a tattoo, so I don't even know what I'd want. I don't know who I'd get to do it, but I'd want it to be someone special. Someone who knows their shit. Not just any fucking Joe Shmo at some dirty tattoo shop."

"It's totally fine, Law. Just forget I mentioned it."

"I mean, what would I get?" And now I have to take a seat on the edge of the skeet ball machine and think it through. "I don't even have a clue. How did you decide on those words on your back?"

She looks over at me and smiles. "Do you want the short version? Or the long one?"

"Long," I say. Automatically. Because I don't want the short version of anything at all when it comes to Oaklee Ryan.

"OK, but let's get hot dogs because I'm starving. I'll tell you over hot dogs."

Ten minutes later we're sitting at a booth drinking Bucked Up on tap and staring down at our exotic hot dog choices. Larry's known for his hot dogs. Apparently. Since this is what Oaklee tells me as we wait in line to order. He's got wild boar dogs. Buffalo dogs—which we turn our noses up at, since, you know, Hanna Harlow's company has ruined that particular animal species for both of us now. He's got one he swears is rattlesnake. But we finally decide on the jackalope dog, which is stupid. Because there's no such thing as a jackalope.

"It's antelope," Oaklee says, noticing my reluctance to eat it. "I promise you. It's just pronghorn antelope. Which is really just a special kind of small deer with antelope-like antlers. They're actually a member of the giraffe family. You've seen them right? They're all over the countryside east of Denver."

I shake my head no, because even though I know they sing about the place where the buffalo roam and the deer and the antelope play in that old-time song, I've never thought about it before.

"Just eat it, you wuss. Take one bite and I'll tell you my tattoo story."

So I do. Because I want that story. I take a huge bite because when I go in, I go all in.

"Not bad," I say, still chewing.

Oaklee takes her bite and chews, nodding her head like this is the most delicious hotdog ever, then wipes her mouth with a napkin and begins her story.

"OK, so when I was in sixth grade I had to do a report on a famous woman I admired. So I chose Ingrid Bergman because my dad loved classic black-and-white movies, so by the time I was twelve I'd seen *Casablanca* a million times and I thought it was just… very romantic. I mean, Rick gave up Ilsa because he knew she was better off without him."

Oaklee sighs. Smiles at me. "I loved that ending, even though it was sad and everyone wanted Rick to go to America with Ilsa instead of Laszlo. I think he did the right thing by leaving her behind. He knew she'd be unhappy and he loved her so much, he couldn't ruin her life like that. So I chose Ingrid Bergman for my report and that's when I found her quote. 'Be yourself. The world worships the original.' And for my eighteenth birthday my dad took me to get my tattoo. Right before I left for college. Because he knew what I wanted and he thought that would keep me grounded when I came up against the wider world and people wanted to try to force me into being something I'm not."

I grin. Truly loving that story. "So why didn't you get the whole thing?" I ask. "Why didn't you add in the 'be yourself' part?"

She shrugs. "I think it goes unsaid. I mean, you can't be original if you're not being yourself, right?"

"You're a smart woman, you know that, Oaklee?"

She grins. "I have my moments."

Yeah, she sure does. "So listen, I've never been against tattoos. I sorta love them. I love yours, that's for sure. It was a very nice surprise to flip you over last night and see that waiting for me."

She blushes. And oh, fuck, yeah. I love that blush. I mean, I do realize that I just met her two days ago, but I don't like to see her sad. Which gives me an idea for later. But first—"So if I say yes, I need to go somewhere good. A real artist, ya know? Not someone who draws cartoons, because that's not what I'm looking for."

"I have just the place," she whispers.

"And I need to think of something worthy. Something I can look back on over the years and say, 'Yeah, I'd do it again.'"

"OK," she says. "So let's see what we can come up with. What is meaningful to you?"

I just blink at her.

"Like, what symbol do you use for inspiration?"

More blinking.

"For instance," she says, understanding that I'm just a dude who doesn't give much thought to symbols, "I relate to… well, it's stupid to say beer, but that's exactly right. It's my life. It reminds of family, and good times, and of course, the business. I don't make all the labels anymore but that's what I did when I was a kid. I made labels. Came up with clever names. Because each beer has a history. Each beer we've come up with has memories attached to it. And yeah, Bucked Up was invented before I was even born, but I was there when it rose to fame. I remember my dad's face when he won that first international award.

154

So if I were going to get more tattoos, I'd use beer as my inspiration."

"You'd get beer bottles?" I ask. "Or labels?" I try to picture her like Larry over there, only instead carnival people, she's got six-packs of beer on her arms.

"No, dummy." She laughs. "Words are my thing. I'd get our beer names done up in the same calligraphy as it is on the label. But no pictures. Just words."

"Interesting," I say.

"Maybe if I was really clever," she adds, looking up at the ceiling, like this idea just popped into her head, "I'd take the beer names and make them into a poem. Then write that all down my back. And all the regular words would be in one font and all the beer names would be in their original font." She smiles and sits back, apparently satisfied with her future tattoo plan. "Yeah. That's what I'd do."

"Well, I don't think I want words."

"Of course not. That's my symbol." She smiles at me. "You just need to find your roots. The one thing that can describe you in a picture. And then go from there. Like my dad, he had an Old West theme. A whole herd of mustangs on his back. Six-shooters on his upper arms. And of course, the infamous bucking bronco as his main front piece."

"He was all bucked up, huh?"

She nods. Tilting her head a little like she's remembering him. All his tattoos. All their time together when she was young.

"So," I say. "Not to be pushy, but what happened to your mom?"

"She's dead to me."

"Dead... to you?" I ask. "Or really dead?"

"It's all the same to me. My dad got a woman pregnant. She never told him about the baby, just disappeared, and then one day he found a four-year-old on his doorstep."

"He did not!" I bellow.

"I swear to God! She brought me to the brewery, dropped me off in the lobby, told the hostess I was his kid, and left me there. She never came back. I never saw her again. It was just the two of us after that."

"So you know her name though."

"Yeah. I looked her up when I was fifteen. She was dead by then."

"Wow," I say. "I don't even know what to say to that."

Oaklee shrugs. "Don't feel sorry for me, that's for sure. I got as good a childhood as any kid could ask for. And my dad might've been a beer-making biker on the outside, but he was an astute businessman. He saw the craft beer trend before anyone else and took Bronco Brews to the next level. When he died I inherited a five-hundred-million-dollar portfolio."

I whistle. You know that whistle people do when they're amazed at something? That's what I do.

"Jesus," I say. "That's a lot of money. Is that why you decided to renovate your building? You just have so much money you don't know what to do with it?"

"Sorta. But also, he'd always wanted to fix the building up. Just didn't have the time or inclination to deal with it. So I figured I'd do it. We'd already planned it all out before he died. So really, all I did was see it through to the end. And you know what's funny?"

"No, but I can't wait to hear it."

"All I did was increase my net worth when it was done. It's like… money makes money."

I hold up my beer to do a cheers, and say, "No truer words have ever been said."

She laughs, holding up hers to clink against mine. "But anyway, we're off topic. If you're going to get a tattoo, you need a plan before you start. Otherwise you might regret it later."

"Right. A symbol." I think real hard but I don't know. "I have no symbol," I finally admit. "I have nothing like you do. Not really. I mean, my childhood was filled with fucked-up parents, drugs and violence. Which isn't the kind of shit you want to memorialize on your body in ink."

"Surely there was something. What did you think about as a teenager?"

I ponder that for a little bit. Then say, "Chaos. That's the only thing I can think of. Just... chaos."

"O-kay," she says. "Well, how would you describe your life now?"

I sigh. Because it's sad that I have no symbol. "Just... making money, I guess."

Oaklee makes a face. Scrunching up her nose in the process. Which I find adorable. "You want to be a TV star. That's something."

"Yeah, but no. I want the show. I want the mountain lifestyle. I want the house and the land, and maybe some horses. I want..."

"You want the peace," she finishes.

"Yeah," I say, nodding. "Yeah. Life was chaos growing up and it still is, just in a different way. So I guess I just want the peace. I want to drop out, ya know? Be away from the hustle and relax."

"And a TV show will give you that?"

I shrug. "I know it sounds crazy, but I feel like it will. Like if I could just sell all the properties I own down here

I could move up into the mountains, sell houses to other people like me—people who need to drop out every now and then and can afford to do that—and I'd be happy."

"Hmm," she says. "Chaos. I kinda like that."

Which makes me guffaw. "What's to like about chaos?"

"Well, some people get handed chaos and shut down. Like your parents. I don't know anything about them, but typically people fall into a life like that because they can't find a way out. The chaos overtakes them. But others thrive on it. It makes them stronger. Makes them rise up. Makes them better than they were before. And you're one of those people, Lawton. You see chaos as a challenge."

I suddenly feel happy. It takes me a few seconds to pull that feeling into a coherent thought, but when I do, I say, "Like you. You're chaos, Oaklee Ryan. This whole game we're playing is chaos. But that's what I like most about you. The challenge."

She looks down, blushing. Her long blonde hair falls over her eyes, but I can still see them peeking up at me from behind the thin curtain. And she says, "Well then. What are we waiting for?"

We don't finish our jackalope dogs or our pints of Bucked Up. Just stand up and walk out. Her hands gripping my upper arm like she's my girlfriend.

CHAPTER FIFTEEN

OAKLEE

We dropped our packages off with the hostess at Bronco Brews and the whole way back over to Shrike Bikes I feel guilty for bringing up the tattoo idea. I mean, if the guy wanted tattoos, he would've had them already.

But on the other hand, Lawton Ayers isn't a man who'd agree to something just to go along. He's the kind of guy who has an opinion. He's the kind of guy who knows what he wants. So he's not the kind of guy who'd mark his body with ink just to make a girl he hardly knows happy.

That rationale makes me feel fine about this.

But the guilt still lingers in the back of my mind.

"We don't have to do this," I say.

We're already approaching the front door to Shrike and my weak attempt to talk him out of the whole idea doesn't even make him pause. He just opens the door, stands aside, and says, "We're doing this."

So we go inside, make our way to the back where the tattoo shop is and stand under the neon pink sign that says Sick Girlz Ink. The buzzing sound from the machine in back fills my ears as I ding the little bell that lets the artists know someone is at the counter waiting.

Vivi Vaughn peeks her head around the corner of a wall. "Be right—hey!" she says, changing her tone mid-sentence. "Oaklee! Long time, bitch!"

Vivian Lee Vaughn. How to describe her? Pink hair done up in Fifties victory rolls. Tall, curvy, big tits, and pouty lips. She is someone you can't help but look at. Add in her full-sleeve tattoos—all hot-pink-and-black skulls and red hearts, filled in with a healthy dose of pale-pink stars—and she's got *Tattoo* magazine cover model written all over her.

"Vivi!" I say. "I have a friend who needs some work."

"I'm just about done, sweets. Be out in a sec!" she calls back.

"So…" Law turns to face me. "Don't tattoo shops usually have artwork on the walls? There's nothing here to get ideas."

"Oh, she's all custom. You tell her what you want, she draws it out on the spot, then she works her magic. You wanted an artist? She's the best in Denver. Her family owns the iconic Sick Boyz Ink up in Fort Collins, so she and her sisters come by it naturally."

"Well, would you look at that?" Law laughs. "I've got two real-life examples of women being chips off the old man's block."

I laugh too, because I've never thought about it that way. But it's true. Viv and I are two bitches at the top of their game in a world given to us by our fathers.

"But she has a scrapbook of her work over here," I say, walking over to a coffee table and sitting down on an overstuffed pink-leather couch. "Wanna see some of it?"

He does, because he joins me, and then we sit there, the book in our laps between us, and flip through.

"Jesus," Law says. "You weren't kidding. Everyone in here is a living, breathing masterpiece."

He's right. Everyone in the book has a well-planned, color-coordinated work of art on their bodies.

"She makes me want more than one." He laughs. "How'd you ever walk away with only that back piece?"

I shrug. "It's all I wanted. But yeah, it's addictive. Especially when Vivi or her sisters do them. You just want to come back as soon as you can and get more to keep it going."

He flips through the book, stopping to look at a few. One is a Dark Knight back piece done up in blues and blacks. The next is Iron Man done up in deep red and gray. And the third is a Sex Pistols chest piece with a huge anarchy symbol superimposed over a girl with a tall mohawk.

He lingers on that one for several minutes.

"Fancy yourself a Sex Pistols tattoo, Law?"

"No, not exactly. But—"

"OK," Vivi says, leading a woman out to the counter to pay. "Be with you folks in a sec. Just gotta button up this gig first."

"No problem," I say, turning back to Law. "What were you gonna say?"

"Well, chaos, right? I'm looking to control chaos. So the anarchy symbol is a good start. That's the patch on the back of the jacket I gave you." Then he points to a few framed comic books on the wall. "But I really like that too."

"Anarchist superhero theme. Didn't see that coming." I laugh. He puts the book down and we stand up to get a closer look at the art on the wall. "Is this a real comic?" I ask. "I've never heard of *Anarchy Found*."

"Yeah, but it's very limited-edition stuff. Only three issues and it was mostly an art piece."

"So you're familiar with these anarchists?"

"I've heard about them back when I was in college. Read bootleg copies online but never seen one in person."

"Hmmm," I say. "Well, that sounds a little bit like roots if you ask me."

"Hey, guys," Viv says, walking over to us. "Sorry for the wait. What can I do for you, Oaklee?"

So I tell her. I tell her all about my new boyfriend Lawton Ayers and what he's looking for. He jumps in when appropriate, trying to explain his vision, but having trouble.

"OK," Viv says, cocking one blonde eyebrow at him. "So you like comic books, and anarchists, and the colors blue and red, and punk rock."

Lawton makes a face. "Is that what I said?"

"That's what I heard," Viv replies.

"I don't think that's what I mean. I want something cool. Something that kinda personifies where I came from, but not who I am now. Something that chronicles that journey."

Viv chews her lip. Eyes drifting up towards the ceiling as she thinks.

"Oh!" I say. "I know." Both heads turn to look at me. "Hold on." I grab the book and start flipping though photographs. "Like this, but"—I flip a few more pages until I find another photo—"with this too."

Vivi looks at me. Then at Law. "This what you want?"

Law takes the book from my hand. Looks at the photo. Flips the pages back to the first one. Then repeats that process a few more times until he starts smiling. "Yes, but…" Flipping pages again. "But with this too." He points to another photograph.

Vivi eyes him for a second, then says, "You're naked now. No ink at all. And you're telling me you want *this*?"

Law nods.

I try to picture how intricate that piece would be and can't.

"What you're asking for is more than a bicep. It's gotta flow over to the chest and finish up on the opposite arm. Probably involve both shoulder blades on your back too. This is a commitment. You're gonna need to come back a whole bunch of times over the next *year* to get this kind of work. Like... you and I are gonna be real good friends by the time I'm done."

He nods again. "I get it."

But I don't. It was just... just supposed to be one. I didn't want to change him that much. I mean...

But Law follows Vivi when she walks over to the counter, picks up a sketchpad, and starts drawing with colored pencils, like this is really happening.

When she's done, she holds it up and Law says. "Yes. Do it."

Vivi looks at me and I don't say anything, because I'm still kind of stunned that he's going to take it this far.

So Vivi says, "OK. Follow me."

So he follows her back behind the wall to get himself inked up.

For me.

And the guilt is back. So much guilt is flowing through me, I put a hand on his arm and say, "Are you sure?"

And he says, "Yeah."

That's it. Just... yeah.

But I don't think he'd be here if I didn't bring it up. I don't think he's ever given tattoos a second thought after his friend told him not to get them. And now he's here making an insane commitment to turn his skin into artwork just to play my game.

My heart starts beating fast. Sweat begins to bead on my forehead and I get a little dizzy as the reality of what's happening sinks in. Vivi leaves the room to go get something.

"Law," I say. "Maybe you shouldn't do this."

"What?" He laughs, sitting down in the tattoo chair. "It was your idea!"

"I know," I say. "It shouldn't be my idea, it should be yours."

He reaches over, places a hand on my cheek, and says, "It *is* my idea. I've always wanted one, it's just… I was told to look professional, ya know. And that was Bric's idea of who I was, not mine. And now my whole life is about to change. In a few days I'm gonna meet up with those Home TV people and after it's all done, I'll be a different guy. The guy I've always wanted to be. The guy I always thought I was. Maybe… maybe that's my problem? Maybe I'm having an early mid-life crisis because I turned into who Bric wanted me to be, not the guy I wanted to be?"

"And this guy you envision yourself being… he has sleeves and a chest piece? Because that's what this will be by the time you're done."

"Why not?" he says. "I mean, if I was happy being this guy I'd just keep doing what I'm doing. I'm tired of being this guy. It's never felt right, ya know? It's always felt fake. Like I forgot who I was and where I came from. And I feel like if I get this piece then there's no way I'll ever forget again."

I smile at him. Tentatively. Almost convinced.

"And besides. We need to get that Hanna Harlow bitch and once she sees the new me, she'll fall right into our trap."

My smile falters. He wants to make me happy, which, for some reason, makes me sad instead.

"You're gonna stay?" Law asks, pulling me out of my building panic. "Or go do something? She says it'll take a few hours, at least. So don't feel obligated to hold my hand." Then he winks at me. "I can take it."

I wheel an extra doctor's stool up to the chair where he's sitting. "I'm not going anywhere. I'm with you."

Vivi returns and gets down to business. Going through all the motions of prepping his arm, then getting all her needles ready, loading one into her machine. She lines up all her inks and then puts on her headgear that directs a bright light down onto her canvas and begins.

Buzzing fills my ears. Lawton jokes, wincing as the needle carves out his design, but watching too. Fascinated with the changes he's making to his body.

For me.

Jesus Christ, Oaklee. You're so wrapped up in yourself. It takes some kind of ego to think this guy would endure pain, mark up his body, and pay a thousand dollars for a tattoo if he didn't want it.

At least I tell myself that. The whole time Vivi is working her magic.

Because that's all I *can* tell myself.

Because if I'm the only reason Lawton Ayers made this decision I won't be able to live with myself.

CHAPTER SIXTEEN

LAWTON

Oaklee eventually leaves the rolling doctor's stool and makes herself comfortable in an overstuffed chair in the corner. But she never takes her eyes off me. Her expression is a mixture of sadness and fear. But every time she sees me staring at her—it's hard *not* to stare at her— she smiles at me. Like she's putting on a brave face.

I know she's worried about this Hanna situation. And she has every right to be because this shit is way more serious than either of us first realized.

I could write it off as some kind of egotistical paranoid delusion—the whole *Hanna wants to be me* thing. But that's not what Hanna is doing. I think that's pretty clear. She's targeting Oaklee. For whatever reason, she wants to either steal her life or take her down.

Why though? I wish I knew.

Vivi doesn't talk much. She's one hundred percent focused on her design. I watch for the first hour. Carefully. Making sure she's doing what I envisioned. And it hurts pretty bad. Feels like a knife carving through my skin.

But eventually my arm grows numb and my trust is complete. Oaklee was right. If you're going to get a tattoo, this is definitely the best place to be.

My phone chimes a text—Eduardo, who tells me he's upgraded her security panel and ordered a metal accordion door to block the entrance to her apartment. I'm about to text him back and tell him thanks when I remember my idea from earlier. So I text back another request too.

"Got somewhere to be?" Vivi asks, not taking her eyes off her work.

"Nope," I say, looking over at Oaklee. She looks drowsy and still a little bit sad. "I'm present."

"Good," Vivi says. "Because I'm gonna need about three more hours before I'm ready to let you go today."

Oaklee stands up and walks over to us, peering down at the work-in-progress. Then she smiles at me, but again, it looks forced. "Are you hungry? I can go grab us some burgers from the bar."

"No beer," Vivi says.

"No beer," Oaklee repeats. "I know. Lawton? Food?"

"Nah," I say. "I've got plans for us later. Better save our appetites." And then I wink. Which makes her smile again, and this time I think it's real. And I so much want her to feel better about things, I decide to make more of an effort to include her.

"So... this upcoming beer festival," I say. "What day is it?"

"Next Sunday."

"What are you entering this year?" Vivi asks, joining in.

"A secret beer," Oaklee says. "Something I've been working on for a while now, but no one knows about."

"To keep Hanna Harlow from stealing it?" Vivi asks.

"What?" Oaklee says. "How did you—"

"Give me some credit." Vivi laughs. "I drink beer. Anyone who didn't notice that Buffed Up was just a knock-off of Bucked Up is an idiot."

"Right!" Oaklee exclaims. "How do people not see that?"

Vivi stops working and looks up at Oaklee. Her headlight shines in Oaklee's eyes for a moment, which makes Oaklee put up a hand to shield them. Vivi adjusts her light and says, "I dunno. It's weird, that's for sure. And I heard she came in here earlier bitching about Shrike Bar not putting it on tap."

"What happened?" Oaklee asks.

"The usual Hanna meltdown. Lots of drama. Lots of promises. Lots of bullshit."

"So what was the decision?" I ask.

Vivi smiles. "No way is that cheating bitch gonna get her foot in this door. She just wants our tap because of the TV show."

"What TV show?" Oaks and I ask at the same time.

"The new Shrike Bikes show. My cousin Oliver decided to take the Biker Channel up on their offer to do a show. Spencer did one years ago and got tired of it. But now that Oliver's in charge, looks like he's in."

"Interesting," I say. I guess I'm not the only guy in Colorado who wants to shake things up.

"Very interesting," Oaklee echoes. "I had no idea people were so into doing these reality shows."

"People?" Vivi asks, back working now. I sorta hate it when she stops. Like… I get used to the constant pain, so a break makes it worse once she starts up again. "Who else is doing a show?"

"Lawton," Oaklee says. Smiling down at me.

"Both of us," I remind her.

"Really?" Vivi asks. "Tell me more about this new venture, Oaklee. You didn't mention it last month when I saw you at that party."

"Oh, this is all Lawton," Oaklee says. "He needs a partner and I needed a favor, so we decided to team up."

169

"It's for Home TV," I say. "They like partners, ya know? And Oaklee is like the perfect local girl to host with me."

Vivi looks over at me, her drawing paused. Then she looks at Oaklee. Back at me. And says, "Yeah, you two are like the perfect couple. I can totally see it. But Home TV? What the fuck kind of show would a beer heiress and a— what do you do again?"

"Real estate," I say.

She laughs. "For real?"

"Yeah, why?"

"I dunno. I'd have pegged you as a musician or something. You look like a rock-star biker. What's up with that?"

I glance at Oaklee and she sighs.

"It's a long story," I say. Because I can tell Oaklee doesn't want to talk about our little boyfriend game. "But my pitch to the Home TV people is about selling multi-million-dollar mountain homes. You know, the great escape dream and shit like that."

"Because why?" Vivi asks.

"Because I'm tired of selling houses. I want do something more... colorful, I guess."

Vivi stops again, looks at me, moves her headlight so it's not shining in my eyes, and says, "So you woke up one day and said, 'I think I'll be a TV star?'"

And then she laughs again. This time a full-on guffaw.

Which makes me laugh, because it *is* pretty ridiculous. And then Oaklee joins in.

"I know," I say. "I get it. But I've been planning this for a long time. And the meeting with Home TV is this Thursday. This is the big one, ya know. The one where they come see me in my natural habitat and decide if I'm a good fit."

"So you need a partner in crime?" Vivi asks.

"Exactly," I say. "And Oaklee is that perfect partner."

"How long have you guys known each other?" Vivi asks. "Not long, from my guess, because you've never mentioned him before and I'm not hitting on you or anything, Law, but you're hot. She'd have mentioned you."

"It's recent," Oaklee says. "But it's perfect." She smiles at me. "I have something he needs and he has something I need and so it's... just... perfect."

"Wait," Vivi says. "What do you need from him?"

Vivi is a smart cookie. She gets that the nervous glances Oaklee and I are trading are a clue that there's more to this story than we're telling.

"Come on," she says. "What the fuck is going on?"

Oaklee sighs. Loudly. Then pulls up the rolling stool and says, "OK, but if I tell you, promise not to laugh at me."

Vivi crosses her heart with one black-gloved finger.

"I'm playing Jordan's Game with him."

"What?" Now Vivi—who is probably not a chick you can shock easily—looks shocked. "You two are playing a sex game?"

"You know about Jordan?" I ask. Probably the wrong question for this particular sideways conversation, but I'm so fucking curious.

"Everyone knows about that deviant." Vivi laughs. "One of the showroom guys tried to buy a game from him a few months back, but he couldn't afford it. So how much you paying for this?" Vivi asks Oaklee.

"That's not the point. And it's not a sex game. It's a get-even-with-Hanna-Harlow game."

"So you two aren't…" Vivi makes a rude gesture to indicate fucking. Oaklee blushes bright pink. Which has Vivi guffawing again. "You are! You little sex kitten." Then she looks at me. "I've tried to set her up with a dozen guys to get her out of this funk she's been in the past couple years and she's turned me down every time. So good on you, Lawton. Way to go!"

Where to take the conversation from there?

Never mind. Moot point. Because Vivi is now quizzing Oaklee on our plan to take down Hanna.

Which, after much cajoling, Oaklee cops to.

Thirty minutes later, Vivi, apparently satisfied she's gotten all the dirt while she's been drawing on my arm with a needle, says, "It's not a great plan. You need more, you guys. You need a class in advanced take-down methods. Baiting her to fall for Lawton?" She glances at me. "No offense, Law. You're totally hot and I'd gladly fall into your trap. But I'm a bit of a slut and not nearly as suspicious as Hanna. She's never going to take the bait, you guys. You need to like… break into her place and find her recipes. That's the kind of proof you need."

"That's ridiculous," I say, laughing off her dumb suggestion.

But when I look at Oaklee, she's quiet.

"You're not considering this?" I ask.

"Of course she is," Vivi says. "Ridiculous is how Oaklee rolls. Listen now, here's a plan you should consider…"

And that's what we do. We listen to Vivian Lee Vaughn, pink-haired tattoo artist extraordinaire, tell us exactly how to earn ourselves three to five years in state prison with a plan so crazy, it's not even worth mentioning here.

I stay quiet. Mostly because Oaklee is quiet too. And also because once you get Vivi talking about her crash course in how to become an outlaw, it's hard to interrupt her.

"That's what I'd do," Vivi says, once she's finally done. And then she rolls back on her stool, takes off her gloves with a loud snap, and says. "So... what do you think?"

"About your crazy plan?" I ask, still dumbfounded at what I just heard.

"No, dummy." She laughs. "Your tat. It's done. For now. You're gonna need to come see me again in about four weeks and we'll do the other arm. Then we'll start on the chest and back pieces. Let me get you some aftercare stuff."

With that she stands up and leaves the room.

I look at Oaklee. She looks back at me. I say, "We're in agreement that her plan is insane, right?"

Oaklee nods, and even though I've only known her two days, I can see those crazy wheels spinning in her head.

"Oaklee," I say. "This isn't an April Fool's joke. This isn't some prank. This is one hundred percent not happening."

She nods her head, still quiet. Then finally, she says, "Agreed," just as Vivi comes back in talking about how I should take care of the tattoo.

Which is fabulous.

It's a group of five people. Teenagers I might've hung out with back in the day. Leather jackets, punk hair, tattoos tattooed on their bodies. All hanging out in a decaying urban setting. The building behind them has broken windows. The old brick crumbling. And on the side of the wall is a spray-painted anarchy symbol in red and blue. All done up in photorealism.

I have to admit, the artist might be insane, but her work defies any opinion I have of her moral compass.

It occurs to me though. The irony that what she just inked on my body is a testament to who I was. And I have to wonder, as I watch her wrap my arm with special tattoo wrap, then get up, listen to her instructions, and pay her a thousand dollars on my credit card, if I have any room to judge.

CHAPTER SEVENTEEN

OAKLEE

"I'll walk you home," Law says, once we get outside Shrike.

"Of course you will," I say, smiling at him. "You're a true gentleman, Law. And I'm sure you'll walk me to my door again, won't you?" I do one of those wink-wink things. To indicate I'm thinking about sex.

He gets it.

"I'm definitely walking you all the way up. I need to show you the progress Eduardo made on your security system today."

"Is that the only reason?" I joke.

He just gives me a sly grin. But it's enough. And it's not that I really even want sex with him tonight. I mean, that would be a bonus, of course. I just want him to stick around. It's been nice having someone to divert my attention away from all this Hanna bullshit. Even going up to Golden yesterday for the beer thing at the Opera House was funner with him there. And today... well. Wow. We packed a lot into today.

"I'm actually pretty tired," he says, jolting me back to the conversation we're having. "So I'll probably just drop you off and we'll figure out where we go next tomorrow."

"Oh," I say. "OK."

"I have clients tomorrow," he says, trying to explain. Because my reaction was clearly disappointment. "I have three houses to show and the inevitable paperwork that will come with those since the market is hot and all three of them are interested in putting in offers."

"That's fine," I say. "I have a ton of things to do tomorrow too."

Which is a lie. I don't really do anything at the brewery. I mean, it's not like I tend bar or wait tables or anything important like that. I have paperwork. There's always that. But none of it is pressing. In fact, most of my days are spent doing busywork. Some beer testing. I do that almost every day just out of habit. I chat with customers at lunch or dinner. I work on new recipes, and new label designs, and new beer names, and new beer recipes. Which is all the fun stuff that comes with running a brewery. And yeah, that's all critical stuff, but... I have no labels to design, or beers to name, or recipes to come up with because I employ fifty-two people for a reason. So they can do all that stuff for me.

So I spent a helluva lot of time thinking about Hanna Harlow. Way too much time thinking about that bitch.

Maybe I'm having an early mid-life crisis too?

It's not like anyone ever asked me if I'd like to run a brewery. It was just assumed. By me, not just my dad. I never even considered another career.

Is that weird?

"Ya know," I say as we cross the street and head towards the front door of the brewery, "I'm looking forward to this TV show interview thing. In fact, I think it would be fun to work with you on this project."

"Yeah?" Law says.

"Yeah. I might be bored, Lawton. Meeting you might've highlighted some deficiencies in my life."

"Social?" he asks. "Or professional?"

"Both."

"You're falling for me, aren't you?"

I laugh as he opens the door to the brewery and holds it for me. "Maybe a little."

He follows me in and then beats me to the elevator to press the button.

But the little button doesn't light up. "Oh, my God, did Eduardo forget to turn the elevator back on or something?"

"Nope," Lawton says. And that's when I notice there's a little panel in the stainless-steel button cover. "Now you gotta press a code to even open the doors."

He presses the code on the keypad, the doors open, and we step inside. Then he repeats the code again to make the penthouse floor light up and the doors close.

"It might be overkill," Law says. "But it's a good idea to have too much security rather than too little."

His concern gives me a warm feeling inside. Like he really is my boyfriend, because this is the kind of stuff boyfriends pay attention to and take care of.

When the doors open again at my apartment he exits with me. "Oh, we forgot to get dinner!" I say, glad he's still here but afraid he's just gonna say goodbye and leave.

"No, we didn't," he says, shooting me a grin. "I got this. Come on. There's a little surprise for you on the roof." He takes my hand and starts leading me up the stairs.

"What? What kind of surprise?" And if his concern over my safety had me feeling all gooey inside, this pushes me over the edge. And I'm glad he's got his back to me as we walk up the steps, because I have a wide smile on my face.

"You'll see," he says, looking over his shoulder at me once we get to the top. We make our way into my bedroom and I grab his old leather jacket off the bed as I pass. Because it's chilly outside. Because I want to wear it. Because it was his and now it's mine.

I slip it on and then climb the ladder, wondering the entire time if Law is looking at my ass.

I hope he's looking at my ass.

Just as I get to the last few rungs on the ladder, I stop.

"Keep going," he urges with one hand on my hip.

"What did you do?" I breathe.

"Just keep going," he says. "You'll see soon enough."

So I climb those last few rungs and step out onto my roof. Law follows me. Stands next to me as I take it all in.

The entire water tower is lit up with strings of white lights. They glow against the backdrop of night, and the city, and the stars like something out of a dream. And the underside is draped with white mosquito netting. Just the way my dad used to do it for special days.

"What is all this?" I breathe, afraid that talking too loud will break the spell.

"The deluxe package boyfriend pays attention, Miss Ryan. So…" He shrugs when I look at him. "I had Eduardo set this up."

"For me?" I say, my hand over my heart.

"Yes, of course for you." He laughs.

"But… it's not even my birthday!"

"Oaklee," Law says, turning to face me as he takes both my hands in his. "There are no rules for special. We can make this life as fun, as cool, and as special as we want. Any time we want. There's no holiday on the calendar called Special Day."

"But you… we… we're not even really dating."

"So? So what? I like you, you seem to like me. And maybe we're not dating for real, but we're definitely partners, right? In your game. In my game." He lets go of my hands and throws his arms up. "We can do whatever you want. And you said this made you happy as a kid, so it took almost no effort at all for me to replicate what you loved."

No effort? Is he kidding? "My dad never climbed the water tower to string lights all the way to the top. I think the whole city can see this tonight."

"Well, Eduardo wasn't happy about that, no doubt." He laughs. "But that's how I saw it in my head when you described it to me, so that's how it got done."

"Eduardo..." I say. "How did you get him to do this?"

"He and I go way back. We work together all the time. He's a cool dude and besides, now I owe him a favor, and believe me, he'll make me do something equally ridiculous when it's his turn to collect. Besides, he's gonna overcharge me for this security, don't worry."

I turn and look out at the city. Wondering who can see this. Wondering if people who look out at my water tower every night are looking out at it right now thinking, *Well, damn. That's fuckin' awesome.*

Because that's exactly what I'm thinking.

Lawton Ayers has blown me away.

I turn back to him and he says, "I got pizza too. So we can eat. It's good cold, so I figured—"

And that's when I walk up to him, grab his face in my hands, and kiss him. Right on the mouth.

He kisses me back, our tongues doing that sweet, familiar dance again. His hands go to my arms, grip my shoulders tightly as the kiss grows. Becomes less desperate and more passionate.

"What's that for?" I ask, reluctantly pulling away to point at the picnic table.

"That," Law says, nodding his head at the table, "is the sheepskin rug off the floor of your bedroom. I didn't think you'd want to be picking splinters out of your back tomorrow morning."

I can't help it. I laugh. "You planned the lights, the dinner," I say, motioning to the pizza box on a small side table nearby, "and the sex?"

"Well, go big or go home." Then he smiles. "You can say no if you—"

I push him backwards. Taking him by surprise so he'll stop talking. I place both hands on his chest, making him take another step back. Then another. Until he bumps into the end of the picnic table and leans back, half sitting, half standing. Grinning at me like a boy who is about to get lucky.

Because he is.

My hands reach for the button of his jeans. His hands slipping inside my leather jacket and under my shirt. I suck in a breath of air because they are cold. But I don't care. I drag his zipper down, my hands reaching inside, my fingers wrapping around his cock.

I feel him grow at my touch and his eyes go from wide with delight to half-mast with desire.

"Tonight," I say, "it's your turn."

He shakes his head. "I took my turn last night."

"Liar," I whisper, crouching down, his cock fully hard now, and kiss the tip of his head as I stare up into his eyes.

"You're going to kill me, Oaklee."

God, I love it when he says my name. It makes me want to melt. I open my mouth, cover his head with my lips, and swirl my tongue around until he closes his eyes.

He opens them again. Almost immediately. And his hands grip each side of my head. His fingers grabbing my hair to guide me, helping me take him deeper.

I want to look at him. I want to see every expression on his face. But it feels so good to just close my eyes and pump his cock with both hands. Enjoying my part in this as much as he's enjoying his.

"God. Damn," he growls, when I press my head forward until the top of his cock is hitting the back of my throat. I might not have porn-star skills when it comes to this kind of thing. But I have a good idea of what turns guys on. And even though I know my limits and the gag reflex is about to kick in, I try harder. I take him deeper. I open my throat, breathe through my nose, and watch his expression. My eyes on his. His eyes on mine. Desperate to keep this moment in a cage forever. Never let it go.

But nothing lasts forever. And I have to back away and take a breath so I can dive back down to repeat the whole thing again. Then again, and again, and again… until I'm sucking his cock like it's food and I'm starving.

"Oaklee," he groans again. "You're gonna—"

But he doesn't finish, because I stop, stand up, and reach under my skirt to slip my panties down my legs.

He watches me. Crooked grin on his face.

And when I place my hand on his chest again, he lies back on the sheepskin rug. His cock so hard, it's standing straight up. Like an invitation for me to climb on top of him and cover him with my wet pussy.

Which I do. Gladly.

"We could go inside," he says, breathless now as his hands slip under my shirt again, tug my bra down, and fondle my breasts. "So the whole city can't watch."

"Let them watch," I say, positioning my hips on either side of his thighs. I sink down. His cock filling me up. My pussy wet, and ready. But the friction is still there. He is big. And Hard. And thick. And I feel everything like this is my first time ever.

"Yes," I moan, placing my hands flat on his chest as I begin to rock back and forth. I want to feel everything tonight.

"Yes," he agrees, moaning back. Both hands still gripping my tits the way they did last night when he brought me to climax over, and over, and over again. "Fuck me," he says. Urging me to go faster. "Fuck me hard, Oaklee."

So I do. I stop rocking and start bouncing. My breasts still cradled in his hands. Holding them as I lift up and slam down.

I want him close to me. Even though I am exactly one arm's width away, it's too far.

And he gets that.

Because he gets me.

So his hands stop squeezing my tits and instead, he wraps his arms tight around my back, pulling me down on top of his chest. Holding me captive as he takes over. Thrusting up inside me with a desperation I've never felt before with anyone.

He takes me completely, just like that. Lying on a sheepskin rug, perfectly balanced on a picnic table, on top of my building, at the tip of the world.

He fucks me as the city watches.

Two people beneath an old water tower. Basking in glowing white lights. Hidden only by the false privacy of mosquito netting. Under the star-filled night sky.

We come.

CHAPTER EIGHTEEN

LAWTON

There is the rush of sexual climax… and then there's the rush of sexual climax with someone you adore.

The difference between the two is so instinctual everyone knows this to be true. There is some connection… something in your chest. Maybe it's the heart, maybe it's the soul—it doesn't really matter what you call it. When you have feelings for someone and you consummate that with a sexual experience everything is heightened.

Her whole body softens and then slips off to the side. Her breasts against my ribcage. Her face tucked into the crook of my neck. Her fingernails tracing some lazy pattern on my chest.

My eyes are closed so I don't really know for sure if her eyes are closed too but I'm certain they are. She's basking in the same post-coital glow as I am.

"So… question," she whispers through her still-heavy breathing.

"Shoot."

"Are you multi-orgasmic as well? Or is that just a talent you bring out in others?"

I smile. Hold in a laugh. Then open my eyes to a surreal fantasy version of the underside of her water tower.

The white lights make it all look so special. It's funny how that happens. How a string of nine-dollar mini lights can change everything. How a sheepskin rug can turn an old wooden picnic table into something so much more. How a leather jacket and a tattoo can change a man in the span of two days. How a woman named Oaklee can make him see himself in a brand-new way.

I wrap my arms around her and roll over so she's on her back and I'm on top. I move my hips. Just a little. Just enough for her to feel my still-hard cock against her inner thigh.

"What do you think?" I ask her.

She's smiling up at me, her brown eyes turned slightly yellow from the glow of the lights, her cheeks pink. Flushed from the exertion of sex. Her breathing slower now, but not her heart. Because I can feel it underneath me.

Still pounding.

Waiting for more.

Trying to match mine.

So we can keep time together.

I think that's what hearts do. Keep time. Keep everything together. Keep this crazy thing called life in perspective.

"One more time here," I say. "Then I'll take you inside so I can get you naked."

It's too cold to make her take her clothes off. Even though I know she'd do that if I asked her to. I can already feel the chill of her beneath me. But my body heat will help. Will protect her from the cold.

The deluxe package includes a boyfriend blanket on a cold night.

She opens her legs, reaches down between them to play with herself, and my hips adjust enough to allow my cock to slide up to her opening. Her fingers are grabbing my shoulder now. And even through the leather I can feel them dig.

I want to take the jacket off so she can leave marks on me. I want there to be nothing between us. But I want her to be on the bottom at least once. So she can look up and see the surreal fantasy version of the underside of her water tower just like I did. So we can share that special feeling of being with someone you adore in a way that can't be repeated.

No one will ever make love to her like this again. Not even me. Because this is a moment and moments pass into other moments and no two are ever alike.

She thrusts her hips upward, trying to force me to enter her. I just grin, because not gonna happen. Not until I say so, at least.

"Come on," she whispers, watching me intently. "Let's go."

"We've got time. There's no rush."

She thrusts upward again. "There is a rush. A rush I want to experience again. Don't make me beg, Lawton Ayers."

"Begging?" I ask playfully. "Is that something you do?"

She giggles, then gets serious real quick. She frowns. Pouts her lips. Widens her eyes. "Please," comes out like a whimper. Like she's been wounded and needs relief. Relief only I can administer.

"Just take a moment, Oaklee. Feel it with me."

Her eyes narrow slightly. Like she's trying to figure out what I'm asking.

"The game is over," I say. "That's what I want you to feel. We passed it by some time ago. I'm not sure when, exactly. But the game is over."

"OK," she says, her face relaxing. The pout is gone. The confusion is gone. And all her expectations seem to melt away. "We're real," she whispers.

She's not asking me, she's telling me.

I nod, and in that same moment I allow my cock to slip inside her.

She closes her eyes and clutches my shoulders tighter. And yes, I so badly want to be naked with her inside so I can really feel the hold she's got on me right now.

I fuck her slow this time. I feel her this time. I relish the way her pussy clamps against my thick shaft. I enjoy how wet she is. How she moans just a little. How her legs wrap around my waist, trying to box me in and keep me close.

She doesn't need to do that. I'm not going anywhere.

I kiss her as we fuck. It's a slow kiss because it's a slow fuck. Our tongues wrapped up in each other. In the simplicity of this night and how everything after this will be complicated.

Because that's just how it goes.

She draws in a deep breath, holds it as her body stiffens and I know what's coming.

She's coming.

And there's nothing more beautiful than watching the face of a woman you adore reach the pinnacle of muscle-twitching pleasure with you on top of her.

So I come too.

Because that's what turns me on the most.

Her pleasure.

CHAPTER NINETEEN

OAKLEE

The moment I orgasm he thrusts his hips and fills me so deep I can't breathe. The muscles in my legs are spasming. My eyelids flutter closed—not sure if they want to stay that way and drag the moment out behind a curtain of fireworks on black, or open wide to see the whole thing in perfect clarity.

They lose the battle and stay closed as pleasure courses through me in waves. My muscles contracting against his cock. The low growl comes from deep within him as he reaches his climax with me, and then the explosion as he comes inside me.

I laugh. I can't help it. I just smile, and laugh, and let the happiness and satisfaction bubble out of me like some wild child who's never been let out to play.

"Jesus," he says, his body relaxing.

I lean my face up into his neck. Smelling the new leather of his jacket, the faint scent of antiseptic from the tattoo, and aftershave leftover from this morning.

He grabs my hair, pulls it—not too hard, but not too softly either—until my mouth is up against his again.

We don't kiss. We don't even move. We just go still.

I can feel him smile. I'm sure he can feel me smile too.

"Now what?" I ask.

"Whatever you want, Oaks," he replies back, kissing my lips softly. Tenderly.

"I'm not talking about—"

"I know what you're talking about," he says, cutting me off. "And my answer is still, 'Whatever you want, Oaks.'"

"But—"

"Shhh," he says. "Stop thinking."

I laugh. "No one can stop thinking."

"It wasn't a request."

"No?"

He continues to kiss me. His mouth more urgent. His lips more demanding. His will imposed.

"No. We're going to take that pizza inside," he says. "Then we're going to fuck in a hot shower so we can get warm. And then we're going eat dinner naked in front of your fireplace."

I just smile.

"Any objections?"

"Can't think of any."

"Good, because that wasn't really a question either."

"You're dumb."

He places both palms flat on top of the sheepskin rug and lifts his upper body up off me. My shirt has ridden up, exposing my belly. And the cold, silver zippers of his jacket drag across my skin and make me shudder.

"Game over, Oaklee."

I get serious. My smile gone. My shuddering body still. I have to swallow hard before I nod yes and say, "OK." Because this… this is real. I think this is real. "OK," I say again.

He gets up, puts his cock back in his pants and zips up. Then picks up my panties, slips them back up my legs so slowly I want to die… and offers me his hand as he grabs the pizza box with the other. We take the long way around to the stairs that lead down onto another terrace on the opposite side of the building so we don't have to climb down the ladder.

Maybe he thinks we do this because it's difficult to climb down a ladder holding a pizza box.

But that's not why I take him the long way.

It's because I don't want to let go of his hand.

We enter through a sliding glass door that leads into one of the spare rooms on the main level.

"What's this room?" he asks as we walk past the large wooden barrels and giant glass jugs called carboys.

"This is my secret beer room," I say, looking over my shoulder to wink at him. "This is where I keep the Assassin Saison."

He pulls on my hand to make me stop. So I do and find him studying everything. "So why do you need both barrels and jugs?"

"Oh, the jugs are for infusing the fruit flavors. I was testing out two different kinds, so instead of making a huge batch in a barrel, I use the carboys for that. Then when it's right, I transfer that to the barrels."

He looks at me and says, "That's fuckin' hot."

"What is?" I laugh.

"That you know how do this kind of stuff. Beer-making. Just thinking about you wearing a lab coat as you drink beer you brewed with your own hands makes me hard."

He pulls me close so quick, my breasts bump up against his chest. I tilt my head up to look at him and the strangest feeling courses through my body. I don't even think I have a word to describe it.

There's several long moments when all we do is stare into each other's eyes. It's weird, but hot. It's strange, but nice. It's...

"We're going out to dinner tomorrow," he says.

"OK."

"I'll pick you up after work."

"OK," I repeat.

"I'm going to monopolize your time from now until you make me stop."

I smile. "OK."

He stares at me for a few more seconds. Then nods his head, satisfied that I understand what's happening, and takes the lead as we leave the secret beer room.

He drops the pizza off on the kitchen island, then twirls me around. My skirt flares out as I spin, and then he's got the leather jacket down my arms. It falls to the hardwood floor with a audible thump. And while I'm still thinking about how sexy that sound is, his jacket does the same.

His tattoo is shiny from the clear antibacterial film Vivi used to cover it up. His t-shirt tight across his chest and upper arm.

I trace a finger down the outside of the film, making his skin quiver.

"Do you like it?" he asks.

I nod, slowly lifting my eyes up to meet his again. "I love it."

"Good," he whispers, his fingertips reaching for the hem of my shirt. When he lifts it up my body begins to tremble. Maybe from the chill in the air, but more likely, it's just... his touch that does that.

"Cold?" he asks, as the shirt goes up over my head and then lands on the floor on top of my jacket.

"Little bit," I say, as his fingers find the waistband of my skirt. One tug later it's over my hips, pooling at my feet with a soft flutter.

He unbuttons his jeans, grabs his cock through his pants. It's clearly hard and ready to go again. And yes. Yes, he is most definitely multi-orgasmic.

"Shower?" he asks, studying my body. His eyes tracing every curve, every bit of me, until they finally rest on mine again.

I nod. Knowing full well it's not a question, but not caring.

He takes my hand again and leads me up the stairs and down the catwalk hallway to my bedroom. Once inside he takes me directly to the master bathroom.

"Nice," he says, stopping in front of the giant clawfoot tub. "We're gonna use that. Eventually. But not tonight."

I picture what a bubble bath with Lawton Ayers might look like. Would he fuck me? Shampoo my hair? Would he finger me under the water as I sat between his legs and leaned back into his chest?

"Oaklee?"

"Huh?" I look over at him. He's sitting on a bench near the entrance to my closet, pulling off his boots.

"Still with me?"

"I'm here. Just…" I blush a little. "Having a little fantasy about you and me in that bathtub, that's all."

He laughs. "We'll get there."

"I'm sure we will," I say, stepping towards him as I reach around behind my back to unclasp my bra. He watches me intently as it comes free and slips down my arms to rest on the hard marble floor at my feet. I keep going. Because I want to be naked with this man. Right now. And wiggle my panties over my hips. Not so seductively that I look like a stripper up on a stage, but pretty close.

His mouth is open, his eyes fixed on my pussy as I reveal it, then step away from my discarded underclothes and turn to the shower. Giving him a nice, long look at my backside as I reach in and turn the water on.

He's behind me then. Hands on my stomach, arms circling me as his fingers dip down between my legs and slip between the soft folds of skin to find me wet.

His lips caress my neck with kisses and I swear to God, I just melt back into him. My legs shake, my back arches, and when I turn my head towards him, his lips are there.

How? How did this happen?

"Stop thinking, Oaklee." It's like he's reading my mind.

"I'm not objecting," I say, trying to explain.

"Doesn't matter. There's time to think later. Now will never happen again so let's just enjoy it."

I don't know if that's sad or romantic. A little of both, I think, because—

"Oaklee," he whispers, playing with my clit.

"Oh, God," I moan.

"Stop. Thinking."

He urges me to step into the shower, the spray of the water hitting me like a hot jungle mist. A moment later he's pressing a bar of sweet-smelling lavender-colored soap along my arm, while fingering me with his other hand at the same time.

We both step under the water, letting it fall down our bodies—making it slick where we have contact. My back against his chest. His arm down the length of my stomach. The soap lather fills the bathroom with the scent of lilacs.

I close my eyes. Be present. Pay attention to all the little details that I don't want to forget. The way his finger feels inside me. The steam flowing up towards the ceiling.

The hardness of his cock pressing against my ass and the way his breath catches in the same moment as mine.

I turn to face him because I can't stop myself. "I want to see you," I say, taking his face in my hands. His eyes are brown. So brown. I don't think I've ever noticed them before. They have flecks of black in them. And rings of green that I never noticed before. His cheeks and jaw are shadowed with today's stubble. Just enough to be scratchy. Just enough to be sexy.

His neck is thick with muscle, but not out of proportion with his tall frame. His hair is dark, the water changing the brown to a near-black. It looks longer now too. Messier. Less suit and more leather jacket. One thick strand has fallen onto his forehead, curling a bit at the end. And that chin dimple appears, pierces my heart with an arrow, and then disappears just as quick.

"I like you too," he says. Because he knows what's going through my head.

He knows me. Somehow, he does.

He sees into me—through me.

His finger withdraws from inside me and his hand rests on my shoulder, urging me to turn. So I'm standing under the water and he's a step away from it.

I feel exposed for some reason.

He is just as naked as I am, but the way he looks at me. With that hunger inside him. Silent, introspective, unmovable.

It makes me shudder even though the water spraying down my back is slightly too hot.

Smiling, he backs up to the marble-field wall, leans into it, one leg bent, the other straight so his body is slanted just a little. Just enough so that when he says, "Come here," and I do, and I reach him—he can lift one of my legs up, slide his full-erect cock inside me, and then grip the firm muscles of my ass and lift me up.

He holds me like that for so long—his gaze trained on mine—I start counting out loud for some reason. "One," I say. "Two. Three—"

And when I get to three he drops me, just a little. Just enough so that his cock sinks so deep inside me, I can feel it—not just in my pussy, but in my gut. In my heart. In my soul.

"How?" I say.

He shrugs, like this question makes perfect sense, he just doesn't have the answer.

"Does it matter?" he finally asks back.

And I decide… "No."

It doesn't.

CHAPTER TWENTY

LAWTON

I know what she wants to know. I just don't feel like thinking too hard about it.

It's insane. It's stupid teenage love. It defies logic and therefore, it isn't real. It's the situation we've been thrown into. It's the game. It's Jordan Wells and Hanna Harlow. It's Bronco Brews, and *Rocky Mountain Millionaires*, and Home TV, and Shrike Bikes, and that stupid Opera House tavern up in Golden.

It's the leather jacket, and the Assassin Saison, and the water tower on the roof decorated in white lights.

It's the lack of elevator security, it's the view of her penthouse from my terrace, it's the alley down below, and the tattoo on my arm covered in antibacterial plastic, and a lingering feeling inside me that...

We did something wrong.

We fucked this up.

Somehow, some way, we missed the most obvious clue.

And yet... it's still the closest thing to perfection I've ever felt with a woman.

So does it matter? Does it matter that when I leave here and tomorrow comes—when I go back to work and take phone calls, and meetings, and show houses, and do paperwork—the fantasy will end?

Will the sting of tomorrow take away the sweetness of today?

That's the question she's asking.

And that's the question I answer when I reaffirm and say, "No. It won't."

"Fuck me hard this time," she says.

I smile.

"Just do it."

I smile bigger.

"Fuck me like the world ends tonight. Fuck me like we'll never fuck again. Fuck me like—"

I whirl around, pressing her back into the hard tiled wall of the shower, back my hips up so only the tip of my cock is inside her. And thrust forward.

Her fingernails dig into my bare shoulders, gripping them like she never wants to let go, and I pound her again. She leans her head down, mouth open, and bites me on the fleshy part of my arm. Just a quick nip. Like she needs to get my full attention even though she already has it. It needs to be complete. It needs to be all-consuming. It needs to belong to her and only her.

I thrust again. Then again, and again, and again. Giving her what she wants. Her bite becomes a kiss. Her fingernails find their way to my back. Dragging up and down, up and down, and I fuck her back and forth. Back and forth.

And then I change my tactics. Stopping completely.

"No," she whines, biting my shoulder again. "No."

I hug her close. My hands gripping her ass so hard, she'll have bruises tomorrow. My chest pressed into her breasts, relishing the feeling of her softness again the hardness of me.

As slow and soft as it's been so far with Oaklee, that's how fast and hard it is now.

I fuck her like the world ends tonight.

I fuck her like we'll never fuck again.

I fuck her just the way she wants me to.

Her orgasm comes with a scream this time. A primal yell that makes me think of neighbors disturbed. Waking up and turning to each other with questions of, "What was that?"

But then I remember she owns this whole building and no one lives here but her.

So I keep going.

I fuck her till she's screaming, and moaning, and whining, and begging me to keep going and stop all in the same breath.

She comes all over my dick for the third time tonight.

I come inside her for the third time tonight.

And even when that's over and I'm sitting down on the stone bench on the other side of the shower, her in my lap, her head on my shoulder, our hearts still beating fast—like that's the only speed they know how to beat— she says, "Again," as she slip out of my lap and drops to her knees to take my cock in her hand. Her eyes gazing up at me like I am her god and she is my servant.

And I swear, I am hard for her. It shouldn't be possible. I am spent in every way possible. But I am hard for her. Before she even gets the tip of my cock to her lips I am ready.

I grip her hair. Tight, because I can't help myself. Hard, because that's how she wants it right now. Rough, because I know the sting will only serve her in the end.

She gags, but I don't stop. I push her face down until she loses eye contact with me. I push her face down until her chin is rubbing against my balls and her nose is pressed up to the skin of my lower abdomen.

Saliva drips out of her mouth. A strand hanging on her lips, then slowly, like a movie in slow motion, it drips onto my balls.

I release her head because if I don't, I'll come down her throat. She pulls away, gasping for breath, hand automatically coming up to wipe away the saliva.

I expect her to be angry. I expect, at the very least, a scowl.

But she smiles and then tips her head back down and we do it again. Then again. And again. Taking breaks each time she reaches critical mass. The moment when she can't hold her breath, or keep her gag reflex in check, or stand another second of it.

And each time she goes longer. Each time she tries harder. Each time... she surprises me in a way no woman I've ever met has surprised me before.

"I'll keep going," I say. "I won't stop. I won't come. Not until you tell me you've had enough." It comes out like a warning because that's exactly what it is. Sexual self-control is something I've perfected. Something I cherish. Something I take seriously. "I can go all night," I say, when she doesn't answer me.

She's breathing so hard now. Gasping for air. Her cheeks are bright red. Her lips slightly swollen from her efforts. Her eyes... still bright. Still excited.

She kisses the tip of my cock again, then opens her mouth—gaze locked on mine—and wraps her lips around my cock. Both of her hands grab my shaft, pumping up and down with a slight twisting motion. They are slick with water and saliva. That, along with the steaming heat from the shower, is the perfect combination to make me come.

But I don't. Not until she gives in. And her actions make it clear she's not giving in, she's just changing tactics.

She goes slow now, and I don't press her. I lean back against the tile wall and let myself relax. Let my body soften just a little. Let my eyes enjoy the beautiful picture she's painting with her actions.

She takes my cock out of her mouth and swipes her tongue up and down my shaft. And Jesus fucking Christ, I might be a liar. Because there's a moment when I think I might lose control after all.

She feels it too. Senses it the way only a woman connected—tuned in to me and only me—could be.

Because she stops. Gives me a minute. Plays the game we're not playing.

She doesn't want to win. Not at my expense. Because this isn't a competition.

She wants me to get what I want, the way I want it.

"You're not real," I say.

She giggles. Flashing a smile at me I don't think I've seen before. Something in between happy and satisfied. Something I want to see more of.

"You're the one who's not real."

"Maybe neither of us is real?"

"Maybe none of this is real?"

I smile now too.

"God," she says. "That dimple you unleash when you smile sometimes. I want to die every time I see it."

"Dimple?" I say, momentarily distracted. "What dimple?"

"What do you mean? That cute-as-fuck dimple in your chin when you smile."

I furrow my eyebrows as she plays with my cock. Her hands never stop. Her eyes once more locked on mine.

"You mean you don't even know you have it?"

"Didn't have it." And then I smile. "Until you, apparently."

"You're dumb."

"But it's funny. I was just thinking the same thing about your smile."

"What about it?"

"It's different tonight."

"No, it's the same smile I've always had."

But I shake my head. "If I can have a secret dimple I only reveal to you, then you can have a smile you only reveal to me."

She stands up, dropping my cock. Which is almost a relief. Because even though we're talking, I'm still very close to coming again. And then she climbs back into my lap, lowering herself down onto me. Pressing hard until I'm deep, deep inside her.

"Let's both come again. And smile our secret smiles as we do it."

I don't even try to understand at this point. I just nod my head and smile until she giggles and pokes a finger at my chin.

And that's her secret smile too. I know it's for me and only me.

Because we come, for the fourth time tonight, together.

Later, after we've gotten dressed—me in my jeans, her in a t-shirt and shorts—and we've eaten our pizza and talked about everything except Hanna Harlow, and TV shows, and beer, and real estate, we climb into bed together naked.

Her body pressed against mine. Her heat is my heat and my heat is her heat.

There's no pressure at all. We fucked, and fucked, and fucked again. So there's nothing left to do but be still in the dark. My arm under her shoulder. Her head on my chest. Her heart beating slow, keeping time with mine because that's what they do.

She says, "Good night, Law."

And I say, "Good night, Oaks."

Like this is just what we do before bed.

Like we've been this couple for decades instead of days.

And it's only then that I remember that feeling I had earlier.

The feeling that I've missed something. Some clue that's so obvious.

But her soft breathing tells me she's asleep and it doesn't seem fair to stay awake without her.

So I sleep too.

Because that's all there's left to do.

CHAPTER TWENTY-ONE

OAKLEE

I dream of smiling. Of laughing. Of happiness. And even though I'm asleep and I know it's a dream, I know why I'm happy.

"Hey, sunshine," a gruff voice whispers near my ear.

I know this is Law. I know it's morning. And I know the next thing he says is going to be about leaving. About work. Or being late.

I open my eyes and smile for real. His face is right up next to mine, his eyes just inches away. The brown eyes with flecks of black and rings of green are pretty much the best thing to wake up to. Ever. "You're leaving, right?"

"Not yet. It's fuckin' early."

Which makes me laugh.

"I was gonna make breakfast first. What do ya like?"

I don't even eat breakfast but I don't want to say that. "Ummm... I dunno. Cereal?"

He makes a face. Which is adorable because out pops the dimple. "No, I mean like, real breakfast. Something hot."

He's hot. His stubble is clearly into the getting-me-wet territory. I didn't see him wake up yesterday morning— God, was that only yesterday?—so I missed the morning stubble.

I never want to miss it again. I reach for his face, my hand finding a home flat on his cheek to feel the roughness. "Bacon?"

I'm pretty sure guys love bacon.

"How about French toast?" he offers up instead.

"Is French toast something on your regular menu?"

"No." He smiles again. Fuckin' dimple. "But it's sweet and I want you to have something sweet to start the day."

I sigh. It's one of those God-I-might-love-you sighs. Contentment, or whatever. "Sure. I'd love some French toast."

"OK," he says, leaning over to kiss me on the cheek. "I'll work on that while you wake up. Meet you in the kitchen in ten."

I watch him get out of bed. Naked. He has a very nice ass. Like… those glutes get worked regularly. And his thighs. Jesus. He looks over his shoulder as he pulls on yesterday's jeans.

Dimple. Only it's a new dimple. This one has a twin and they are both in his lower back, right above his ass.

"You OK?" he asks. "Not having regrets about last night or anything, are ya?"

I shake my head no as I study his new tattoo. It's gorgeous. Still wrapped up in that clear barrier Vivi put on it last night. The colors are fantastic. Bright and new. Just like this relationship. "Do you get a lunch, Lawton Ayers?"

He laughs. "I do. Eventually. But I got clients today, so there's no telling when it'll be. I'll be back for dinner though. Still wanna go to dinner tonight?"

I nod my head. Let out a long breath of air. And wonder how I'm gonna get through an entire day without him.

Then wonder… how did that happen over a weekend?

"Ten minutes," he says, walking back over to kiss me again. "Don't keep me waiting."

I watch him leave the bedroom. I wonder if he knows how hot he is. He doesn't act like it. He doesn't have a stuck-up air to him. Even though he's rich, handsome, and smart. Which is like the stuck-up trifecta.

But Lawton is a guy who comes from nothing. I can't forget that. He's got it all now, but if that new tattoo on his arm is any indication, it was a long journey to get here.

I can hear him downstairs as he goes through my kitchen cabinets looking for things. A frying pan. A spatula. I hear the fridge open and close several times. Getting out eggs and butter probably.

"Five minutes, Oaklee!" he calls from downstairs.

But I stay in bed a little longer. Thinking about how nice it is to have someone else in this penthouse for once.

That comes with a bunch of feelings. Mostly about loss, and sadness, and pain. And not all of them can be attributed to the fact that my father used to live here with me and now he's dead.

Some of them, I admit, come from the fear of failing. That I might fuck up this new beginning and it'll all go away.

Because—I swing my feet out of bed, my hands flat on the mattress, my head bowed—because I'm pretty bad at relationships. I've never had a long-term one. And maybe I tell myself that it was Hanna who stopped me from falling in love. That I was always afraid she'd try to take what I had. Always be there waiting to kill anything good that came into my life.

And that's partly true, I guess. Because she is a sneaky bitch who is way too obsessed with me and my life. But it's not the whole truth.

The whole truth is... I'm just very bad at relationships. I don't take orders. It's hard to put the needs of others first. It's a challenge to consider other people's opinions instead of just my own.

But I don't feel that way with Law. I like considering him. And he's not really a bossy guy. At least not outside of sex. Then he does have a bossy side.

"Two minutes, Oaks!" Law yells. "Get your ass down here!"

And apparently that carries into breakfast.

But it's all so hot, I don't care.

"Coming!" I yell.

I pee, pull on my shorts and t-shirt from last night, and walk down the stairs, kicking myself for not getting down here immediately, because I can see those back dimples as he flips French toast at the stove.

I walk quietly over to him and wrap my arms around his torso, pressing my face into the back of his shoulder. "Delicious," I say.

He turns his head just enough for me to see him smile, then looks back at breakfast. "Go sit. I'll bring it to you."

I back off. Reluctantly. And take a seat on the barstool up against the island where he's set a place for me.

He plops two pieces of French toast onto a plate, pours some syrup over them, then sticks his fingertips into a bowl of powdered sugar and sprinkles that over the top.

When he sets it down in front of me I feel... special?

Yes, but no. That's not it.

"Eat," he says.

"Aren't you eating?" I ask, my fork already cutting into the bread.

"I never eat breakfast," he says, bending over so he can place his elbows on the counter and lean forward. He just smiles at me. Like serving me a homemade breakfast is the perfect start to his day.

Cared for?

Yes, but no. That's not it either.

"Me either," I say. "But for you I make an exception."

He laughs. "Well, it's not even up for discussion. If I'm here, you're eating breakfast. It's good for you."

"But it's not good for you?" I ask, shoving the fork into my mouth. "Mmmm," I hum.

"Well, you're not insisting I eat, are you?"

"Should I be?" I ask, my mouth still full. "I mean, would you listen?"

"Of course I'd listen. Listening is the least I can do for you."

Adored?

That might be it. But it's so ridiculous.

"You don't have to eat it," he says.

"No," I say back quickly. "I want to." Because I do. He made it specially for me. He wants me to eat it. So I want to eat. "It's the least I can for *you*."

He pushes forward on the island. Slowly coming towards me. I swallow my food and hold my breath for a moment. Then his lips touch mine and we kiss.

If I wasn't sitting down I might faint. That's not even an exaggeration.

When he pulls away, he licks his lips and says, "You taste good."

What the fuck is happening? Am I falling in love with this man?

"So do you," I whisper back.

Which makes him sigh. "I gotta go home and take a shower and get to work. Got a nine o'clock showing down in Greenwood Village."

"Then what?" I ask. "What will you do then?" Because I have a sudden need to understand his day better. I want to know everything.

"Then…" He thinks for a moment. "Then I have a showing in Cherry Creek at noon and I round out the day with another one in Park Hill at three. In between there's lots of paperwork and shit. Pretty boring stuff."

I picture all this. Him taking people to these million-dollar houses. Talking to rich people. Probably couples, but maybe not. Then I realize something. "You know, if we get this TV show we can do that stuff together."

He nods. "I think that would be good fuckin' fun, Oaklee Ryan."

We stare at each other for a long moment. "I think I'm very fuckin' glad you're my boyfriend this week."

He laughs and backs off. Standing up straight. Shoves his hands in his pockets and just stands there, looking at me as I look at him. His hair is messy, that stray curl I noticed in the shower last night still hanging over his forehead. Like that's where it lives when he's not taming it back into a more professional style.

"Well," he says, "I get to be your boyfriend next week too, so there's that."

"And then what?" I ask.

"Then we're partners forever," he says.

And I'm not quite sure if he's just talking about professionally. Or if he means we're going to like… really give this romance thing a go.

"So I'll pick you up for dinner?" he says.

I nod. "I'll be waiting."

He walks around the island and sits down on the couch to pull his boots on. Then he grabs his t-shirt and pulls it over his head. Slips his arms into the leather jacket and stands there looking like a Greek god in need of a motorcycle.

"I'll check in with you later, OK?"

I nod, because I'm actually speechless. Then catch myself, because I don't want him to walk out without me saying anything. "Yeah. I'd love that."

He winks at me and turns. Walks to the elevator, presses the button, then looks over his shoulder at me. "Respected," he says.

"What?" I ask, shaking myself out of the stupor he's put me in.

"That's what you feel. Because I know you've been asking yourself that since you came downstairs. It's respected, Oaklee."

And then the elevator dings, opens, and he walks inside.

I watch them close. Watch him disappear.

And wonder how long I have to wait before I can marry this man. How soon is too soon?

Because yeah, I feel special, cared for, adored, and respected when I'm with Lawton Ayers. But that's what he's making *me* feel. Not what I'm feeling back.

What I feel back scares the shit out of me.

Because Hanna Harlow is still out there. I still have to deal with her. She's still stealing my recipes. She'd steal my life if I let her.

If I love him, then now I have something else she can take away from me.

And I hired Jordan Wells to give me a boyfriend for Hanna. Not me, her. So I could get close to her and figure out how she's doing all this. Why she's doing all this.

And I just know—I feel it deep down in my gut—that if she sees Lawton like this… like he is now and not like he was on Saturday at the Opera House tavern… if she sees the real him she's gonna want him just as much as I do.

Because how could she not?

And that terrifies me. What if he likes her better than me? What if he falls for her charm just like all those other boyfriends did?

There's a part of me—a rational part—that says he won't. She's got nothing I don't already have too, after all. She's pretty, but no prettier than I am. She's smart, but no smarter than I am. She's successful, but no more successful than I am.

But there's another part of me—the insecure part—that says he will. Because she's more outgoing than I am. She holds her shit together when things get hard. I blow up. She's satisfied, and happy, and on her way up.

And I'm lost, and sad, and falling pretty fast in this whole beer business. I haven't won a beer festival award since my father died. I'm surviving on what's left of his fumes and she's gassed up full, ready to win the race.

So there's like a few minutes, as I sit and eat the rest of my French toast, that I dwell on all that. On how she always takes things away from me. On how she always beats me to the finish line.

But I snap out of that thought.

Remember who I am.

Remember what I'm capable of.

And decide to fight for what's mine this time instead of letting her take it from me.

I will fight for Lawton. And I will fight for my beer recipes. And I'm gonna enter Assassin Sour Saison in the festival this weekend and win that prize too.

I do not care what it takes, I'm going to fight that bitch.

CHAPTER TWENTY-TWO

LAWTON

It feels weird to be in a suit after this weekend. Which is also weird, because I wear suits every day and leather jackets… never. But I miss it. I want it back. I want to take off this tie, take off this starched-collar shirt, take off this life and put on something else.

But work. This fucking job. I have clients to meet and paperwork to file, and deals to close and… yeah.

So that's how I spend my morning. Driving down to Greenwood Village to show another half-acre-lot mansion. Being polite to clients as they discuss the pros and cons of the amount of veining in the marble countertops. Listening patiently as they tell me they'd like to offer a hundred and fifty thousand dollars under fair-market value so they feel like they're getting a deal. Force myself to smile and say, "That's an excellent idea, Scott. Let's make it happen." And then drive away and do it all again in Cherry Creek and Park Hill.

I don't actually get a lunch so I'm glad I didn't try to make plans with Oaklee. Not unless you count pulling through the Carl's Jr drive-through and eating the number three value meal in my car as I sit in traffic a lunch.

Which I don't.

I have an urge to text her all day but I don't know what to say. Rather, I do know what to say, I'm just not sure it's appropriate. Because what I want to say is, "God, I miss you."

But that's very stupid because… I don't think I've earned the right to say that yet. I need to earn the right to have these feelings for her. People don't just fall in love over a weekend. Especially when they came together for business purposes only. Especially when both business propositions are flat-out crazy.

I mean, she hired me to bait her nemesis into a fake relationship so I could… could what? Steal something from her? Get her to admit something on tape? I don't see her end game in this and I don't think Oaklee sees it either.

This game was a… a whim. A last resort. She's grasping at anything to save herself from drowning under an obsessed nemesis.

And me.

Jesus. I'm no better because I want her to be a figurehead in my new venture with the TV show.

And both of these things are equally ridiculous.

When I get back to the office Zack is out, the receptionist has gone home for the day, and it's too quiet as I finish up what I need to do so I can put this place behind me and go back to the little game I'm playing with Oaklee.

My cell phone buzzes on my desk and when I check the number, the area code for LA pops up, so I answer it.

"Lawton Ayers," I say.

"Please hold for Michaela Cummings." And then I get three hold beeps.

I get why people do this. They could actually be that busy, and Michaela Cummings is the executive I'm working with over at Home TV, so she probably is so busy she can't be bothered to press some buttons on her phone to make a call.

But sometimes I think it's just a tactic. So the person receiving the please-hold-for call thinks something important is about to happen.

"Lawton!" Michaela says into my ear. "How's things? Are you ready for this meeting?"

"Hundred percent, Michaela. Hundred percent. I'm your man. This show is gonna be great."

"Perfect. Perfect. Perfect." She says it three times. Like she's actually doing something else out there in LA and wants to make me think I've got her full attention as she does it.

I roll my eyes, kind of annoyed. It's been a long day and I don't particularly feel like stroking egos. "So what's up?" I ask.

She whispers something to someone, then says in her normal voice, "Just calling to make last-minute arrangements. We're moving the meeting up to Wednesday. Are you available Wednesday?"

"Uh, sure," I say. "Yes. I can do Wednesday."

I can't really do Wednesday. I have five fuckin' appointments that day. But I can't tell her that, either, now can I?

"How about…" She pauses for a long time. Like ten whole seconds. "How about noon? Does noon work? I think we're catching a return flight to LA at three. So… noon?"

Noon. Is she flying in that morning? I don't get it. And if her flight leaves by three, then how long does she think this meeting will last? Ten minutes? Twenty tops?

"Noon is… great. We'll have lunch—"

"Sorry, no time for lunch, Law. Just the quick meet-and-greet and then we gotta get back to work. You understand though, right?"

"Totally," I say. "No problem. Shall we meet at my office?"

"Sounds great. Email me the details and my assistant will handle things from there."

"OK—"

But the phone goes dead in my hand. I put the handset back on the base and stare at it for a moment. Wondering... wondering if this is really the new second-chance life I thought it was going to be.

But then it rings again, and my hand automatically picks it up. "Lawton Ayers," I say, expecting it to be Michaela's assistant.

"Mmmmm, Lawton Ayers. It's a very nice name."

"I'm sorry?" I say to the unfamiliar voice.

"This is Hanna Harlow, Lawton. I was wondering if you had time to meet up with me tonight. Perhaps have some dinner? Chat a little? We didn't get much time to talk on Saturday and I'm thoroughly intrigued by your sudden appearance in my old friend's life."

At first I can't really put all those words into something that makes sense. The announcement that this is Hanna throws me. Especially the blatant way she purrs her name. Not to mention the seductive tone of her voice as she makes her intentions clear.

"I'm sorry, Hanna. I'd love to, but I have plans with Oaklee tonight."

"Cancel," she hums. "She'll understand."

Which makes me laugh. "Uh, no, I really don't think she would."

"I know what she's up to," Hanna says.

"Good for you," I say.

"It's not going to work, ya know."

"I have no idea what you're even talking about, Hanna. But I gotta go."

"Last chance then."

"Last chance for what?" I'm annoyed now and it shows.

"To broker some kind of deal for poor little Oaklee. She's not going to like what's about to happen to her."

"What the fuck does that mean?"

"Come to dinner with me and find out."

I sigh.

"Just text Oaklee and tell her you're running late. I promise, you'll be home to her in time for bed." And then she pauses, and adds, "If that's what you still want after our... *talk*."

I don't even know what to say.

"Lawton?"

But I don't like her cocky self-assurance. Especially when she's been stealing Oaklee's beer recipes. It's like... she has a secret. Something we missed. And wasn't that the feeling I got last night? Wasn't I just thinking about how something was right in front of me and I couldn't see it?

So I say, "Where?"

"My bar. In Boulder. Look it up on your navigation. Buffalo Brews on Pearl Street. See you in an hour."

And then she is the second person to hang up on me in the span of five minutes.

Lovely.

I sigh again as I press Oaklee's contact in my phone.

She picks up on the first ring. "Hey! You about ready for dinner now? What time will you be here?"

"Hey, Oaks. I... I just got a call from Hanna Harlow who says I need to have dinner with *her* tonight so she can

215

tell me about her big plans for *you*. I said yes, but I can cancel."

Oaklee is quiet for too long on the other end. I start to wonder if she's still there. "Oaklee?"

"What the fuck?"

"I'm sorry, I'll cancel—"

"No, you're going. I mean, what the fuck is she doing?"

"Well, I guess she's going to tell me, right? That's why she wants me to drive all the way out to Boulder and meet her."

"At her bar?"

"Yeah."

Oaklee goes quiet again.

"I'd rather have dinner with you, so… just say the word and I'll call her back and cancel."

"No," Oaklee says. "No. She's up to something and you need to find out what it is. So you're going to dinner with her, and if she hits on you, you play along, OK? The Boyfriend Experience. Just try to figure out why she's doing all this. Like… what did I ever do to her?"

I make a face. It's some cross between sad, exhausted, and resigned. "Sure," I say. "I'll do what I can."

"Call me when you're done."

And then she hangs up on me too.

CHAPTER TWENTY-THREE

OAKLEE

I pace back and forth after I hang up with Law. Chewing my thumbnail, packed up tight with anxiety over this little move Hanna just pulled.

What does it mean? What is she doing? I mean, obviously she wants Lawton. I don't think Law is interested in her, so I'm not too worried about that part.

But how long before she works her devil magic and has him wrapped around her little finger just like everyone else?

There's a part of me who thinks this whole boyfriend experience is enough to keep him, but is it? Is it really? I mean, we have a deal. He helps me figure out Hanna and I help him get this TV show.

He needs me.

But I don't want him to need me. Not that way. I want him to *like* me. And not just as a business prop, either. I want him to like me for me. I want him to be with me. Date me. Maybe even... love me.

Eventually.

Some day.

Maybe.

It could happen.

We have a connection, I think we both feel that. And we had so much great sex last weekend, it was like an avalanche of orgasms.

So we definitely know we're compatible.

I stop pacing and look out my window at his terrace.

God, I'm fucking insane. I should've never let him take this job. And I should've never agreed to be his partner. Because now we're all mixed up in business. I'm practically having a workplace affair.

My office phone buzzes on my desk, so I walk over and pick it up.

"Oaklee," I say. It's someone from down in the brewery since this is a dedicated line.

"Um... Oaklee? This is Dana? From the bar?"

"Yes, Dana?" She's been with me for three years as the daytime bar manager and she still says this every single time she calls my work phone.

She sighs. "OK, everyone told me not to say anything to you, so don't tell anyone it was me."

"What the hell are you talking about?" And she sounds like a Valley Girl so every sentence sounds like a goddamned question.

"The news, Oaklee. I know you're upset about that Buffalo Brews woman. Haley or something?"

"Hanna," I growl.

"Yeah, her. Well, she's on the news right now telling people she's got the number one craft beer in Colorado."

"What?" I say, getting hot with anger. "Everyone knows that's not true. Bronco Brews is still number one."

"I know, but there's an article out on the *Westword* website today. About next weekend's festival and all. And they have already declared her the winner because she has some secret beer, and she gave them a sample to try."

"She has a secret beer?" I say.

"Yeah."

"Shit. OK, well, thanks for telling me, Dana. And don't worry, I won't tell anyone it was you."

"Thank you!" she chimes, then hangs up the phone.

I reach for the remote on my desk, turn the TV on, then start flipping through the local channels looking for Hanna Harlot's face.

"I can't tell you what it's called," Hanna says to the camera on Channel Five. "Not until next weekend. But *Westword* has already—"

I turn it off. I'm too pissed to watch.

Online I find the *Westword* site and yup. Sure enough, there's Hanna's stupid face. If they're already talking about her on Monday's Featured Brew column, and the new print issue doesn't come out until Thursday, they are probably going to give her the fucking cover this week.

That stupid bitch!

I just stare at the article. Read some of it, but her bragging is so over the top, I just can't stand it. How she came from nothing. How she bootstrapped herself up the ladder in a man's world. How no one helped her and she did it all herself.

I want to barf. I want to scream—"She cheated off me!"

I want to strangle her.

And tonight, Oaklee, she's having dinner with your boyfriend. Because you told him to do that.

I'm dumb. Very, very stupid. Because clearly Hanna is playing a game I have no knowledge of. I don't know the rules, or the plays, or the pitfalls—or anything. I'm clueless.

And—I reluctantly admit—I'm losing.

She's talking about her secret beer, I'm not. Score one for Hanna.

She's on TV, I'm not. One more point for my nemesis.

219

She's the Featured Brew in today's *Westword* Online. They're calling her beer the best in Colorado and the contest isn't for another six days!

And… she's having dinner with *my boyfriend* right now.

I can't. I can't let her do this. She has broken my life up into little pieces and now it's time I put all those pieces back together again.

CHAPTER TWENTY-FOUR

LAWTON

Boulder is tucked up against the foothills of the Rocky Mountains about thirty miles northwest of Denver. But once you get there it's immediately clear that Boulder and Denver, while connected via sprawling suburbia, have almost nothing in common.

Denver has a view of mountains but it's not in the mountains. Boulder is where the mountains begin, and the large rock formation to the west of the city, called the Flatirons, is the iconic symbol of Boulder.

It has a small-town feel, it's a college town—the University of Colorado campus takes up a significant portion of the valley—and it's best known for its 420 activities, the unofficial-official day where everyone gets together and smokes pot on campus. But the football team—the Buffalos, of Buffs, as they are called around these parts—aren't bad either, and the science departments are top-notch.

Pearl Street, where I'm headed to meet up with Hanna, has its own culture. Just as Denver has the 16th Street Pedestrian Mall, Boulder has the Pearl Street Pedestrian Mall.

If you're going to be a craft brewer in Boulder, opening a brewery on Pearl Street isn't a bad idea. Hipsters and families alike flock to the four square blocks of downtown trendiness every day.

After fighting the evening traffic on the Boulder Freeway, I finally make my way into downtown, pay for parking, and walk the two blocks into the shops.

And while Oaklee kinda prepared me for who and what Hanna Harlow is—I am not prepared for what I see when I walk up to the entrance of her brewery.

It's three stories tall, red brick, historical and... there's a giant buffalo head painted on the front.

The balls on this woman are almost unbelievable. Not quite, because I'm seeing it with my own eyes, but she's got stones most men would kill for.

I sigh, wanting very much to just turn around, go back to Oaklee's place, and fuck her all night.

But I go inside anyway. Because it's my job.

It's a lot smaller than Bronco Brews. Just a very tiny reception area where people are crowded against the walls as they wait for a table or a seat at the bar to open up. And just one hostess, who looks a little overwhelmed staring down at the seating chart on the small podium.

"Excuse me," I say, leaning over to make sure she can hear me over all the noise. "I'm here to see Hanna Harlow. I'm Lawton Ayers."

The girl, who can't be a day over nineteen, looks up at me with a frazzled expression as she tried to make sense of my words. Then it must all click together, because she smiles and yells, "She's waiting for you upstairs. Just go on up." I look around for the stairs, then the girl points. "Over there!"

I thank her, but she's already looking down at her seating chart again. So I push past servers, and customers, and people waiting for a table, and pull the door to the stairs open, sighing with relief as the noise level falls when the door closes behind me.

Of course she's upstairs. Because that's where Oaklee would be.

This whole thing is creepy. Like, what is wrong with this woman? Why is she so obsessed with Oaklee? And why can't anyone else see it but us?

When I get to the top of the third floor, the door is locked. But there's a buzzer next to it, and when I push it, one of those industrial bells rings for several seconds on the other side.

The door opens before the bell even stops—and there she is.

Hanna Harlow looks so much like Oaklee in this moment, I take a step back. Her hair, her makeup, her clothes... all of it. Oaklee.

A chill runs up my spine.

"You came," she says in a soft voice.

"You invited me," I say back.

We stare at each other for a long moment, her eyes meeting mine. Then she steps aside and says, "Come in. Please."

I take a deep breath, tug on my suit coat, and enter.

Her apartment isn't on the top floor of a downtown Denver building and it's got no views of the mountains, but everything else... God. It's all the same.

How is that possible?

Same floor-to-ceiling windows. Same open-loft layout with the kitchen in the center. Same stairs, same catwalk surrounding the perimeter, and there's even framed beer labels on the walls like Oaklee has.

I let out an incredulous laugh.

"Yes," Hanna says. "It's eerie, right?"

I just turn to look at her. Wondering how she can stand there, letting me see her for what she is, and still remain calm. Like this is all normal. "What the fuck is wrong with you?"

"Hmmmpph," she says, blowing air through her nose. "You know, I figured you were a smart guy. A millionaire by the age of thirty. A guy who came up from nothing, just like me, and made it. That says a lot about a person, ya know. So I made some assumptions. But maybe I gave you too much credit?"

It's my turn to huff. "Well, I certainly didn't give you enough."

She stares at me, silent for several painful moments as the animosity between us builds. Then she says, "So you've made up your mind already? Or are you interested in the other side of the story?"

"What other side?" I laugh. "I mean…" I pan my hand to her. Then to her apartment. "You even have a fucking buffalo painted on the front of your building."

More silence from her as she watches me. Then, "So you're going to stay and hear me out? Or you're going to leave and take all your preconceived notions with you?"

"Whatever," I say, taking a few steps further into the apartment. "Talk then. But I'm pretty sure there's nothing you can say that will explain"—I hold up both my hands—"this."

"Well," she says, walking over to the countertop where there's two bottles of Buffed Up waiting for us. She uses a bottle opener to pop off the tops, then turns, hands me one—which I take on instinct—and says, "You'd be wrong, Lawton Ayers. There's twenty-eight years to this story that you have no clue about. Because none of it fits into the bullshit narrative that Oaklee Ryan sold you."

CHAPTER TWENTY-FIVE

OAKLEE

Shrike Bikes is closed by the time I get over there, but Sick Girlz is open and there's a side entrance though the alley, so that's where I go in. The shop is busy. Buzzing from the back tells me that there are several artists working tonight and there are two groups of customers sitting on various couches and chairs waiting for tattoos.

But Vivi is at the front desk, filing her hot-pink nails, when I walk in. "I'm ready," she says, jumping up off her stool and coming around the counter holding a black, drawstring bag.

I nod, then turn around and walk out, my pink-haired friend at my side. "You're sure about this?" I ask her.

"Nothing to it," she says, walking over to my car and getting in the passenger side.

I get in too, then look at her, unsure if I should really go through with this. "The last time you said that we ended up in jail."

She shrugs. "Hey, that's the price you pay when you need things you don't have."

"Vivi—"

"I got this, OK? We're good. She's not gonna know. And you've got Lawton over there, right?"

"Yes, he's probably with her right now." God, I'm so angry about that.

"Then at least we know she's busy. Trust me. You absolutely need to do this."

I do trust her. Mostly because Vivi is badass, but also because she's well connected here in Colorado. If we do get in trouble like we did last time, she has ways out of things. She has people who will swoop in and take care of shit.

So I take a deep breath, start the car, and pull out of the alley and make my way up towards the freeway.

She talks about all kinds of things as I drive, like this is no big deal. I just listen, say nothing, and chew on my thumbnail as we enter Boulder and I find parking a good six blocks away from Hanna's Pearl Street storefront.

She takes off her leather jacket as we get out of the car, hands me a pair of leather gloves, and once we put those on, we're both dressed in black from top to bottom.

"I feel like a cat burglar," I say as we walk. Vivi is swinging her little black drawstring bag like we're just out for a stroll.

She looks at me. I catch a brazen gleam in her eyes. A glint of light reflecting under the yellow street lamps. "Meow," she purrs. And then she hits me in the shoulder and says, "Relax. You need proof, Oaklee. And that's what we're going to get tonight. My plan is perfect. Nothing's gonna happen and even if it does—"

Here it comes, I think to myself.

"—I'll just call my cousin Oliver and he'll fix it."

I decide to agree with her. Because what choice do I have? I need to put a stop to Hanna Harlow before she ruins me for good.

We don't bother entering Pearl Street like all the other pedestrians because we have no intention of walking through the front door. No. We head straight to the alley and a few minutes later we're standing under a fire escape attached to the Buffalo Brews building, looking up at it.

"OK," Vivi says. "This bitch uses a subsidiary of my cousin's security company and I worked there for three years as a teenager and know all the backdoors. So it was super easy to hack while I was waiting for you to show up. Now all you gotta do is boost me." She makes two fists around the bars covering the alley windows on the first floor and says, "I'll grab it, get it down, and then we can go up together."

"That's gonna make a shit ton of noise," I whisper.

"That's why I have this," she says, opening up her bag so I can see the can of WD-40 inside. "Trust me. This is not my first fire-escape rodeo, Oaklee."

And for a second I wonder what Vivi Vaughn does in her spare time? Is breaking and entering just another Monday night to her?

Questions I probably should've asked myself before I agreed to her plan, but it's too late now. I crouch down, she puts her foot on my shoulder, and then she's climbing up the side of the building like a monkey. Two minutes later she's on the second-floor landing, spraying the hell out of the fire escape with WD-40.

"OK, I'm gonna ride it down, you get on, and we'll climb back up. Ready?"

And before I can say anything in reply, she's on her way down.

It makes noise. No doubt. But it doesn't squeak. When she reaches me, we both look up, then around. Just to see if anyone heard and will come see what the fuck is going on.

I almost wish someone would see us so we'd have to run away, probably laughing like girls gone wild, and forget this whole crazy plan.

But none of that happens, because if anyone did hear the fire escape come down, they don't bother looking.

So I take a deep breath, climb up after her, and resign myself to the insanity of Vivi Vaughn because this is the first step in getting my life back.

When we get to the second-floor landing we both look in the window. It's dark in there, too dark to see anything.

I try to open the window, but it doesn't budge. "Locked," I whisper.

"No problem," Vivi says, fishing through her bag of tricks for something else. And then, like she's a spy in a *Mission: Impossible* movie, she removes a glass cutter, fastens it to the glass, and pivots the arm around in a circle. It makes a little bit of noise, but I'm surprised at how fast and quiet the whole act of cutting through a window actually is.

A few taps later and the glass circle she traced is now a hole. One more second and she's got her hand inside, flipping up the lock, and then I'm staring at an open window.

"Let's go," she whispers, taking one last look around the alley before she sticks her leg in and enters.

My heart is beating so fast, I have to take several deep breaths to calm myself. But then I hear voices down below. People are coming down the alley, so I have no choice.

I slip my leg in after her, and disappear inside Hanna's building.

CHAPTER TWENTY-SIX

LAWTON

"No?" I ask Hanna. "So everything she's told me about you is wrong, is that what you're saying?"

"Look," Hanna says. "Every story has two sides, OK? And whatever she told you, I'm sure you think it's all real because you think you know her. Or, at the very least, you met her first and only got her side, so naturally that's the one you believe."

"Right," I say, blowing out a laugh with the word. "OK, so tell me then." But just as the word comes out of my mouth, my phone buzzes in my pocket. I fish it out and look at the screen.

Oaklee: *Take her downstairs to the bar. Or dinner. Take her anywhere but her place. And do it quick.*

I look at Hanna and say, "Excuse me a minute. I have to answer this text."

"Sure," Hanna says. "Take your time. I've got all night."

So I text Oaklee back. *What are you talking about?*

Oaklee: *Just do it! I need her to be out of her place like now.*

Me: *Where are you?*

Oaklee: *I'm in her apartment. I'm watching you two talk right now.*

Me: *WTF Oaklee!*

Oaklee: *I have to find proof. Vivi is here with me, so don't worry. We'll be fine. Just get her out of there!*

I turn back to Hanna, who is sipping beer from the bottle of Buffed Up. "Everything OK?" she asks.

"Sure. But… I'm hungry. So how about we go grab some food while you tell me all about how I've got you wrong?"

"I can order us something from downstairs—"

"No," I interrupt her. "I haven't been to Boulder in a long time. Let's go somewhere. Somewhere nice."

She eyes me suspiciously. And she should, right? Because Oaklee and Vivi have broken into her apartment and are about to steal things and they are probably like twenty feet away from where we stand right this moment.

"I'm starving, Hanna. And I want something good in a place I can relax. Because I ate a burger in my car for lunch today and bar food just isn't gonna do it for me tonight. So you can come with me, or not. But I'm gonna go eat."

She stares at me for another long moment, then sets her beer down on the counter and says, "Fine. We'll do it your way. How about Joe's Italian? It's got wine and white tablecloths. Will that suffice?"

"Sounds perfect," I say. "Let's go."

Joe's is just two blocks down on Pearl Street, so we walk. Hanna is quiet as we wait for a table. Biding her time until we're actually seated and have the menus out in front of us. I order a whiskey because I feel like this story might require one. And once we've ordered our entrées, she says, "OK. I would like you to give me the benefit of the doubt and check all your opinions of me and preconceived notions of what's going on between Oaklee and I until I'm done talking. Can you do me that one favor?"

"Sure," I say, sipping the whiskey. Because why not.

Hanna takes a deep breath and starts talking on the exhale. "I first met Oaklee at college, but I knew of her long before that. I mean, everyone knows about Bronco Brews, right?"

"I guess," I say.

"Especially teenagers teaching themselves how to drink. It's kind of a rite of passage to become familiar with your local celebrity brews and Colorado has no shortage of local brewers. So I knew of Oaklee because kids talk. And she was our age, she was pretty, and, well, you can probably guess what the boys at my high school used to say about Oaklee."

"Is that why you fixated on her?"

She holds up a finger. "Hold that thought. I haven't even started this story yet. I'm just telling you I knew of her before I actually met her. So we get assigned to the dorm at school freshman year and it's pretty cool to room with her because she's like… sorta famous in her own way."

"So you knew about her and you were roommates, and you were both microbiology majors?" I ask.

"I see where this is going, but I was always going to use my degree to brew beer. I just couldn't get accepted into microbiology with that as a goal. So I lied and told them I wanted to use it to eradicate diseases."

"Why not?" I ask. "I mean why did you have to lie? Because starting this story with a lie, Hanna, it's not looking good for you."

"Well, here's a newsflash. Science majors are competitive and back then microbiology was filled with people who wanted to use it for beer-brewing. Oaklee was always going to get in. Her father knew professors at CSU. They give out scholarships there. She had an automatic in. I didn't. I had to take the major seriously so they would take *me* seriously."

"Oh, come on, Hanna. That's bullshit. Why not just admit you thought she was super interesting and decided to model yourself after her? Because it's so obvious. I don't think I'm interested in hearing any more if this is going where I think it's going."

"It's going where you think it's going, Lawton. Because that's the truth. She copied me, not the other way around."

I laugh so loud, people look over at us. "So that's your story? You're the victim? She stole your beer recipes? She stole your beer names, and labels, and"—I point out the window, down the mall where her shop is—"Buffalo Brews and Bronco Brews aren't categorically similar, and Buffed Up isn't a ripoff of Bucked Up? Is this what you're going to tell me tonight? Because if so, I don't think I can stand it."

I check my watch, noting that it's been twenty minutes since I got Hanna out of her apartment. And I wonder if that's enough time for Oaklee to get what she needs. Because I don't want to hear any more.

"That's because you're missing the most vital piece of information, Lawton. The same piece of information I was missing up until that first year of college."

"Which is what?" I ask.

She stares at me. Takes a deep breath. Lets it out. And then says, "I am not Oaklee's enemy. And if you listen to my story from beginning to end, you'll see my side. You'll see her for who she really is. A wild girl with a streak of mean. A girl who came from privilege, was given the world, has more than most, and wants to keep it that way. You'll see that what she's been telling you... is all *lies*."

CHAPTER TWENTY-SEVEN

OAKLEE

Vivi and I watch through a cracked door on the far side of Hanna's apartment as Law gets my text and makes an excuse to get her out of the apartment. And as soon as they leave, we go into sneaky thief mode.

Vivi goes straight to her office and starts hacking into her computer. I look around, stunned at what I'm seeing. Because... it's my apartment. I mean, sure, it's smaller and the art on the walls is her brand, not mine. But...

"This place is fucking creepy," Vivi says from the office. "And I'm in. What should I be looking for?"

But this *is* my apartment. In like... a Bizarro World way.

"Oaklee!" Vivi whisper-yells. "Tell me what to look for!"

"Recipes," I say, peeking my head into the office. "Look for anything that resembles a beer recipe. What yeast she's using, anything you can find on her graphic design... stuff like that."

Then I go back to the main living area. Comparing and contrasting her design to mine. Her kitchen is smaller. Everything is smaller. But it's so clear. It's so... *me*.

I feel sick all of a sudden. Almost violated. And I know that's stupid, because none of this stuff is mine. This isn't my apartment. All my stuff is safe back in Denver.

But...

"Found something," Vivi says. "Come and look."

I walk into the office and round the desk to see what Vivi has on the computer.

And even though I came here with a goal in mind—to find evidence of her stealing my father's recipes. My recipes, now—I am not prepared for what I see on the screen.

Handwritten recipes, scanned into her computer. In *his* handwriting.

"She must have the originals around here somewhere," Vivi says, getting up from the desk chair. I take her seat, while she starts going through file cabinets.

"These are mine," I say.

"I know," Vivi replies. "Print them. But we need to find the hard copies too. We'll take those with us, since they're yours anyway."

I scan the list, not trying to figure out which recipes she has, but which ones she does *not* have.

Because she has them all.

Every single beer we've ever developed is in this list. And all of them are in my father's handwriting.

"I can't fucking find them," Vivi says.

"That's because she scanned them," I say softly. "She stole these from my apartment, scanned them, and left the originals with me."

"Delete them," Vivi says. "Every single one."

I know I should get up, walk out of here, and forget I ever saw any of this. I know what we're doing is illegal and I could go to jail. I know that none of this, even if I take it with me, would be admissible in court.

I understand all this. But I highlight every one of those recipe files and my finger hovers over the delete button, ready to take this final action.

But then my phone buzzes a text.

"Shit," Vivi says. "See if that's Lawton."

It is Lawton. I know this even before I see the message on the screen. *We're heading back. If you're still there, get the fuck out now!*

Vivi reads it with me, then presses my finger on the delete button, grabs me by the shoulder, and says, "Get up. I gotta cover my tracks real quick."

I do. And I just stand there, watching her fingers fly across the keyboard. Deleting her footprints. Covering up that we were here. And then she logs off and gets up, carefully placing the chair up against the desk, and says, "Let's go."

We leave the apartment the same way we came, that hole in the glass the one thing we can't erase. The one piece of evidence we *must* leave behind.

And a few minutes later we're back down in the alley, sending the fire escape ladder back up.

The whole way home Vivi is talking. Wild theories coming out of her mouth. Crazy explanations for why Hanna Harlow has all my father's original recipes.

"She broke in," she says. Which is the most obvious answer. Especially since my security was so lax. Why was I so naive? She has everything of mine. Everything. And I still have no proof.

"Maybe she hacked you remotely?" Vivi offers, as another theory. "Do you have all those files on your computer too?"

I nod. "My father did it that way. He'd write them out, then scan them into the computer so he could have them on his tablet while he was downstairs."

"She could've hacked you. We can do a forensic trace. There's no way she could've been careful enough to hide all her tracks. Not unless she hired hackers at least as good as me and my cousins."

"Well, why wouldn't she?" I ask. "I mean, what's stopping her from hiring the best? If I was gonna go to all this trouble I'd hire the best. And they could be anywhere in the world, ya know? People go on that dark web or whatever, and they can get anyone to do anything. So even though I got all the answers I needed to prove I'm not crazy, that she really is stealing my corporate secrets, I have no proof. None. So there's absolutely nothing I can even do about this."

Vivi is driving home. She just jumped into the driver's seat and said, "Keys," and I handed them over. So she makes a pouty face as she gets us back on the freeway towards Denver.

"Maybe Lawton found out something useful?" she offers as a way to make me feel better.

"Shit." I laugh. "She probably sweet-talked him into believing her lies. He's probably dating her by now. They probably have a date for dinner tomorrow too."

I'm only half joking.

"Well, don't jump to any conclusions until we talk to him, OK? Lawton knows what she's doing. He's not going to fall for it."

I just stare out the window as we drive, silent, until we're getting off the freeway and making our way back into LoDo. She pulls up to the alley entrance to my building and turns the car off. Looks at me.

"Thank you," I say. "I would've never done any of that without you."

"I wish we had actual proof you could use. But at least you know now. She *is* stealing from you."

"Yeah," I say back. "But how much more does she plan to take before she's done? Because I don't have much left."

CHAPTER TWENTY-EIGHT

LAWTON

I just sit and listen to Hanna's story. Without comment, just the way she wanted it, from beginning to end. And when she finally stops talking, she pauses. Takes a breath, then another, like she's trying to catch it.

"Well," she finally says.

I just shrug. "What do you want me to say?"

"How about, 'Maybe I don't have the whole story?' How about, 'Maybe I was wrong about you?' How about, 'I should pick and choose my friends more carefully?'"

That last part comes spitting out of her mouth like venom.

All I can do is shrug. "It's your word against hers, isn't it? And you say she knows all this?"

"She does," Hanna says, raising her chin in defiance. "I tried to tell her everything years ago. And all she did was turn on me. Told me she never wanted to see or talk to me again. Threatened me with bodily harm. Said she'd get her friends to take care of things if I decided to take this issue any further. And if you've known her for any length of time, then you've seen what she's capable of. You know what kind of friends she has."

"Well, from what I've seen you two have the same friends. So what's that say about you?"

"Bullshit. She hangs out with those Shrike people. They're all criminals. You like those fancy boots you have? That overpriced leather jacket with Spencer Shrike's signature inside the sleeve? You do know he's a killer,

241

right? All those people are a bunch of violent liars. The whole twisted circle is a cross between a mob family and Colorado royalty."

"And you went over there trying to take over her tap. Trying to get Buffed Up to replaced Bucked Up. I mean, come on, Hanna. This is all so much bullshit."

"She's crazy. And somewhere deep down inside, you know I'm right."

I just shake my head. "I really haven't seen that side, Hanna. I don't know what to think about your story, but I'll take it back to Oaklee and ask her."

She stiffens. Breathes in through her nose. Sets her jaw and glares at me. "She's going to deny everything."

"I mean, I don't know what you want from me tonight. I don't even know why you asked me out here. None of this is even my business. I'm just a guy dating a girl you hate. That's all I see."

"Well, you know what I see? I see a man who wears a suit every day walk into a bar on Saturday trying to pretend he's a biker. Trying to play the part Oaklee Ryan assigned to him. I see a very successful man bowing to the will of a very sick woman. And that's sad, Lawton. Sad. Because I like you just the way you are. I know she brought you to the Opera House to bait me. To see if I'd take you away. And how stupid would I have to be to fall for that old trick?"

"Why, because you've done it so many times before it's old?"

"Is that what she told you? That I stole her boyfriends?" And then she laughs. "This," she says, waving a hand at me. "You, dressed in a suit. That's my type, Lawton. That biker costume she dressed you up in last weekend, that's all her. Pretty soon she's gonna ask you to get a tattoo."

"What?"

"It wouldn't be the first time. Hell, she's done some pretty crazy things to catch a guy. I wouldn't put anything past her. And she's got something up her sleeve for you, take my word on that."

"Like what?" I laugh.

Hanna shrugs. "How should I know? But just wait. Something will happen. She's with you for a reason and you'll figure that out sooner than later, because Oaklee Ryan didn't get what she has by accident. She's ruthless. She has no conscience. And she's a very good little actress, Law. A very good liar."

And then Hanna pushes back her chair, places her napkin on the table, and says, "I've got the check, don't worry about that. It was nice talking to you, Law. I hope you take a good long look at what I've told you. And I hope you figure out you're just a pawn in her game before it's too late and she ruins everything you've built over the years."

She leaves me sitting there. Just replaying her whole story back in my head.

And reluctantly, I have to admit, some of it makes sense.

No, a lot of it makes sense. Like… all the weird *why* questions that have been running through my head these past few days suddenly make sense if I subscribe to Hanna's logic.

Questions like… why would Hanna do all this crazy shit?

But if what she told me is true—and it's certainly plausible—then all of it fits.

The competing breweries. The recipes. The beer names and even the stupid buffalo head mural on the front of her building.

Is Oaklee that crazy?

I mean… she has pulled some stunts. There's no denying that. And why would all her beer friends not see what I see? Why would they let Hanna get away with all this? Why, for that matter, would the entire craft brewing community let her win festival after festival? Give her taps where Oaklee once ruled?

If none of what Hanna just told me is true… then… Jesus. She's insane.

But if it is true… then that makes Oaklee the insane one.

I push back from the table, leave the restaurant, walk back to my car, and drive back to Denver. More confused than ever.

Who do I believe? The girl I thought I was falling in love with over the weekend?

Or the one who just gave me a rational explanation that counters everything Oaklee has been telling me?

I don't know. And even though before I had dinner with Hanna I was planning on spending the night fucking Oaklee's brains out and falling asleep in her bed, holding her tight—that's not what I do.

I go home.

Alone.

CHAPTER TWENTY-NINE

OAKLEE

I text Law when I get upstairs and then stare at my phone as I watch the little notification to say it was delivered. Which it is. But those little bubbles telling me he's texting back don't appear.

I don't know what to think about that.

Well, that's not true. I have lots of things to think about that.

One. He's still with Hanna and he can't answer me yet.

Two. He's still with Hanna and doesn't want to answer me at all.

Three. He's driving home, so he saw the text but can't text and drive. Which makes sense because that's dangerous and I don't want him crashing his car on the freeway trying to calm my fears that he has, in fact, decided Hanna is way more interesting, and pretty, and successful, and he'd like to fuck her instead of me.

Four. He's fucking her right now.

God, I'm so stupid.

I go over to my terrace and open the doors. The night air is cool and the wind is strong, but I don't care. I just stare at his apartment down the alley and watch, hoping that any minute now—

The lights flick on.

He's home! I text him again. Asking if he got my message. Which I know he did, because it was delivered.

I chew my thumbnail as I wait for the comment bubbles...

Nothing.

What's happening right now? Are fears two and four justified?

I know I shouldn't call, but I can't stop myself. I press the green button on my phone and it starts ringing. And just when I think it's gonna go to voicemail, he picks up.

"Hey," he says, his greeting short and sharp.

"Heeeey," I say back, my greeting soft and long. "So... what happened?"

"I should be asking you that, Oaklee."

"What do you mean?"

"What did I tell you about Vivi's stupid plan last night? I mean, Jesus Christ. What the fuck were you two thinking?"

"I needed proof, Lawton. And I got it. She has all my father's recipes on her computer!"

"You broke into her computer?" He sighs. And it's clearly an exasperated sigh.

"I didn't. I don't know how to do that shit. Vivi did."

"Vivi did," he says. "So she's a hacker, she's a tattoo artist. Any other special skills I should know about Vivi Vaughn, Oaklee?"

"What do you mean?"

"You know what I mean. Hanna told me all about her family."

"Hanna told you," I scoff. "What exactly did she say?"

"That she comes from dangerous people, that's what she said."

"Well..."

"I looked her up, so don't bother. Everything Hanna said seems to be true. Her cousin is some infamous rapist—"

"Bullshit!" I yell. "He is not! That's all bullshit!"

"Her uncle killed a guy back in the day. And pretty much every newspaper in Colorado—not to mention several national and international publications as well—has done extensive exposés on the crime syndicate she's connected to."

"Crime syndicate?" I laugh. "Come on. And you believe her?"

"All I know is that you and Vivi broke into Hanna's apartment—*while I was there*—and... and... what the *fuck*, Oaklee?"

"Calm down," I say. But I have a very sick feeling in my stomach. "What exactly did she say tonight? Because you didn't answer my texts and now you're angry with me."

"Damn fucking right I'm angry."

"I saw the proof, Lawton. She has stolen everything from me! And she's gonna continue to take, and take, and take until I have nothing left."

"You know"—he sighs again—"she told me quite a story tonight."

"What story?"

"A bunch of shit you left out."

"Like what?"

"And it would be nice," he continues, like I'm not even talking, "if you'd tell me all that stuff yourself so I don't have to play the game with you anymore."

"All what stuff? What exactly did she tell you?"

He's silent on the other end of the phone. I can see his shadow through the sheer curtains covering his terrace window. He's pacing back and forth.

"Lawton," I say, my tone irritable now. "Tell me what the fuck happened tonight."

"Ya know, I'm tired, Oaklee. It's been a long day. Hell, it's been a long weekend. And I have work tomorrow and the meeting with Home TV was pushed up to Wednesday for some reason, so I'm just gonna go to bed and I'll stop by your place tomorrow after work and we'll discuss where things go next."

"'We'll discuss where things go next?' What's that even mean?"

"I mean this game. I mean this TV show. I just don't know. You're wild, Oaklee. You broke into her fucking apartment tonight!"

"So what are you saying? That you believe whatever that lying bitch Hanna told you? That you're not going to help me? That I'm not going to that meeting with the Home TV people with you?"

One more long sigh from Lawton. And I know what he's going to say before he says it. "Yeah. Maybe. I don't know. We'll talk about it tomorrow night. OK? I gotta go."

And then he hangs up because I get three quick beeps letting me know the call was dropped.

I just stand there. The air cold now, not just cool. The wind wild now, not soothing. And look at my phone.

She did it again. She's gonna take him away from me now too. All because I told him to go have dinner with her.

So it's my fault, isn't it? I practically gave him to her. Practically pushed them together. Made him dress up

248

like… like the kind of guy he isn't. The kind of guy I like, which is the kind of guy Hanna likes too.

Isn't it?

And even though I'm not one of those girls who cries over a man… I want to cry. The tears sting in my eyes. The wind whipping across my face, trying to erase them.

But when I go back inside there is no wind.

So my tears fall freely as I crawl into bed and hide my face in the pillow.

And pretty soon I'm sobbing. Full-on ugly cry. Because no matter what I do, I can't compete with her.

She's always one step ahead.

Always there, ready to kick me when I'm down.

I can practically feel her boot connecting with my stomach as I lie in bed feeling like…

Like I just lost something a whole lot more important than a stupid beer recipe.

CHAPTER THIRTY

LAWTON

I hang up on her and I feel bad immediately because I want to believe her. I want to be on her side. I like her, for fuck's sake. Was... was what? Falling in love with her just yesterday. Which is ridiculous, but that's what people think when they first meet.

And don't know each other, I tell myself in my head.

Because we don't know each other. She doesn't know anything about me and what I think I know about her might not be true.

But that Hanna... she sure can spin a tale. And if she's lying she is a sociopath. Because it came across so... so authentic. No one is that good of a liar. No sane person, anyway.

She didn't come off as insane. Sorry to say.

I hold my phone in my hand and look out the window. Out at Oaklee's apartment. I see her walking inside. Like she was out there looking at me while we were talking.

My thumb is on her contact. Ready to press it and try to explain how I'm feeling... but I don't know how I'm feeling. That's the problem. And I really am too tired to get into it tonight.

Tomorrow, I decide. Tomorrow I'll make a date with her at lunch and we'll go over all this. I'll tell her everything Hanna said and see how she reacts.

I take one last look at her apartment and then the lights go out.

I turn away from the window, flick my lights out too, and get in bed.

When I wake to my alarm in the morning it feels like I spent the entire night thinking and didn't get a moment of sleep. But it's not true. I did sleep because I just woke up. I just feel like I didn't.

I go through the motions of getting ready for work, utterly dead inside. And it's not just Oaklee and Hanna, either. It's everything. I don't want to go to work. I don't want to sell real estate anymore. I'm not even sure I want this TV show. Something feels off there too. Like... that phone call yesterday. Changing the date. Kinda hanging up on me.

Something's wrong.

But I don't have any options right now. Not good ones. So I put on the suit, careful of the tattoo, because I removed the clear antibacterial barrier in the shower and now it's touching the starched fabric of my shirt.

And even that is bugging me. Like... what the hell was I thinking? Getting a tattoo? Jesus Christ, I really am having a mid-life crisis at thirty. It's pathetic.

My phone rings just as I'm gathering up my wallet, ready to leave for work. I check the incoming call and see 'unknown number' on the screen.

Afraid it might be Home TV, I tab accept and say, "Lawton Ayers," with as much enthusiasm as I can manage. Which isn't much.

"Lawton, it's Hanna."

Jesus. That's all I need.

"Hey, Hanna," I say, reaching for the front door with my one free hand. "I'm on my way out to work right now. Can I call you later?"

"I'm afraid this can't wait." Her tone is clipped. Almost angry.

So I pause in front of my door and say, "What's up?" knowing in my gut that I'm not going to like what's up one bit.

"I don't know if you're aware, but I have a rather sophisticated security system in my home."

"Nope. Didn't know that." I say it calmly, but I already know where this going.

"Well, I do. Or I did. Because as it turns out, my contract with the security company was cancelled last night."

"Hmmm, that's weird," I say, rolling my eyes. Fucking Oaklee.

"Very strange, yes. Especially when I do a little digging—digging I probably should've done before I hired them—and do you know what I found?"

"Hanna, I don't have time for guessing games. So just get to the point, please. I'm on my way to work."

"That my company was really a shell for Shrike Security."

"The mobster-slash-royal family of Colorado?"

"That's the one."

"OK?" I say, pinching the bridge of my nose.

"And someone was in my apartment last night."

"If you're alluding to me being there, then yeah, that's no mystery."

"That is not who I'm alluding to, Lawton. As you well know. Because I have my own private security, aside from the one I contract with. So not all the cameras were turned off last night. And guess who was in my apartment while we were out for dinner?"

I don't bother answering this time. It's rhetorical anyway.

"Your girlfriend."

"Well, that's super weird."

"She sent you to keep me busy, didn't she?"

"No, Hanna. You invited me over, remember?"

"I don't know what you two are up to, but I told you what was going on last night. And I'm going to give you five seconds to make a choice, Lawton. And if you make the wrong choice I will be forced to escalate matters. Because someone was on my hard drive and deleted all my beer recipes. So choose."

"Choose what?" I ask, thoroughly annoyed now.

"Her. Or me."

I laugh. I just can't deal. "How about I choose neither of you? Huh? How about I pretend I never met you or her? And the two of you can both just fuck off and fight your little war without this soldier, How about that?"

Hanna sucks in a breath on the other end of the phone. Lets it out. "I wish it were that simple, Lawton. But it's not. So if that's your choice—if you're not on my side—then I'm afraid we're done here."

"Great," I say. "We're done."

I press end on the phone, open my front door, and take the stairs down to the parking garage because I'm so pissed off right now, I need to expend the energy.

I'm clicking the key fob to unlock my car when a blow to my head knocks me down to the hard concrete.

When I look up, stunned and confused at what just happened, I see two men in cheap suits standing over me.

Late thirties, maybe. One has close-cropped brown hair and a neck tattoo. The other one has a pony tail and long face that makes me think of a horse.

"We were hoping we'd all be friends," Neck Tattoo says, cracking his knuckles for effect. He glares down at me as his leg swings back, and then the kick to the stomach has me doubled over again.

"But it's not turning out that way," Horse Face says, swinging his foot to deliver the third blow.

But here's the thing no one gets about me. They see me in this suit. They comment on my nice manners. But I'm built like an MMA fighter for a fucking reason. So just as that foot is coming towards me, ready to connect, I grab it, twist, and stand up at the same time. This makes Horse Face's whole body twist, and now he's off his feet, in mid-air, hands out trying to break his fall so he doesn't crush that horse face of his on the goddamned concrete.

He doesn't quite make it and there's a sickening crunch as his mouth connects with the ground and blood puddles under him like a newly forming lake.

I look at Neck Tattoo, do one of those let's-go-motherfucker motions with my fingers, and say, "No, it's not turning out that way."

He attacks. And he knows two things as he does this. One. I am trained. Two. So is he. Because he goes for my leg, lifts it up high, like he's gonna trip me backwards. But whatever he thinks he knows about me, he's wrong. Because this is my signature defense. The second he tips me off my center of balance, I flip my body around, plant both hands on the concrete, and kick him in the face with the free foot.

He goes reeling backward while I'm getting to my feet and then we attack each other. He goes high, because he's taller than me, and reaches for my head, going for a snap down.

I deflect both hands, ram my head into his gut, and do a double-leg takedown. He's on his back, I'm on top of him, and even though I know I've got him now, this motherfucker jumped me like a pussy. So I don't take the high road and let him off easy. I ram my knee into his mouth, his fists flailing at my face. One connects with my eye so hard I almost black out, but now I'm pissed.

I double-punch him. Cheekbone, forehead, cheekbone, forehead. Over and over until he's choking on his own blood.

I get up, breathing heavy, and look around for Horse Face. He's running for a car, gets in, starts it up, and then squeals the tires as he aims the vehicle straight *at me.*

This is my cue that it's over. I need to bail, and because the door to the stairwell has a security lock on it, I go for that. I reach into my pocket for the keycard as I run, and swipe it.

I look over my shoulder as I enter the stairs, but they're done with me. Neck Tattoo is stumbling towards the car, and two seconds later he's inside and they disappear up the parking garage ramp.

"Motherfuckers," I say, still out of breath.

I look down at my shirt and find it bloody from the blow to the face I took. So I take the stairs two at a time, all the way up to my floor, then go back inside my apartment and scream it again.

"Motherfuckers!"

It's fucking Hanna, I know it. That's what her little phone call was about. That fucking bitch sent thugs to rough me up.

This shit is crazy. These *girls* are crazy.

I take off my suit, wash the blood off my face and hands, pull on yesterday's clothes because they're lying in a heap on the floor, and then go back out. Heading straight to Bronco Brews to tell Oaklee this fucking game is over.

CHAPTER THIRTY-ONE

OAKLEE

It was a sleepless night. Tossing and turning doesn't even begin to cover how I spent the last eight hours. It was more like… I wanted to throw up. I wanted to turn back time. Stop Law from going over to see Hanna. Stop this stupid game before it started and just tell him… I like him. We should give it a real go.

Because I knew. That's the worst part. I knew Hanna would ruin things and I sent him over there anyway.

What the fuck is wrong with me?

I get out of bed early, stand in front of my terrace window as the sun comes up, and focus on his terrace down the alley.

Did he sleep?

Is he thinking about me?

But then I make myself take a shower, get ready for work and go through the motions of making coffee. But it just sits in front of me. Untouched.

I have to fix this. I don't know how I'm going to do that, because I don't know what Hanna told him. And even though he said he'd call me after work and we could talk about it then, I don't think he meant it.

My phone rings in my office. So I walk in there, pick it up, and say, "Oaklee." It comes out sad and pathetic.

"Oaklee, this is Janice downstairs."

Janice. Great. She's one of the brewmasters, which means this call is not what I need right now. "What can I do for you, Janice?"

"Well, there's people outside and I don't know what to do."

"People? What people?"

"I didn't open the door, don't worry. But they said something about an appointment with you this morning."

"Appointment?"

"Do you want me to let them in and send them up?"

"No," I say. With all this crazy drama going on and Lawton getting me thinking about security—"No. I'll come down and take care of it myself. Thanks."

"No problem," Janice says before hanging up.

Who the fuck? This had better not be Hanna. I'm really not in the mood for that kind of confrontation right now.

I get in the elevator, take it downstairs, and as soon as I step out I can see a group of people standing out at the front doors. We don't open until lunch, so I have no clue what this is about.

I unlock the door and open it up to find two smartly-dressed women and two equally well-dressed men. "Can I help you?"

"Oaklee?" the woman with the blonde bob says.

"Yes," I say.

She offers her hand and I reach for it out of instinct. "It's Michaela!" she says. Like I'm supposed to know who she is.

"OK," I say.

She tilts her head at me, strange expression on her face. Something in between confusion and curiosity. "We talked on the phone yesterday?"

"We did?" I say. "I'm sorry, I'm confused. What's this about?"

Michaela looks over her shoulder at her entourage, then back at me. "What do you mean? We talked yesterday. You pitched the show to me because you knew I was coming to town for a meeting. And we made arrangements to go over things."

"Things?" I say.

"The *Brewery Smackdown* show?" she says. Like this should ring my bell.

"I... I have no idea what you're talking about."

"Home TV," Michaela says. And now she's irritated. "I was very excited about this concept and that's why we flew in this morning to meet with you and your partner."

"With Lawton?" I say, still confused. "And what do you mean *Brewery Smackdown*? The show is about mountain homes, not a brewery. And certainly not my brewery."

Michaela laughs nervously. "Lawton Ayers?"

"Yeah, he and I have a meeting with guys this week about the *Rocky Mountain Millionaires* show. I have no clue where you got the idea I was doing a show on the brewery."

"You called me," Michaela says. "Can we go inside?" She looks over her shoulder again.

"OK," I say, opening the door. "My office is upstairs, so... would you like to go up there and sort things out?"

"That would be great," one of the men says. He looks very annoyed. But I can't tell if it's with me for not understanding, or with Michaela for fucking this whole thing up so bad.

I take them up the elevator, feeling nervous and self-conscious because everyone is on the wrong page, and then lead them into my apartment. "Can I get you anything?" I ask. I want to play good host because if I fuck up Lawton's deal, he'll probably never talk to me again. "Something to drink?" I offer.

"That won't be necessary," the man says. "Are you Ms. Ryan?"

"Yes, I'm Oaklee Ryan."

"And you own this Bronco Brews?"

"Yes," I say.

"Did you call our corporate offices on Saturday morning?" the second woman asks.

"I'm sorry, who are all you people?"

"I'm Mike Brown," the man says. "Executive Producer at Home TV. I oversee all the new show concepts. This is my assistant, Jake Slocum. And this is Michaela's assistant, Lisa Stevens. We're here because somehow you knew we were coming to town to talk to Lawton Ayers about his mountain show, and you wanted to pitch us an idea about dueling local breweries before we decided to commit to him."

My stomach sinks. "Let me guess," I say. "Would these two breweries be Bronco Brews and Buffalo Brews?"

"Yes!" Michaela says. She's excited now that I seem to be on the same page. "We love, love, love this idea, don't we Mike?"

"I was intrigued enough to get on a jet at five AM this morning to fly in for your meeting, but I have to say, this was not the reception I was expecting."

"Jesus Christ," I whisper. "This isn't happening. Look, there's been—"

But that's as far as I get in the way of an explanation. Because the elevator doors ding and then the doors open and Lawton appears.

Face all beaten up.

Raging mad expression on his face.

And yelling, "What the fuck are you two doing to each other?" Before I can tell him that Home TV is in the house.

CHAPTER THIRTY-TWO

LAWTON

I regret my outburst as the words are leaving my mouth for three reasons.

One. Oaklee didn't do this to me, Hanna did.

Two. She's in the middle of a business meeting and I just yelled the word *fuck*.

And three. I look like I just got in a street fight. Because I did. So the two women actually look afraid of me and the two men just angry.

"Uh..." I say, in the ensuing silence. Four unknown well-dressed people stare at me with wide eyes. "Um..." I force a smile. "I'm sorry." Then look at Oaklee, who is shaking her head at me on the sly. "I didn't realize you had people up here."

"Lawton," Oaklee says. "You're bleeding! What the hell happened to you?"

I look at her... acquaintances, then back at her and say, "Um... I can come back later."

"Wait," a tall man in a very expensive suit says. "You're Lawton Ayers?"

"Uh..." And for some reason I know the right answer to this question is no.

But Oaklee says, "Yes. This is Lawton. He's the one you have a meeting with, not me."

"Meeting?" I say. "No. I have no clue what you all are doing, or talking about, or... anything. So I'm gonna go." I point at the elevator as I look at Oaklee. "Over to

Jordan's office and have a little conversation with him about the contract we signed. I'll come back later, see ya."

But Oaklee runs over to me and grabs my arm, tugging me back into the fray. "Lawton," she whispers. "These are the Home TV people. They're here for your meeting. I don't know how they got my name—did you mention me?—anyway, doesn't matter. They're here about the show."

"We can hear you," one woman says. "And we've already explained. We're not here for Lawton Ayers. We're here for you."

I spin around because I recognize her voice. "Michaela?" I say. "Michaela Cummings?"

She purses her lips and nods. "Yes. I'm sorry for the confusion, Lawton. And I don't know why you're here. But this isn't your meeting. We're here because Oaklee Ryan contacted us about a show based on her brewery."

"That's not true!" Oaklee says, grabbing my arm tighter. "I did not! I don't know what's happening but I never called these people! I wouldn't even know where to start the process of getting a TV show!"

The other woman opens up the cover to her tablet, shaking her head. She stabs the screen a few times with her fingers and then holds it up so we can see. "Oaklee, we have emails from you. An entire pitch for dueling craft breweries in Denver. You even said you knew we'd be in town this week and set up this morning's appointment."

"But I didn't!" Oaklee says, looking up at me. "I swear! That wasn't me!"

"Then who was it?" the man asks.

"They came from ORyan@broncobrews.com," the tablet woman says. "Is that your email?"

I look at Oaklee.

"Lawton—"

"Is that your email?" I ask her.

"Yes, but—"

"Jesus fucking—"

"OK," the man says. "Ms. Ryan, we're very interested in hearing more about this show. We've been looking for something like this for a while now. Otherwise we wouldn't be here. So are you going to pitch us or not?"

"It's Lawton's show!" she says. "It's not my show. You guys want Lawton."

"No," Michaela says. "Look, Lawton." She turns to me. "We appreciate all the hard work you've put into this concept of yours, and to be honest, we're only taking your meeting tomorrow because we were coming to hear Oaklee's pitch. We were going to cancel on you. Sorry, but we're not looking for another million-dollar-home show at the moment."

"The deal is off?" I ask. Stunned. Unable to believe this whole fucking scene is happening.

"There was no deal, son," the man says. "OK? It was just a pitch and while it started out interesting, we're just not moving forward. And to be quite frank, Mr. Ayers, you're really not the kind of personality we're looking for."

I look at Oaklee, that last bit echoing in my mind.

She's shaking her head. "It wasn't me," she says. "This was Hanna, Law. This has Hanna written all over it. She did this! She ruined your—"

"Enough," I say, stopping Oaklee before she can say anything else. "You know what, Oaklee. I came over here to tell you one thing and that's all I'm going to say and then I'm going to leave. Game. Over."

"Wait! Lawton! Let me explain!"

I whirl around. "Explain?" Then I laugh. "Ya know, I believed you, Oaklee. But the things Hanna told me last night have me questioning everything. And you know what? I don't think I even care who's telling the truth." I shake my head. "No, that's not right. I don't care. I don't care at all. I'm getting out of this contract right now. Good luck with everything. And I hope you and Hanna can work your bullshit out. Because the two of you are toxic. To yourselves, to each other, and to everyone around you."

"Lawton!" she calls.

But I just walk to the elevator, push the call button, and get inside without saying another word.

I'm done with this girl.

I'm done with the TV show.

And I'm done with this game.

The drive over to Jordan's office near Capitol Hill only takes a few minutes, and that's not nearly enough time to calm me down after the shitstorm morning I've just had.

I take the elevator up to his floor and stop at the receptionist. "I'm here to see Jordan Wells."

"Do you have an appointment?" she asks.

"No," I say curtly. "But he's going to see me. Tell him Lawton Ayers is here and I want to talk. Right. Now."

"Um…" She stares at me, and I don't know if I'm scaring her because I look like a thug who just got in a fight, or if I'm kinda pissing her off because I'm being overly aggressive. "OK." she says. "Let me just check with his assistant and see if he's available."

She gets up, walks through the glass doors that separate the offices from reception, and disappears off to the right.

I pace back and forth in front of the desk, gaze wandering to where the girl just disappeared. She returns, followed by another woman a little bit older than her, comes back through the glass doors, and says, "Eileen can help you, Mr. Ayers."

"Why don't we go back here," she says, waving her hand at the glass doors, "and I'll check his schedule."

I'm about to say something snarky back, but decide to take a deep breath instead. "Fine. But I need to talk to him immediately."

I open the door for her, let her lead the way, and follow her back to another reception area where she takes a seat at her desk and punches a button on her desk phone. "Jordan?"

"Jesus Christ, Eileen. What the fuck is it?" Which tells me either he's either having a very bad day, or Oaklee is already bending his ear about what just happened.

Eileen shoots me a pained expression. "Lawton Ayers is here to see you."

I know Oaklee is filling Jordan's head with lies right this moment. So I just take off down the hall in search of Jordan's office.

"Hey!" Eileen yells. "You can't go back there!"

"The fuck I can't," I mumble under my breath. I peek into offices as I walk, looking for—

There he is! The door opens for me and a tall guy blocks my way. There's two other men in the office with Jordan, all of whom look like they're in the middle of a serious conversation.

"Dude," I say, walking forward towards Jordan's desk. "Duuuuuuuude."

"I'm sorry! He got past me!" Eileen says from the doorway.

Then one of the guys gets up and says, "And I'm out of here." And he is, because he leaves.

"What the fuck is going on, Lawton? Oaklee Ryan just called me, seemingly distressed. And why the fuck are you dressed up like a... a..."

"A thug?" I finish for him.

But he just smiles at me. "No. Like a hot dude. Is that a... did you get a *tattoo*?"

"Oh, that's funny. Real fuckin' funny, Jordan. Do you have any idea what kind of game this chick wants me to play with her?"

"Uh, yeah." He looks over at one of the other guys. The one in the suit who may have had a gun out when I came into the office, but maybe I just imagined that, because I don't see it now. Jordan laughs, like this is actually funny. "Little bit of wine, little bit of food, send her flowers at work, maybe a little bit of dancing, and then cap it all off by taking her to her sister's wedding or something, right?"

Sister's wedding. That's almost funny. "Uh, no," I say.

"Class reunion?" Jordan asks.

"No," I say. "And when I say no, I mean no to all of that shit. Do you have any idea what she thinks the job of a boyfriend really is?"

"Tell me," he says, laughing. "Because I've been wondering what her real reason was for this game since I took the contract."

Every stupid thing I've done for her in the past four days comes tumbling out of my mouth. Her crazy nemesis.

Her idea to change the way I dress. The fucking tattoo. The break-in. And how she just cost me the goddamned TV show.

"I've had it," I say once I'm done with my rant. "I want out of this contract right the fuck now."

And that's when Oaklee opens the door, Eileen protesting behind her, and yells, "He's lying!"

CHAPTER THIRTY-THREE

JORDAN

"OK," I say. "Let's all just calm—"

"Lying?" Law rages. "Lying?" He looks at me and growls, "Get me out of this contract, Jordan. I'm done."

I look at Oaklee, who is now pouting. But she says nothing.

"Oaklee?" I say. "What's going on?"

She shrugs and it's clear she's holding back tears. "I—" But she just starts shaking her head.

"You what?" I ask, trying to be gentle so I don't push her into *actually* breaking down.

"She just ruined my fucking TV deal."

Oaklee is still shaking her head. She whispers, "I had nothing to do with that."

I don't actually know what to say here, so I just wait them out. Law takes a seat in a chair, his leg bouncing up and down like he can't control the adrenaline rush. Oaklee just looks down at her feet, and I'm sure she really is crying now. So I look over at Darrel, who simply shrugs.

Finn, who is standing guard at the door, says, "Your dad's coming."

"Shit," I say. "Everyone shut up and let me handle this."

My father always knocks, it's the professional thing to do. But he is the boss, so that knock is just a warning that he's coming in.

"Dad?" I say. "What's up?"

He looks around. At Oaklee first, then Law. Because he knows Darrel and Finn. Then he says, "Everything OK in here? The whole office heard the shouting."

"Sorry about that," I say. And then I whisper, "It's a very emotional divorce."

Which makes my father's eyebrows crinkle, because I'm not actually a divorce attorney. But hey, he goes with it because I sometimes do weird shit.

"Try to keep it down. We're taking depositions in the conference room."

"Sure thing, Dad. Sorry about that."

He leaves and I say, "I'm fucking working here, Law. OK? You do not come barging into my office demanding anything. Especially when it has to do with a game."

"Fuck you," he says. But he keeps his voice down. "I want out of this stupid shit."

"I didn't have anything to do with that meeting this morning," Oaklee cries, desperate to be heard. "It was all Hanna and you know it. Why would I sabotage you, Lawton? I like you. I thought you liked me. Why on Earth would I fuck all that up over something I don't even want? And how the hell would I even get the information to set up the meeting in the first place? You're being unreasonable and I don't know what Hanna told you last night, but whatever it was, it's all lies."

"All of it, Oaklee?" He huffs out some air.

And right now I feel more like I'm moderating a couple's therapy session than pretending to facilitate a messy divorce.

"OK," I say. "Oaklee, did you buy the Boyfriend Experience for someone else?"

"Yes." She nods. "But that's not even how it turned out! He's *my* boyfriend experience! I don't even want him to keep the game going."

Jesus. I hope she doesn't want her money back. I was counting on that cash for the down payment I need.

"Good," Law says. "Because I'm out. I'm done with you two. What you and your sister are doing to each other, I don't want any part of it."

"My sister!" Oaklee yells.

"Shh," I hiss. "If my dad come back in here—"

"Sorry," Oaklee says. "Where the hell did you get the idea she was my fucking sister?" And to her credit, she whisper-yells that entire sentence.

"She told me the whole story last night. How your father cheated on your mother and then abandoned them both. And when he died she contested the will and—"

"I will fucking kill her!" And this time it's not a whisper-yell, it's the real deal.

We all look at the door, and yup. Two seconds later my father is knocking and entering again. "*Jordan*," he hisses.

"Sorry," Oaklee says. "I lost control. It won't happen again."

My father gives me one more stern look. A look that says, *Do not fuck with me right now*. And I'm actually kinda happy about that. So I smile when I say, "Last time, promise."

I watch him go. Actually stare at the door even after he's gone. And feel sad all of a sudden. Lawton and Oaklee are whisper-fighting over whether or not she has a sister called Hanna, but I let my thoughts linger on my dad for a few more moments.

Until Law says, "She sent two assholes to fucking beat me up this morning!"

"Who?" I say. "Oaklee?"

"No, fucking Hanna."

"OK," I say, pinching the bridge of my nose. "Run this all by me again. And this time keep your fucking voices down." I point to Oaklee to go first and when Law interrupts, I point to him and say, "Shut up. You already had your say so just let her talk."

So she does. Her tale comes spilling out as quick as Law's did. It's a tale of betrayal, and misplaced trust. A jealous woman taking away a life hard earned. And even though she does admit to the breaking and entering last night, I find myself... on her side.

Because sometimes one can only take so much before they run out of rational options. They map out a diplomatic course of action. They focus. They aim themselves on their road, stay in their lane, play by all the rules... and what good does it do?

I can relate to that part.

People make mistakes, but should one mistake define them forever?

I glance up at Darrel just as Oaklee gets to the part about this morning and find him watching me. He nods. A small nod that no one else sees. Not even Finn.

But I do.

And I know exactly what that nod means.

CHAPTER THIRTY-FOUR

OAKLEE

I pace back and forth in front of Jordan's desk as I tell my side of the story. It's a story Law already knows, because it's the one I've been telling him all along. I have no idea what Hanna told him, but he must see through it. I must make him see through her lies. I've given up way too much of my life to this crazy bitch already.

I will not give him up too.

So when I'm done explaining things to Jordan, I take the seat next to Law, turn my body so I'm facing him, look him in the eyes, take a deep breath and say, "I'm sorry. I know this is all my fault. I was the one who wanted to play this game, but I don't wanna play any more, Lawton. I'm sorry if you think I didn't like you as you were. Because that's not true. Yes, it was my idea for you to get that tattoo, and if you felt pressured... if you felt that I somehow talked you into it, I'm sorry for that too. I'm sorry for the boots you're wearing, and the shirt, and the jeans. I'm sorry if you feel I didn't accept you for who you were. I do. And I had nothing to do with the TV people showing up this morning. That was not me." I stop to catch my breath. "It has to be her."

I pause. Waiting for him to say something. He just stares at me, thinking, I guess. Running everything though his mind.

I look at Jordan, who just shrugs. Then he says, "Lawton. I really am starting to feel like a marriage counselor here. You need to say something."

Law looks at him, then back at me, and says, "How crazy does a bitch have to be to tell me a lie like the one she told last night?"

"What did she say?" I ask. "Sisters? I mean, that makes no sense at all. All anyone has to do is look at her birth certificate."

"She had one, Oaklee. With your father's name on it."

"That's bullshit! We're the same fucking age for God's sake!" I'm careful not to raise my voice and bring Jordan's father back in here a third time. "My dad never said anything! And she never said anything! I didn't know who the fuck she was until she showed up in my college dorm room! And she met my father, Law. She came to my house a couple times that first year. You'd think my dad would've acted weird... or... or something! But he didn't. This is all lies. All of it. She's insane! We are the same fucking age! It's not even *biologically possible*!"

And then I know what he's gonna say, so I point at him and growl, "If you accuse me of being her twin, I will... I will punch you in the eye."

Law lets out a long breath of air, then looks over at Jordan. "So..."

"So..." Jordan says. And he's smiling. Like... what part of this is funny? I want to slap him. But then Jordan turns to one of the other guys in the room. The one in a suit. He nods to him and that guy smiles as well. He says, "OK, we're on it. Come on, Finn, we've got shit to do."

And the two of them leave the office, and the three of us just look at each other.

Jordan is the first to speak. "Well, I think I owe you something for taking this game in the first place, Lawton. So, if it's OK with you two, we're gonna take it from here."

"Take what?" I ask. "From where?"

"He means," Law says, "he's going to fix this for us."

"If that's what you want?" Jordan asks.

"How? How do you fix crazy?"

"She knows Oaklee and Vivi Vaughn broke into her place last night, Jordan. It would not surprise me in the least if she's pressing charges right this minute. She says she has surveillance."

"Oh, shit!" I say. "Vivi said she took care of that!"

Jordan presses a button on his desk phone, says, "Eileen, get me Oliver Shrike on the phone, please."

"Sure thing," Eileen says back.

Jordan looks at me, then Law. He says, "I can take care of all of this. Luckily, Oliver will be interested in protecting his family. So he'll most likely go along. But if any of this twin shit is true—" He looks at me.

"It isn't!" I insist. "She's lying about all of it! She is not my stupid sister! She's just a jealous freak who wants to steal my life."

"If it's all lies," Jordan continues, "then she's one crazy bitch and we need to be careful. Sociopaths don't react the way we would. They have no guilt, they have no conscience, and they will most definitely strike back."

Just as he says that, my phone buzzes in my pocket. I take it out and check the screen. "Shit. Now what?"

"Who is it?" Law and Jordan ask at the same time.

"The brewery." I tab accept and say, "Yes?"

"Oaklee?"

I roll my eyes, because *she* called me, right? But I don't want to get pissy at people who have nothing to do with my very bad morning. So I say, "Yes, Dana. What's going on?"

"Um… you might want to turn on Channel Five if you're near a TV."

My stomach sinks again. "What now?" I whisper back.

"Hanna's doing an interview. You're really gonna wanna see this. Because… just turn it on."

She ends the call and I spy a remote on Jordan's desk, so I grab it and turn the TV on, navigate to Channel Five, and see Hanna Harlow's face on the screen.

The little banner at the bottom says, *Buffalo Brews releases special-edition beer for festival this weekend.*

And then I hear the name of her beer.

Which is the name of my beer.

And that's it. I can't help it. I give up. I can't win.

She stole my secret Assassin Sour Saison and this time she didn't even bother changing the label or the name.

She just stole my beer and announced it to the world as hers.

I look around the room, unable to focus on anything. And just say, "I gotta go," as I turn and walk out.

CHAPTER THIRTY-FIVE

LAWTON

Oaklee walks out. She's like March—came in like a lion and went out like a lamb.

I look over at Jordan, who's frowning. "Follow her," he says. And then his phone buzzes and Eileen says, "Oliver Shrike is on line three for you, Jordan."

"Thanks, Eileen." Then he looks at me, surprised I'm still in his office, and says, "Go fucking follow her!"

I nod, turn, and leave.

She's waiting at the elevator when I get out in the reception lobby. Her arms crossed at her chest. Her head tilted up as she stares at the electronic sign above the door, waiting for it to ding.

"Oaklee—"

"Just... not now, OK?" She doesn't look at me.

Jordan's father walks up between us. Leans forward to push the button, even though it's already lit. And then he and I meet eyes.

The elevator dings, the doors open, and Oaklee walks in. Wells Senior and I follow, each standing on either side of her. Oaklee pushes the button for the lobby, Wells pushes floor seven. Then the doors close and the three of us stand there in awkward silence.

Wells clears his throat. "You know, my wife and I went through a rough patch when Jordan was a teenager. He..." Wells laughs. Like he's reliving a memory of his son and it makes him happy. "He was a handful, that kid. Still is. But he's turned into a good man."

Oaklee and I both turn our heads to look at the tall, well-dressed older man. Our eyes meet and then we turn away.

"But if you love someone, sometimes the fight is worth it."

The elevator dings floor seven and the doors open. Wells steps out, then turns back to us, his hand pressed against the door, holding it open. "Only the two of you know if the fight is worth it. But in my experience, more often than not, people are worth fighting for."

Then he smiles at us, turns away, and walks off.

The doors close and both Oaklee and I sigh as we descend to the lobby.

When we get out of the elevator and start walking for the door, I take her arm, gently, and make her stop. "Look, I'm sorry, OK? Can I come back to your place so we and figure this out?"

She's still upset. Her eyes are glistening with tears. But she nods and says, "Your house. I don't know how Hanna got all this information, but I can only assume she's bugged my apartment. And there's no way I've giving her another private moment of my life. So I'm not going home. Ever again until I can call in a specialist to search it."

She walks off to wherever she parked her car. I watch her until she slips around a corner. And then I walk off in the opposite direction.

When I pull into my garage, Oaklee is waiting for me, her car probably parked in her own lot down the alley. She leans up against a thick concrete pillar looking defeated and sad.

I get out, walk over to her, and take her hand. She starts crying again. So I pull her close, hug her tight, and say, "We'll figure this out. Don't worry."

Oaklee shakes her head no. Because she doesn't believe me. I've fucked this whole thing up and now... her trust is gone. Maybe not her trust in me. I'm not sure about that yet. But her trust in my ability to make things right is definitely on hold right now.

And I don't blame her.

"Come on," I say, pulling back. "Let's just go upstairs and relax."

"Don't you have work?" she asks.

"Fuck work. I called my office and cancelled my day after Hanna's thugs tried to kick my ass."

"I'm sorry about the TV show, Law."

"Forget about it. Things happen for a reason. I truly believe that. So... fuck them. Maybe you should take them up on their offer?"

She huffs. "No, thank you. I never wanted a TV show. It was only going to be fun because we'd have been partners."

I squeeze her hand as we get into the elevator. "We're still partners, Oaks."

She looks at me and gives me a half-hearted nod, trying to smile through her tears.

"We're still partners and we're gonna get that bitch, OK? Because if all that shit she said last night was a lie—"

"It was! My father wasn't that kind of man. He was honest, and good, and even when he made mistakes he owned them. He took responsibility. And she is not my fucking sister!"

"Then Hanna Harlow is a psychopath."

"Yes," Oaklee says. "She is. But you know who else is kinda crazy?"

"You?"

This makes her laugh. Which makes me feel a little better about being such a raging dick this morning.

We get out of the elevator and walk to my apartment door. I open it, wave her in, and then she turns. "Me," she says. "Yes. But not just me. Now she's fucking with Vivi Vaughn. And there's not a sane person alive who would do that. So that just proves she's not only insane, she's stupid too."

Then she walks over to my kitchen, opens up the freezer, looks around for a moment, and withdraws a bag of frozen vegetables. "Your eye is swelling," she says, walking towards me and taking my hand. She leads me over to the couch, points to it, and says, "Sit. I'm giving you a complimentary deluxe girlfriend experience."

God. I think... I think... "I think I love you, Oaklee Ryan."

That makes her smile, but she pushes me backward with a palm to my chest. I sit and she climbs into my lap, pressing the frozen bag of broccoli against my brow.

It stings. But it's not the worst sting I've ever felt. And anyway, having her in my lap is worth the sting.

Our eyes meet. Both sets sad. Because we lost things today. We're still losing things in this moment.

But then she kinda grins at me. And I kinda grin back, because how could I not? And she says, "You're worth fighting for."

"No," I say, reaching up to place my hands on either side of her face. "Not me, us. We're worth fighting for."

"She stole my beer, she stole my label, she stole my name… and she stole your TV show. What else could she possibly want?"

"Forget her," I say. "Just for a little bit. Just… just be with me right now."

Her shoulders slump and her lips pout in the most adorable way.

But I know she's not trying to be adorable, she's very sad right now. And none of this is her fault. So I say, "Ya know, a long time ago, back when I was this guy"—I motion to the tattoo on my arm—"I had lost everything. My parents were gone, I was living on the street, doing drugs. I had no life, no future to look forward to. I was smart, but didn't think it was gonna get me anywhere. So I wasted it. I wasted years just… pretending none of it mattered. That I was strong enough to handle the world alone.

"But then Bric came along and he told me something one day. Something I'd never forget. He said, 'A fighter never quits and a quitter never fights. You were born a fighter, so act like it.'

"And at the time I blew him off." I laugh. "I literally gave him the finger and told him to fuck off. But a few weeks later I was in juvie again. And Bric came to bail me out. He sponsored me. Gave me a scholarship to a very nice private school here in Denver, and convinced the judge I was ready to change, even though I wasn't. And when we got in his car that day, as we were leaving the courthouse, he said, 'That's how you quit, Lawton. That's how you let everyone else win.'"

Oaklee screws up her face. "What did he mean?"

"He meant… He meant that I was responsible for all the bad things that happen. Not anyone else."

"But"—Oaklee sighs—"I didn't ask for this, Lawton. I didn't do anything to Hanna Harlow except *exist*."

"No, that's not what he meant. He meant I can only control me. No matter what anyone else does *to me*, only I can control how I react *to them*."

She sighs. Bows her head and looks at her hands resting on her legs. "Why were you in juvie?" she asks, peeking up at me through her hair.

"That time?" I laugh. "I had a fight club going. Like… back-alley MMA cage fights. I beat the shit out of a guy one night. Put him in the hospital. But they got me for the illegal gambling, not the fight. He was eighteen, I was only sixteen. But they nailed me for the gambling ring I was running."

"So you made poor choices," She sighs again. "I'm sure I've made poor choices too, but I swear to God, Lawton, I don't know what I did to Hanna to make her hate me so much. To make her want to steal from me and lie about my father like this. For whatever reason, I'm her target. It's like… her mission in life is to ruin mine. And I don't understand. I just don't understand why."

"She's sick, Oaklee." I tap her on the head. "Up here. And we can't control that. We can only control how we react to her."

She pouts her lips. "You're *my* boyfriend experience, not hers."

I chuckle, then lean forward and kiss her on the mouth, my hands holding her face. And my laugh is real. Even though everything in my life has just been upended—I still have her.

And that's all that matters.

"I'm sorry," I say. Because I feel it needs to be said. "I'm sorry for making your life more difficult. For not coming over last night. For not reaching out this morning. For losing my temper and stressing you out. And for the record, Oaklee... you didn't change me." I look her in the eyes as I say this because it's important. "Clothes can't change me. New boots can't change me. And this tattoo is me from start to finish. This *is me*, Oaklee. This is just who I've always been. You simply made me see that. You," I say, "asked me to be myself and no one else. This is me."

She smiles the real smile. The one I saw the other night. The secret smile only I can see.

And then she says, "The game is over, but we can still win."

CHAPTER THIRTY-SIX

OAKLEE

I want to be closer to him. I'm sitting in his lap, my face only inches from his. My body pressed to his chest. My hands on his shoulders. Every part of me is already close, and it's not close enough.

I need skin on skin contact. I need him inside me. "I need you," I whisper. And then I reach down and pull my shirt over my head. He looks at me in a way no other person has ever looked at me.

It's hunger.

It's desire.

There's a yearning inside him that perfectly matches the longing inside me.

I reach behind my back and unclasp my bra. Letting it fall free. Letting my breasts free too. His hands come up automatically. Cupping and squeezing them, our eyes still locked.

"This wasn't quite the experience you were looking for," he says.

"No," I say back. "I got way more than a boyfriend. I got a partner."

He slips my bra down my arms and drops it carelessly to the floor. Eyes locked with mine. I tug on the hem of his shirt and bring it over his head. He helps me take it off and drops it on top of my clothes, starting a pile.

I place my hands on his chest. Palms flat so I can feel him. Feel his chest move up and down. Feel his heart quicken with excitement.

And then, just for a second, I have a stab of fear. Fear that Hanna will come and take him away. Fear that she will spend her life trying to ruin us. Fear that she will succeed.

"Hey," he says. "Don't go there. Not now." He leans forward to kiss me. Make me forget everything but him, and me, and what it means to be us. And then he stands up, taking me with him. I wrap my legs around his middle. My breasts pressed to his chest. Our bodies closer now, but still not close enough.

He walks me over to the kitchen island and sets me down in front of it.

I grin, shy. Because I know he's going to fuck me now. How he'll do that, I don't know. All I know is he will make me come, and come, and come again. As many times as I let him.

His fingers are on the button of my jeans, but I place my hand over his and say, "No, you first."

He grabs me by the waist, turns us in place, and then leans against the counter as I unbutton his jeans, drag them down his legs, and take his cock in my hand as I kneel at his feet.

It's a very submissive position, I know this, but that's not why I'm doing it.

I'm not submitting to him. I don't expect him to submit to me, either.

We are equals, Law and I. I know this. It's something he never has to say. It's something between us. Respect? I dunno. I don't think it needs a word because it's just a feeling.

I put him in my mouth because I want to. That's all there is to it.

I want to.

He leans his head back. His hands gripping the counter. Making his upper arms twist with shadows that highlight the long muscles of his biceps. I let go of his cock, press my face up to his groin as far as I can manage, and place my hands on his thighs as I bob back and forth, dragging my tongue up and down his shaft as we find our rhythm.

His breathing becomes heavy, laced with lust. His eyes close as I watch his face. His legs relax as he braces himself against the marble countertop.

I want him to come. I want him to be first for once. I want this so bad it becomes my mission.

"Oaks," he whispers, his voice husky and low. "Let me—"

"No," I say, pulling away for a moment. "No, Law. This time, *you* will let *me*."

"But—" He tries to fight it. I know he wants to make his case. I know he wants me to come first. That's what good boyfriends do. They let their girl go first. They open the doors, and pull out the chairs, and allow them to be first in everything.

Because the perfect boyfriend puts himself second.

But that's not how it's happening today.

Today he is first and I am second.

Because that's what the perfect girlfriend does too.

I press my face up to his skin again, this time taking him deeper than I've ever taken him before. I swallow down the reflex to gag, and in doing so, send him over the edge.

He jumps off, willingly. His body stiff, his cock throbbing as he spills his release into my mouth and down my throat.

I watch his face as I swallow. His eyes open just in time to see this final gesture of my commitment.

And then he smiles and says, "You're going to come twice for that," like it's a threat, and not a promise he wants to keep.

I stand up, his hands already unbuttoning my jeans. Dragging the zipper down. His fingers between my legs and then inside me before I can take another breath.

My body goes limp, but he's there to catch me. He will always be there to catch me.

And before I know it, my back is pressing against the cold stone countertop. My pants are gone, dropped to the floor. My legs open, his hands on my knees, spreading me wide.

And then his face... his face is there. His chin pressing against my pussy as his tongue does a wild little dance across my clit.

I'm primed. Climbing the peak to the first climax is easy. It's right there... right... there.

And the moment his fingers slip inside me. The moment his mouth closes over my clit and he begins to suck...

I come.

After that we take our time. He strips naked—I'm already naked—and he fucks me all over his apartment. On the counter first. Grabbing me by the knees and pulling my ass along the stone until his cock slides easily into my slick opening. He pounds me. He fucks me slow. He makes me come, and come again.

Then on the couch. Me in his lap. Kissing, tasting each other as I move, his hands on my hips, guiding me back and forth until neither of us can take it anymore.

Then against the wall. His hands under my ass, gripping me so tight, I'll have bruises later. His thrusts so hard his balls slap up against my ass, which only drives me wilder.

Later, we take a shower. His hands all over me, soaping me up. Massaging my tired and quivering muscles. My hands doing the same for him.

Because we're equals.

And this is how you equal.

CHAPTER THIRTY-SEVEN

LAWTON

We are lazy and mostly naked for the rest of the day. Trying to forget the bad and remember the good. I love her in my arms. I'm riddled with guilt for making her cry this morning, even though she says it was Hanna who upset her, not me.

It was me. It's been a long time since I let anger and frustration get the best of me, but that's what took over this morning and I regret it, because it hurt her. She felt alone when she broke down. Abandoned. And that's something I know a little bit about. No one wants to be tossed aside.

But I'm here for her now. And she's smiling at least.

"You hungry?" I ask her. She's wearing a pair of my boxers and one of my t-shirts. I found an old one tucked away in my closet from another era in my life. An Oaklee-appropriate Nirvana Bleach one with all that "We're bad motherfuckers" wording on the back. Which totally suits her, because she's filled to the brim with bad motherfucker.

"I could eat," she says. "Should we order in?"

"Nah," I say. Because I have another reason I want to get out of here. "Let's go somewhere. Come on, get up." I slap her thigh and make her squeal.

And just as she's about to slap me back, my phone rings on the coffee table.

We both look at the screen. Unknown number.

"Let's ignore it," Oaklee says.

"Fuck that. Fuck her." I pick up the phone, tab accept and put it on speaker. "Lawton Ayers."

"Lawton," Hanna purrs. "I didn't think you'd answer."

"What do you want?"

"What's wrong? Things not going your way today?"

"Actually," I say, "things are going pretty fucking great for me." I wink at Oaklee.

Hanna makes a noise with her lips. Like she's annoyed. "The Home TV people called and made me an offer since Oaklee wasn't interested."

"Good for you," I say, watching Oaklee's expression.

"They want both of us."

"Sorry, I'm not interested. I give up on TV shows."

"Not you," Hanna hisses. "Oaklee and me. They like the idea of dueling breweries."

"Fuck off, bitch," Oaklee says. "There's no bribe big enough in this world that could make me go in business with you. You're just a fucking liar, you know that? A crazy fucking liar."

"Oh, how cute," she croons. "The two of you are spending quality time together before Oaklee goes to jail."

I look at Oaklee and shake my head at her. Mouth the words, *Keep cool.*

"What do you want, Hanna?"

"I want Oaklee to say yes or I'm going to the police with that video of her and Vivi Vaughn breaking into my building last night. Do you hear me, Oaklee? Mike and Michaela are coming back for the festival on Sunday to see us duel it out in person before they make this offer. And you'd better be entering a beer so I can win, bitch."

She's fucking crazy. Totally lost her mind.

"Do you hear me?" she yells. "Do. You. *Hear. Me?*"

Oaklee grabs the phone and puts it up her mouth. "How the fuck am I supposed to enter a beer when you stole it from me? Maybe I should call the cops on you, ya psycho! How about I go through my footage of *you* breaking into my apartment and send that to the police? How about we pitch that for the pilot of dueling breweries?"

I know it's probably a bad idea to poke the sleeping bear, but she's not really sleeping, is she? So I'm smiling right at Oaklee when I say, "Back the fuck off, Hanna. You got what you wanted—"

"Oh," Hanna says, interrupting me with an incredulous bark. "Got what I wanted! No. No, no, no. I have so much more I need from Oaklee."

"You're not getting anything from me, bitch! And what the fuck is wrong with you? Telling Law that made-up story about my father and that *you're my sister?* You are on some seriously good drugs if you think either of us is buying your insane fantasy!"

Hanna tuts. But her bravado is returning just as Oaklee is losing hers. "You didn't know him like I did, Oaklee. It's sad and painful when a parent dies and you realize he had a secret life, but—"

"Fuck you!" Oaklee screams. "Fuck you! Fuck you! You're a goddamned liar!"

"Listen," Hanna hisses. "You will do this TV show with me and you will enter one of your pathetic beers in this weekend's contest so I can win—"

"You're going to win with my beer! How fucking insane are you?"

I take the phone away from Oaks and say, "Fine, Hanna, you win." And then I end the call.

"Why did you do that?" Oaklee yells. "She's such a fucking raging bitch."

"Because you really did break into her apartment. And you and I both know that whatever security you have in your building, Hanna won't be on it. So we have to play this right."

"I fucking hate her," Oaklee protests. "I feel like killing her."

A text comes through just as Oaklee says that. "Hanna," I say, looking at the screen.

"God, why can't she just leave us alone?"

"She says there's an appointment at your brewery tomorrow at noon." Which makes me laugh. "Oh, and that's super cute. They have an opening now because my appointment was cancelled."

Oaklee looks horrified. And then she slumps back into the couch cushions, resigned that she probably has to see this through and play along.

"Don't worry," I say. "They have to catch a plane at three, so…"

She doesn't smile.

So I lean over, put my arms around her, and hold her.

I sure hope Jordan comes through for us.

CHAPTER THIRTY-EIGHT

OAKLEE

My mind can't stop. It races with plans, and plots, and insane ideas on how I might take down my archnemesis.

I consider all the ways I could kill her. Hire a hitman. I'm sure Vivi could find me someone willing to kill for money. Or kill her myself. Strangulation is my first choice. Or set her brewery on fire. Then the Home TV people would all go away and I wouldn't be forced to take that meeting.

But even though I'm crazy, I'm not insane.

She wants me to do something like that. She's waiting for me to fuck up.

So I plot blackmail. I make plans to break into her place again, steal that footage of Vivi and me breaking into her place, and get rid of all traces we were ever there. Because she's going to hold that over my head for the rest of my life if I don't do something drastic.

But drastic is stupid. It's impulsive and dangerous because there's a good chance I'll fuck things up even worse.

Eventually I have to leave Law's apartment and go back over to my building to take care of a few business things, but I don't go up to my office. I use the computer in the restaurant office to do what I need, and then I go back to Law's and spend the night there.

The next morning he has to go to work and I have to face Hanna and the Home TV people. Which means I have to go back up to my apartment and give her more footage of me, because clearly, there's a bug in there, or a camera, or whatever. Because I've been thinking about this all night.

Law came over to my place last Friday and we talked about our game. I told him what I needed, he told me what he needed, and those Home TV people said they got a call on Saturday.

Which means Hanna heard that whole conversation.

And boy, does that bitch work quick, or what?

When I get to Bronco Brews, it's only nine AM. I thought about staying away until the meeting, but then I got a call from Jordan telling me he had a security specialist coming over to sweep my apartment.

"Hey, Oaklee!" Justine, the hostess on the schedule today, says. "Your nine thirty is here early." She nods to a guy sitting over on a bench tapping something on his phone.

"Thanks, Justine," I say, then walk over to the man. "Are you Dennis?"

He stands, offers me his hand, and says, "The one and only. Where do you want me to start?"

"Follow me," I say, walking to the elevators where the brand-new security will ensure that Hanna never gets up here again, because Eduardo put the whole system on lockdown and changed the code, just in case.

When we get up to my apartment I say, "Check everything."

But he's already got his large black bag open, fishing out electronic sweeping equipment to look for bugs and cameras.

So I go over to my desk and start thinking about my plan again.

Kill her.

Or set her brewery on fire.

Those are the only things I have so far and neither of them is the answer.

That's the thing about revenge, right? You sink so low to get it.

I will become Hanna if I do something stupid.

And it's no use fighting her lies. I mean, my sister? Come on. She's so insane. But all it takes is a rumor, right? People don't care about the truth. All it takes is one interview with Hanna talking shit to change minds. She could tank my whole brewery business with one lie. And even though none of what she told Law is true, he believed her. Even if it was only for a night, he believed her.

And everyone she tells this story too will believe her as well. Even if it's just for a day. One day is too long.

So I can't kill her. And I can't defend myself from her lies because she hasn't gone public yet.

How fucked up that I can't fight back until she lashes out. And if she never tells that lie to the public it becomes a deterrent. It becomes the most powerful weapon in her arsenal.

Right now what we have is a classic case of mutually assured destruction. We have bombs aimed at each other that neither of us can use without destroying ourselves at the same time.

How the fuck do I get out of this?

How do I take away her power and not blow myself up at the same time?

The phone buzzes in my office so I pull myself out of my thoughts, get up, and walk over to press the speaker button. "Yes?" I say

"It's Dana! So like, you've got people down here," she says in her Valley Girl accent. "Do you want me to send them up?"

"No," I say. "I'll be right down."

"All finished," Dennis says, coming down the stairs from the catwalk.

"Find anything?"

He just smiles. I take that as a yes.

"Thank you," I say.

"It's just my job," Dennis says, meeting me at the elevator.

We get in, I take him downstairs, where he disappears into the kitchen to leave by the back alley.

I focus on the people waiting for me in the reception area, tug on my bedazzled t-shirt to focus myself, and then walk forward with a smile to greet Hanna and the Home TV entourage.

I smile big, playing along like a good little girl doing what she's told.

There's air kisses, and handshakes, and laughing, and... yeah.

I'm pretty much living my worst nightmare.

Hanna is eating it up.

I want to barf.

But I rally, because I have no plan. I have nothing. Even though she did all this unspeakable shit to me, she holds all the cards and we both know it.

I take them upstairs. I play hostess. I get out my beers and line them up on the counter, much the way I did for Lawton last week. Hanna, ever prepared for a throwdown, brought hers with her and there's a few curious looks between the executives as they come to the same realization that Law did.

"Wow," Michaela says. "They are certainly similar. You two don't mess around, do you?"

I make myself smile.

"You know why that is?" Hanna asks, beaming with delight at her coup.

"Why is that?" I ask, leaning forward a little, because I cannot wait to hear her answer.

"It's because Oaklee and I are... well, she's my nemesis."

I want to say, *Ah ha!* But I don't, because... well, I think it's pretty obvious.

"And I'm hers," Hanna continues. "And you know what they say about your nemesis?"

"No," I growl. "What *do* they say?"

Hanna smiles at me, and I swear to God, I think it's real. "They say... they challenge you to be your best self. They make you better. We, Oaklee, make each other *better.*"

"Yes," Michaela says. "That's so fascinating! This is what we're eating up right now, ladies. This... this... this diabolical sense that you two want to kill each other. And yet that anger and hatred makes you so much more interesting. So much more successful. This show is going to be fabulous!"

Yeah, this Michaela, she can suck my tit.

"It's like Larry Bird and Magic Johnson," Mike, apparently a basketball dude, says. "They played, not only so their teams could win, but so they could beat each other. And when one was not playing, the other faltered."

"Is that so?" I ask. "I don't follow basketball." *And this is certainly not like that at all,* I don't add.

Because this is… this is Charles Xavier versus Magneto. This is Superman versus Lex Luthor. This is Batman versus Joker.

And Hanna Harlow is Magneto, Lex Luthor, and Joker all wrapped up into one neat insane package. She has me imprisoned in Kryptonite-infused metal and I don't even have a fucking Batarang to defend myself.

We're talking nemesis to the highest order. We're talking insane radioactive assholes with planet-sized egos. Larry Bird and Magic Johnson look like toddlers fighting over toys compared to me and Hanna.

I need to find her weakness. Because so far, nothing I do or say affects her at all. It's just one lie on top of another. And it all comes out of her mouth sounding like… like absolute *truth.*

She is charismatic in the worst way. So evil, people want to believe there's something underneath all that hate and anger—because otherwise they have to believe in the Devil himself… and that scares the shit out of them.

She is the reason we love to watch the Joker. And it doesn't even matter that we know he's insane, that everything that comes out of his mouth is lies, that he's going to betray anyone and everyone who gets in his way—even those on his side.

We want to believe he's good underneath or we have to admit that evil is real.

How do I fight that?

I need a whole team of superheroes by my side to beat her ass down. I need all my superfriends to show up and help me. I need…

Now, hey there. Wait just a second…

304

That's not a bad idea...
In fact, I think I just came up with a plan.

CHAPTER THIRTY-NINE

LAWTON

The week passes so fast, and Sunday—the day of the festival—comes so quick, my head feels like it's spinning with all the shit that's happening.

I'm not gonna lie—Oaklee getting offered a TV show instead of me... well, it did sting for a few days. But then I thought about her. How she must feel, being stuck with Hanna all day long for the last three days. Unable to speak her mind. Unable to tell anyone how much she's been wronged. Unable to find... justice, I guess.

And then I got over it.

Because I realized something important this past week. That I'm not the man I thought I was. That I was never that man. And that my problem wasn't that I'm dissatisfied with my career, I was dissatisfied with myself.

The TV show was never going to fix me.

"OK," Oaklee says as we walk up to the festival grounds. "I think I'm ready for this."

"Ready to lose and take one for the team?" I ask, shooting her a lopsided grin.

"So ready," she says, squeezing my hand. "I just want to get this over with."

"Just so we're clear," I say. "No matter what happens today, you're my hero, Miss Ryan."

"Ah, stop it," she says. "I'm giving in. I'm not a hero."

"You might be giving in, but you never gave up." I kiss her hand as we enter the crowd and make our way over to the beer-tasting stage. The whole competition is live. There's probably thousands of people here and even though it's a two-day thing, this competition is the main event. There's a decent prize attached to it too. The winner gets a trophy, ten thousand dollars in cash, and their beer on tap at all the city concessions. That means Coors Field, that means the Pepsi Center, Elitch Gardens, the zoo, the museums... all of it.

Oaklee is oddly calm and quiet, considering what's about to go down here today. Everything is on the line. Her future could not be more precarious.

We stop to the side of the stage where the tasters have all taken their seats in front of sample trays of beer.

I see all of her friends from the Opera House tavern last Saturday.

Ace, Rosco, and Beckett are huddled together looking nervous as they talk in low voices. Duke and Cormac just stand next to them saying nothing. Bear and Jack look like they want to throw up. And all the girls are here too. Tallulah, May, Piper, Beatrix, Juniper, and Magnolia. Each of them as solemn-faced, edgy, anxious.

Seeing them so wound up jumpstarts my nerves again too, so I say, "Are you sure—"

"Yes." Oaklee cuts me off. "I'm sure."

"But... but Bronco Brews. Your dad. Your whole life, Oaklee. It could go up in flames."

She swallows hard, but nods her head. "I know. But it will be worth it to end this stupid game she's playing with me. It will, Law. And if things go that way... then... then I'll have no regrets. Because it's the last chance I have to save myself from a life controlled by Hanna Harlow."

I nod. Understanding her desperation.

Then look around to find familiar, friendly faces.

All our friends are here. Vivi and Chuck. Jordan and his two associates. Even Jordan's assistant, Eileen, showed up.

"Where's—"

But as soon as Oaklee says that, we hear them.

A thunderous roar from down the street. It grows louder and more powerful as they come into view, their motorcycles rumbling, shaking everything they pass.

The whole crowd turns to look at the precession, Spencer Shrike, the outlaw patriarch himself, taking up the vanguard, as more than thirty bikers pull up alongside of the park and stop.

They don't turn the bikes off. They just sit there, like an army of darkness in leather and chains, twisting their throttles to announce their arrival—as if they needed the announcement.

Ready for whatever happens next.

"Showtime," Oaklee says, wiping her hands on her skirt. She takes one step away from me, then turns, kisses me on the lips, and whispers, "See you on the other side."

CHAPTER FORTY

OAKLEE

I have to wipe my hands on my skirt twice as I make my way through the crowd to the stage where all my fellow brewmasters are gathered, waiting for the tasting to start.

I glance quickly around, gathering my courage, as I climb the stairs and approach Hanna.

She's smiling with overflowing joy and happiness as she talks with one of the judges. Throwing her head back to laugh at what must be a joke.

I glance over at my peers, who look back at me with nearly blank expressions that aren't easily decipherable. It could be fear, or hatred, or maybe just anxiety.

I guess I'll figure out which soon enough, but there's no time for that now. The host is already introducing today's judges. All local celebrities—which makes this contest a little different than most—and a little more interesting too, because people come out to see them just as much as they do to drink beer in the park.

Hanna sees me coming and instantly her gregarious manner she was faking for the judges switches into something she reserves for me alone.

It took me a while to figure out what that was. But all week, ever since that meeting with the Home TV people where she admitted to being my nemesis, it's been on my mind.

Last night I put my finger on it.

Hatred. Served with a smile.

It's as simple and complicated as that.

She just hates me.

"Oaklee," she says, her voice laced with fake sugar. Like… little yellow and pink packets of sugar-*ish* words come spilling out of her mouth automatically. "Well, don't you look pretty wearing your usual outfit."

"Yup," I say, looking down at my short, fluttery skirt, my old Frye boots, and bedazzled t-shirt that says "I give no fox" in pink and yellow rhinestones right across my tits. "This is me. What you see is what you get."

Hanna's grin goes sideways, her eyes half closed as she meets my gaze and says, "Yes, that was always your problem. You're transparent, Oaklee. You should try a poker face every once in a while."

"You mean lie? Like you?"

She lifts one shoulder up, tilts her head towards it, smiling. A shrug that says, *Guilty, but no one cares.*

A cheer from the crowd makes both of us look at the stage. The local celebrities are all sitting down at the tasting table and the first beer is being served.

"I'm sorry it had to be this way," Hanna says, looking back at me.

"Me too," I say. "I'm sorry this is the day you finally lose and have to deal with what you've done."

She laughs loudly. So loud several of the closer judges look over at us. "God, you're adorable, Oaklee. Always putting up the good fight. Never having the sense to quit while you're ahead."

"Well, you're wrong about that."

She stares are me. "How so?"

"I *do* know how to quit when I'm ahead. And that's why I'm selling Bronco Brews."

Her eyebrows knit together. Fiercely. And for once I'm the one who wants to laugh at her. Because her confusion—even if it's only for a few seconds—is perfect.

Watching her have doubts... well, that's priceless to me after all these years.

"What do you mean?" she asks.

"What you hear is what you get, Hanna. You heard me. I'm selling."

"Bullshit," she snaps.

I look around and find the Home TV people all staring up at us from the front row. All four of them wave. They are in love with this stupid *Brewery Smackdown* show. I wave back at them as I say what Hanna refuses to. "No," I say. "Not bullshit." And then I point over at Spencer Shrike and his train of buddies. There are dozens of them. All dressed up in leather, all tattooed, all looking back at us like the mobster royal family they are. "I'm selling Bronco Brews to Spencer Shrike, Hanna. He's here to sign the contract."

"But..." Hanna stammers. "The fucking show!"

"Fuck the fucking show," I say. "I never wanted that, you did. And I hate to break this to you now, because I know you were expecting this to be a very fun day, but I feel it's my duty to warn you."

"Of what?" Hanna snaps.

"That stealing my beer recipes was one thing. But stealing *his*"—I point at Spencer and his entourage—"is something else altogether." I smile at her and then whisper, "So you're gonna need to take those off the market, pronto, honey. Or"—I point at the crowd—"you see them?"

Her gaze follows my pointing finger until she sees who I'm referring to. An involuntary gasp escapes before she can corral it. Because it's her family.

Oh, yes.

I went there.

"You have a lovely family. Did you forget I saw them at graduation, Hanna? I didn't. So I drove out to your family farm the other day and had a really great chat with your mom and dad. They're so proud of you, even though you cut all ties to them years ago. You know, when you decided you were my sister." I kinda spit that last part. "I told them all about our TV deal and invited them here as a way to surprise you because you wanted to make amends and you're not very good at admitting you're wrong, ya know? Which they totally understood. So they came. Surprise!"

"You fuckin'—" But that's as far as she gets, because I'm not done yet.

"And so... well, you know Spencer isn't the killer you seem to think he is, so your family is safe. But he does have a billion-dollar bottom line, so... you *aren't*. He will take you to court, Hanna. Expose all your lies. And you see them?" I point again. This time to two men in suits, dark sunglasses, and the totally cliché white earpiece dangling down their necks. I now know them as Finn Murphy and Darrel Jameson, Jordan's 'associates', but I don't tell Hanna that. "That's the FBI, Hanna. They're here to arrest you for industrial espionage and I invited your family to see it happen."

She turns her head to look at me. And if eyes could shoot venom, I'm pretty sure that would be her supervillain power. "Bullshit," she growls.

"Oh, no. This is some shit, for sure, but it's not bullshit."

"I will put you in prison. I have footage of you—"

"No, honey. You don't. Because you see that guy over there? The one standing next to Vivi Vaughn? That's Oliver Shrike. Yes, related. And he's a notorious black-hat hacker who not only broke into your security system and found out that footage didn't exist, but also found receipts for the men you hired to breach my computer and steal my father's beer recipes."

This is when things finally start to sink in for Hanna Harlow. Because she doubles down. "You have no proof. I covered my tracks. You have no proof."

"Oh, but I do," I say, pointing over to our peers. "You see them? You see Jack, and Ace, and Rosco, and Bear, and Beckett, and Duke, and Cormac? You know those guys you've been blackmailing these past several years? The ones who knew you stole my beer and you threatened to steal theirs too if they said anything? Yeah." I laugh. "They were hard to convince. Scared shitless of you, Hanna. But the minute I mentioned Spencer Shrike was buying my brewery and would not be putting up with business as usual, they decided there were bigger monsters to worry about and told me everything."

"What the fuck do you want?" she hisses.

I shrug. "I got what I want. I don't want anything from you. I'm selling the brewery, getting the fuck out of this insane Home TV deal, you're getting arrested, shamed in front of your family and peers, and then you're either going to prison for industrial espionage or..."

I let that hang there for a few seconds. Just to enjoy the look on her face.

"Or *what?*" she finally growls.

315

I snap my fingers and Jordan Wells appears at my side, along with his assistant, Eileen, holding a folder out for Hanna to take.

"Or," Jordan says, "you sell Buffalo Brews to Oaklee for the sum of one dollar, agree to never brew or sell beer again, and we call it even." He points to the folder. "It's all in there. I acted as your lawyer and covered all the bases, so all you have to do is sign."

He reaches into his suit coat pocket, pulls out a pen, and holds it out next to the folder.

"You're all insane," Hanna whispers.

"No," I say. "You're insane. And I hope you get the help you need, but honestly, Hanna, I don't care what you do after this. As long you sign these papers and I never see your face again, you're free to go."

"But... my beer..."

"*My. Beer.*" I spit those words out between clenched teeth. "You have no beer. It's. My. Beer. And I swear to fucking God, Hanna, I will take you down. I will ruin your life. I will do everything I just laid out and I will smile as I do it. I don't want to sell my brewery, but I will. If it means I take you down, I will sell everything. I will gladly give up all I've built—all my father built—for the chance to get even with you. So think very carefully. Think very hard how you want to spend the next ten years. In prison, shamed and sad. Or free to think about what a sick, disgusting liar you are and try to get the help you need. But either way, I'm walking off this stage free of you. You lost. I won. And you'd better come to terms with that real fast, bitch. Because I'm gonna count to ten and then this deal is over."

She looks like she wants to kill me. Reach up, wrap her hands around my throat, and strangle the life out of me.

You know, kinda like the way I've felt about her these past few years.

I start counting. "One, two, three…"

Her emotions go through several incarnations. Rage, hate, fear, then finally sadness and surrender.

Because just as I get to the count of nine, the host on stage announces that Buffalo Brews Assassin Sour Saison is up next for tasting… and she signs.

And that, my friends, is how you take down your super-nemesis.

Sometimes the only way to win the game… is to quit the game.

CHAPTER FORTY-ONE

LAWTON

I hold Oaklee's hand as we walk the few blocks over to Shrike Bikes in Five Points. Kinda swinging it. Smiling. Just... fuckin' happy, I guess. And what's not to be happy about?

Assassin Sour Saison won the competition, hands down. Even though those judges were local celebrities and don't really know shit about beer, they knew it was different. They knew it was unique. And they knew it deserved to win.

And yeah, it was under the Buffalo Brews label, but Oaklee made Hanna admit on stage that it was Oaklee's recipe and then tell one more lie.

That she and Oaklee brewed it together.

Then Hanna announced the sale and gave the winning trophy and check for ten thousand dollars to Oaklee in front of the whole city.

Happy. Fucking. Ending.

But hold on there. We're not quite done yet...

"OK, what the hell are we doing?" Oaklee asks, once she figures out where we're headed. "You said we were going up to the mountains today."

"I gotta pick something up from Shrike. Just cool your jets, Oaks."

Oaklee never wanted to sell the brewery. She'd rather die than sell her father's life's work. But she would've. If only to get away from Hanna Harlow. But it didn't come to that.

And Spencer Shrike would've bought it, even though he didn't want a brewery. He would've. If only to help his niece get out of a bind. But it didn't come to that either.

Buffalo Brews up in Boulder had a name change and it's in the process of being renovated. The Home TV people propositioned Oaklee and me together for another show once all this shit went down and they realized the smackdown was a non-starter. *Rocky Mountain Renos.*

We said no.

I open the door for Oaklee when we walk up to Shrike, hold it for her as she walks through, and then enter behind her, slipping my sunglasses up on my head.

"There he is!" Chuck bellows from across the showroom. "We got the cameras out for this one!"

"What?" Oaklee says, looking up at me, confused.

A whole crew of people come over to us. Holding microphones over our heads. Three different cameras filming as we meet Chuck in front of the cash register.

"Just go with it," I say, squeezing her hand before letting go to first shake Oliver's hand, then Spencer's.

I feel like a kid meeting his idol for the first time when he grips my hand and says, "You promise to take good care of her?" as he nods his head.

For a second I think he's talking about the bike I'm about to buy. The one he made custom many years ago and is now selling to make room for more.

But then I realize he's talking about Oaklee.

So I nod back, and say, "I promise."

"You bought this?" Oaklee says, looking up at me.

"I did."

"Because…"

"Because I've always wanted one. And now I've got all this money... so... why the fuck not?"

She sighs. Smiles her secret smile. Which makes me smile mine. And then she says, "Well, this is a nice surprise."

But this isn't the surprise.

"The money transfer went through this morning," Spencer says. "So let me tell you all about my little princess here before you take her away."

"Shoot," I say. "I want to hear all about her."

"She's a little temperamental in the mornings. So you gotta warm her up properly. And she likes to be clean, so make sure you give her a bath after you're done riding her. And her paint chips easily, so you need to bring her in for refurbishing often. I don't want my baby girl to go without her pampering."

He goes on and on like that and the whole time I'm just smiling. Because all these instructions sound a little bit like the deluxe boyfriend package.

It takes hours to get Spencer Shrike to hand me the keys to his baby. But eventually Oaklee and I have it outside, new matching helmets purchased and on our heads. Leather jackets on our backs, boots on our feet... ready to begin the road trip to our future.

And by the time we get up to Indian Hills and pull down the dirt-road driveway to the mountain mansion I closed on last week...

We are fully ourselves.

When we get off the bike I take her hand and lead her around the outside of the property. Showing her the barn, and the confiners that surround the house like a wall. Then I take her inside and show her that too.

The kitchen where we'll cook dinner.

The dining room where we'll eat it.

The master bedroom where we'll sleep at night.

The master bath, where a claw-foot tub awaits our first bubble bath together.

And all the other bedrooms, empty for now, but which one day, hopefully, will be filled with kids.

It's a weekend house. For now.

I sold my condo and moved into the Bronco Brews penthouse with Oaklee. I'm finishing up the condo renovations on the lower floors and getting ready to put them on the market.

I know. I know. I said I didn't want to be a real-estate agent anymore.

But I do for this. Maybe I'll quit after I'm done. Maybe I'll sell my half of the business to Zack.

But then again, maybe not.

I don't have that feeling anymore. The one that demanded I make a change. The early mid-life crisis is over.

So I decide to just live the life I've been given with the woman I love.

Maybe Oaklee and I didn't get the experience we signed up for a few weeks ago, but we did get an experience, didn't we?

The deluxe version, for sure.

The Shrike Bikes show has me on as a guest four times this first season and they're talking about making me a recurring regular next season.

And Oaklee is back, better than ever now that Hanna is out of her life. She's already thinking about the label design for her fall and winter seasonals.

I think her mid-life crisis is over too.

Vivi Vaughn started my second tat on my other shoulder. It's me in a suit, surrounded by a bunch of familiar faces.

That day at the festival is now a local legend. We don't admit to anything, of course. But rumors fly about how we took down Hanna and saved the Colorado craft beer industry.

I think it was the hipsters who talked.

And that's fine. Let people talk. Let them turn it into something more than it was if they want.

We don't care.

We're too busy planning the Husband Experience.

JORDAN

I live in a seven-million-dollar, ten-thousand-square-foot historical mansion next door to the Denver Botanical Gardens. I bought it last fall in foreclosure with the hope of...

What?

What was I hoping?

I live here now because I'm liquidating. I have hopes and dreams too. I need things. It's all I've got left and I don't want it unless...

There are seven bedrooms, eleven bathrooms, two media rooms, two offices, two kitchens, a game room, a library, and a ballroom.

And I live here alone.

There's nowhere to drop my keys as I come in the front door because the place is empty. A family lived here before their luck changed. And they left everything behind when they sold it. Even photographs. The happy couple on their wedding day. Pictures of their kids, and I can only assume they did that because they have digitals in Dropbox or some shit, because that part is pretty cold.

Pretty.

Fucking.

Cold.

(But who am I to judge?)

They left everything like it was a holiday home and whatever they kept there was just... extra. Like they went shopping and bought two of everything and so all this was just... the spare set.

Except it wasn't.

But it's all gone now. I packed up the photographs in a box and gave them to Lawton. Did he ever return them? I have no idea because I never asked. Then I sold all the furniture in an estate sale last month and bought a desk, a bed, and a couch from IKEA and had it all placed in the fifteen-hundred-square-foot office on the main floor.

I'm pretty sure the IKEA delivery people thought I was crazy, but I don't care. And anyway, it might be true.

I live in the office. I don't even bother using the main kitchen because I don't cook and the office has a wet bar—because all gentlemen who own ten-thousand-square-foot-homes have a wet bar in their office—and it even has a dishwasher to wash the cut-crystal glasses I drink bourbon out of every night before bed, so who cares about the industrial-sized chef's kitchen on the other side of the house?

On the desk there's a laptop and on the wall there's a fifty-five-inch TV, except I don't have cable, or Netflix, or Hulu, or even Prime, so why I bought the TV, I couldn't tell you.

If anyone saw me these days I'd get a label.

If I was lucky that label would be... eccentric. But more likely than not, they'd call me...sad.

And that would be accurate.

I am sad. For all the things I lost. For all the ways I've tried to make up to the people who matter. For all the things I'll never have—things that have nothing to do with the size of a TV or the number of bathrooms in a house I don't even really live in, or a wet bar in the oversized home office.

326

I feel sorry for that family who lost this house. I really do. Because at least they treated it like a *home*. At least it was loved.

I don't love it.

I kick off my shoes as I enter the office and pour myself four fingers of bourbon. I sit on the couch, facing the window that faces the front yard—visible because of the fancy landscape lighting—and think about the game that just ended.

Sometimes people ask me why I do this. Why I make up these games. Why I fuck with so many lives. And I say... why not?

I take a sip of my drink, still staring out the window, and ask myself that question now.

It's not because of Oaklee. I don't owe her anything. Whether she knows it or not, she got her boyfriend experience. I don't owe Law, either. Though I do still need him. If I want to get what I want, that is. I need him, but I don't *owe* him. So that's not why.

So why? Why do I do this? Is it some deep craving for forgiveness?

Probably. But that's not enough. Not for the kind of shit I pull off.

So why? What is the payoff?

I've been thinking about this a lot lately. A lot.

And there's really only one answer.

I like it.

I smile just thinking that truth.

I like it.

I hired Darrel to work with me for a reason. And Finn, too. They are both decent enough on the outside. But inside... inside Darrel and Finn are just like me. Two morally bankrupt motherfuckers looking to make a new fortune.

I wield a powerful hammer having Darrel and Finn on my side. Some might say it's not fair, but he who writes the rules of the game wins, right?

Except... I'm cashing out.

All the way out.

Because there's only one thing left for me to want.

That fucking building.

I pick up my phone and call Lawton, ready to make my move. I've liquidated everything I have—except the house, because, well, I haven't quite given up on that. I have one more game to play and it involves this house.

Lawton answers, "Yeah," and for a second I forget I called him and hesitate. "Jordan?" he asks.

"So hey," I say. "I'm ready to make an offer on Turning Point. Did you find out who the owner is?"

"Uh, yeah," he says, hesitating.

"So how much do they want?"

"They're not selling. And man, I tried my hardest too. I pulled out all the stops for you, brother. But these people are holding tight."

"Dude, I pulled together fifteen million dollars cash. Did you tell them all-cash offer?"

"Yeah, they don't care. I'm telling you, they're not selling."

"Who the fuck are these people?" I ask.

"Well, see, that's the interesting part. They know you."

"What?"

"Yeah, some woman named Augustine and her husband Alexander."

"Augustine and Alexander bought my building?"

"It's their building, dude. They're not selling. I'm sorry, I know that club meant a lot to you, but I'm sorry. I tried my best and…"

I end the call. Stare out my window. Sip my drink.

And rage inside at the audacity of those two showing up from my fucking past, in my fucking town, buying my fucking building, and then letting it sit there for almost two fucking years as they wait for me to realize…

I just lost my own game.

Fuck that.

It's time to play dirty.

END OF BOOK SHIT

Welcome to the End of Book Shit. This is the part of the book where I get to say anything I want about the book and you can read it or not. :) They are never edited and always written last minute right before I upload the files to the distributors so there will be typos and you should ignore them!

One of the best things about writing (for me, anyway) is thinking a story will go one way and have it go somewhere else unexpectedly.

Vivi Vaughn didn't really exist before this book, but then… of course she did. Sick Girlz was inevitable, it's only logical that Veronica Vaughn's brother, Viv Vaughn, would have Bombshell daughters too. Her name always began with a V because for some reason that whole clam is fixated on that. And she was born to be a tattoo artist because Sick Boyz was her inherited empire, just like Bronco Brews was Oaklee's.

I'm not going to lie, I had A LOT of fun writing this book. Like almost too much fun. I got to reimagine Spencer and friends way into the future, I got to put a Shrike Bikes showroom in the old Chaput photography building next to Coor's Field, which means I got to go back to the Five Points neighborhood AND I got to stick Oliver in here as well. So even though this book isn't about the Rook & Ronin people I got to kinda pretend it was.

I also got to talk about leather jackets, and

331

motorcycles, and tattoos again. It made me realize how much I missed that world.

Which brings me to a bit of good news I just got a couple days ago. Some of you may already know, but for the benefit of those who don't follow my personal Facebook profile and didn't see the post…

I have signed a TV series option deal for the books Slack, Guns, and The Company (which used to be called Come, Come Back, and Coming For You) with MGM Television. They optioned those five books and have first right of refusal locked in for the entire Rook & Ronin/Company series. And this was ALL due to the hard work my partner, Johnathan McClain, did when he pitched the books, the world, and the TV series project to MGM last fall.

So… this world was one of the first I ever built but it's still going. It's got a lot of life left in it.

It's also the very first "official" tie-in between the Turning Series, Jordan's Game, Rook & Ronin, and The Company. And there's even a mention of Anarchy Series in here too. So FIVE Huss worlds in one book.

I'm laughing out loud right now. Because I know you're not supposed to do this. I know this. Readers are picky and lots of them like to start with book one and read everything in order and HATE finding out later there's so much more that came before.

But I can't help it and I didn't plan it. It just rolled out this way.

OK, so how about the new world. Jordan's world is just getting bigger and bigger and I have a feeling that Law and Oaklee are gonna be one of the favorites.

I'm not really a drinker so this whole craft beer set up kinda took me by surprise when I came up with it. But the more I thought about it the more I liked it. I love creating new "brands" in books. Like Shrike Bikes. Which has stood the test of time. And I started doing this immediately in my very first series I Am Just Junco. In Junco's world there's a movie star called Jax Justice (It's Science Fiction, BTW) who even crosses over into the Anarchy series at one point. And there's a rock star called Cora and I have Junco drinking craft beer in book two (it's called Little Sister) and there's a whole bunch of culture in there. Because that's how you build a world in science fiction. So when I started writing romance that's all I knew. I just figured that's how it's done. And I like reading books like that, so I figured hey, why not make up brands in this romance stuff too? And that's who we got Shrike Bikes and that's how we got Cookie's Diner (which made an appearance in Pleasure of Panic) and that's how we got Sick Boyz tattoo shop.

So building Oaklee's world of Bronco Brews was almost inevitable. But in addition to all that, I actually have a real-world experience with this beer brewing stuff. When I was up at Colorado State University doing my undergrad in equine science I had to take a microbiology class to graduate. And microbiology was already my thing, I loved it. But my professor was this kick-ass little lady who worked with mosquito-borne diseases over at the CDC on campus. And when SHE was doing her college she actually took microbiology with one of the brewmasters for New Belgium Brewing (which is one of the first craft breweries to make it "Big") and they happened to be based in Fort Collins, so she invited him over to our class to give a lecture on how he uses yeast to flavor beer.

So Bronco Brews is like a little Easter egg in my life. It's almost like... no matter how hard I try everything leads back to Fort Collins for me.

Another funny little fact in this book was the whole "hipster" scene in the Opera House Tavern up in Golden. BTW – there is a bar in an opera house in Golden, it's just called something else. I am not a hipster and I only have a cursory knowledge of the "hipster" culture so I had to look most of it up online. (Don't take any of it too seriously if you're a hipster! Lol) But the funny part is that I have this too-school-for-cool (who somehow manages to be super cool anyway) twenty-one-year-old son. My ONLY knowledge of hipster culture is hearing my son proclaim (long and loud) about how he isn't one, OK? Like... that's it. That's all I knew.

HE IS NOT A HIPSTER!

But I know my son. Right? So I started looking up different things... like what do hipsters listen to? And what to hipsters wear? And what do hipsters care about?

And I found Modest Mouse. Who I can't stand, BUT have listened to A LOT because it's my son's FAVORITE BAND and h would play them in the car.

I was like... huh. That's weird.

So I'm feeling pretty good about Modest Mouse because I know them, so they make it into the story.

Then I look up what they wear and I see... Hawaiian shirts and old-school Adidas.

And I'm like... what? Because my SON, who ISN'T a hipster, also had a weird fixation with Hawaiian shirts and old-school Adidas.

And then I get to the names... and I'm like... HOLY SHIT! My son is a hipster! Because his name is Odin. lol

So this story isn't over yet. Because two weeks ago he and his girlfriend take me out to dinner for Mother's Day. And we're sitting in Bourbon Brothers in Colorado

Springs and I'm telling him this same story above. Pointing out how he is 100% hipster in every way imaginable.

He couldn't even deny it. (He did try and deny it. He blushed and laughed and said no! But his girlfriend was like, "I told you! I told you!")

So that was pretty funny. And he would be mortified if he knew I was talking about him in the EOBS (even though he doesn't even know what an EOBS is) ;)

So I just had too much fun with this story. Too much fun. And I hope that's what you take away from it. It's not some super serious mind-bending twisted mystery or anything. It's not some work of literature. It's just FUN.

Jordan is up next. It IS a standalone book. And it IS a MFM love story. And it IS a little bit darker. And it IS just ONE POINT OF VIEW. Just Jordan. He deserves an entire book so that's what he gets. It's called Play Dirty and you can get it at the link below.

Thank you for reading, thank you for reviewing, and I'll see you in the next book!

JA Huss
May 25, 2018

Thank you for reading, thank you for reviewing, and if you want the next book, The Boyfriend Experience, you can find all the links to buy it at:

http://jahuss.com/series/jordans-game

ABOUT THE AUTHOR

JA Huss never wanted to be a writer and she still dreams of that elusive career as an astronaut. She originally went to school to become an equine veterinarian but soon figured out they keep horrible hours and decided to go to grad school instead. That Ph.D wasn't all it was cracked up to be (and she really sucked at the whole scientist thing), so she dropped out and got a M.S. in forensic toxicology just to get the whole thing over with as soon as possible.

After graduation she got a job with the state of Colorado as their one and only hog farm inspector and spent her days wandering the Eastern Plains shooting the shit with farmers.

After a few years of that, she got bored. And since she was a homeschool mom and actually does love science, she decided to write science textbooks and make online classes for other homeschool moms.

She wrote more than two hundred of those workbooks and was the number one publisher at the online homeschool store many times, but eventually she covered every science topic she could think of and ran out of shit to say.

So in 2012 she decided to write fiction instead. That year she released her first three books and started a career that would make her a New York Times bestseller and land her on the USA Today Bestseller's List twenty-one times in the next four years.

Her books have sold millions of copies all over the world, the audio version of her semi-autobiographical book, Eighteen, was nominated for an Audie award in 2016, and her audiobook Mr. Perfect was nominated for a Voice Arts Award in 2017.

She also writes book and screenplays with her friend, actor and writer, Johnathan McClain. Their first book, Sin With Me, will release on March 6, 2018. And they are currently working with MGM as producing partners to turn their adaption of her series, The Company, into a TV series.

She lives on a ranch in Central Colorado with her family, two donkeys, four dogs, three birds, and two cats.

If you'd like to learn more about JA Huss or get a look at her schedule of upcoming appearances, visit her website at www.JAHuss.com or www.HussMcClain.com to keep updated on her projects with Johnathan. You can also join her fan group, Shrike Bikes, on Facebook, www.facebook.com/groups/shrikebikes and follow her Twitter handle, @jahuss.

87376915R00201

Made in the USA
Middletown, DE
03 September 2018